Please return/renew this item by the last date shown

 BATH & NORTH EAST SOMERSET

# SEVERAL STRANGERS

## Writing from Three Decades

CLAIRE TOMALIN

VIKING

VIKING

Published by the Penguin Group
Penguin Books Ltd, 27 Wrights Lane, London w8 5tz, England
Penguin Putnam Inc., 375 Hudson Street, New York, New York 10014, USA
Penguin Books Australia Ltd, Ringwood, Victoria, Australia
Penguin Books Canada, ..., Ontario, Canada m4v 3b2
Penguin Books ..., te Bag 102902, NSMC, Auckland, New Zealand

Penguin Books Ltd, Registered Offices: Harmondsworth, Middlesex, England

First published 1999
1 3 5 7 9 10 8 6 4 2

Set in 10.5/13pt Monotype Minion
Typeset by Rowland Phototypesetting Ltd, Bury St Edmunds, Suffolk
Printed in Great Britain by Clays Ltd, St Ives plc

A CIP catalogue record for this book is available from the British Library

ISBN 0−670−88567−3

# Contents

# CONTENTS

## CONTENTS

vii

# CONTENTS

# PART ONE

# APPRENTICESHIP

Collecting reviews from three decades has brought me face to face with several strangers who went by my name. Jane Austen was right when she wrote, 'Seven years . . . are enough to change every pore of one's skin, and every feeling of one's mind.' I started my working life in publishing with only a vague sense of where I was going or what I wanted to do. This changed as I was launched into journalism and literary editing, where I felt I found my natural habitat and friends. I moved to the *Sunday Times*, and it turned into a battlefield. Finally I became a full-time writer, solitary and obsessive as most writers are.

The thread that has persisted through these separate lives has been reviewing. The first books I chose for myself were connected with women's history and domestic themes. I got the books mostly because no one else wanted them. Since then the sideline has moved closer to the centre. At the time my own first book appeared, in 1974, a publisher friend said with weary condescension, 'Not another book about the bluestockings?' He was a man, of course. Today both sexes are running publishing firms, and male historians are as interested as women in marriage, divorce and children, and in the interaction of public and private lives. Women's history has stopped being a sideline.

Looking up old work has meant thinking back over my career, and made me realize how inseparable work and personal experience have been. I was thirty-five – half way through life, we used to think – when I wrote the earliest review in this collection. What held me up for so long? And how did I ever start? The introductions to the reviews offer answers to these questions, and give some account of how a woman of my generation found herself embarked on a literary life.

I was twenty-one when I took my degree at Cambridge and found a room in London. It was a basement in the house of the artist Roger

Hilton, in Shepherd's Bush, for which I paid £2 a week. My walls were hung with his abstract paintings; the sound of his wife Ruth's violin filtered down, and I babysat for their two small children. There was also a good deal of wild life. My kitchenette in the old coal hole was haunted by giant spiders, and when the cat gave birth to kittens in the back room a ferocious tom, their father we supposed, came in through the window and tore the little ones to shreds. But neither spiders nor murdering cats dented my happiness for long. I was in love with Nick, also just down from Cambridge, and he was living in a room round the corner, in a house belonging to another artist, Patrick Heron.

This was the summer of 1954. I had gone through three years reading English without much thought of the future. I was an innocent, dreamy, not to say dozy, and there was full employment. I had been writing poetry from the age of seven, and although some of my verses appeared in undergraduate magazines, and one poem in Karl Miller's *Poetry from Cambridge,* I did not connect this with the world of careers. I meant to find myself a serious job, but knew I did not want to be a teacher, a civil servant or anything in the theatre. I could not imagine writing fiction, and did not even think of journalism then, because newspapers seemed so masculine, and I had a low opinion of women's magazines.

My·father pronounced that shorthand and typing were always useful to women, and offered to put me through a secretarial training course. I took it, and afterwards applied to the BBC: I was bilingual in French, with good secretarial skills, and a First, but the response was a short letter informing me 'that the competition for General Trainees is confined to men'. (I still have the letter.) I wrote to *Time and Tide,* was interviewed and turned down again, quite rightly, because it was obvious I had not read the magazine. Then my father mentioned me to someone he knew in publishing, and I found myself invited for an interview with an editor at Heinemann.

The Heinemann offices were at No. 99 Great Russell Street, a steep-staired Georgian house almost next door to the British Museum. Three flights up, through an outer office and I was in a very small room where a thin fair-haired man with a quizzical face just fitted behind his desk. His name was Roland Gant, and he would be my boss if I got the job. A few minutes into the interview a younger man, thick-set and wearing heavy glasses, came in without a word and put a piece of paper on Roland's desk. He was James Michie, the poet, and he had been in the outer office as I walked through. Later he told me he had been awarding me marks for my looks. Seven out of ten, he gave me, just enough for the job of secretary/editorial assistant, at £5.10s. a week. This was how things were done in 1954.

My desk was in the outer office, where sacks of manuscripts were dumped every day. Roland and James looked through them and decided who should read what. One of my tasks was to pack them up again for Mrs Tegan Harries, a reader who never appeared in person. From her rasping telephone voice I imagined her as a county lady down on her luck, cigarette dangling over the typewriter as she tapped out her reports in triplicate. The other reader was Moira Lynd, who did come in, from Hampstead, and took books away with her. She was a charming woman, combining political opinions of the extreme left with a good nose for a best-seller. She had refused to learn to type for fear of being given the sort of work I was expected to do, and she wrote out her reports by hand in the office on Wednesdays. Each line sloped more sharply as her pen travelled down the page, so that there was always a large gap in the bottom right-hand corner. Some of the novels that came in were still hand-written too. They were not viewed with favour, but we read them.

I did type letters, but very few, and I can remember only one occasion when Roland dictated to me in French to test my foreign shorthand skills. My impression was that it was more of an ordeal for him than for me. He was a sweet-natured man, a writer and a book lover, and he saw that I liked reading better than typing. My first Reading Room ticket at the British Museum was arranged by him; in this way he was responsible for a great deal of happiness in my life.

It was a cheerful office. One of my jobs was forwarding mail to authors. Roland had been in intelligence during the war, and when he noticed an elaborately formal letter addressed to Graham Greene he said, 'Let's steam it open.' So we did, with the office kettle. The letter was offering Greene a knighthood. Two weeks later an official rang to ask if all letters to Greene had been forwarded, because he had received no answer to an important one. They had indeed, I answered firmly. He said he would post a duplicate in any case. Later I found the original on one of the filing cabinets; and later still we knew that Greene had refused the knighthood, and we thought all the better of him.

Soon I was helping out with reading and reporting on novels. I remember Moira recommending the first volume of Anthony Burgess's Malayan trilogy, and everyone enthusing about Dodie Smith's *Hundred and One Dalmatians*. My reports were neatly typed, but I made no discoveries. Wanting to prove I was not a blinkered highbrow, I wrote a favourable report on a steamy love story about a concert pianist which I thought might sell; Moira damned it, and she was right. Editorial jobs came my way too. I was asked to work on the *Complete Poems of D. H. Lawrence*. I sent the chairman, A. S. Frere, a note asking if I should restore the word 'fuck' where earlier editions had printed a dash. I was told he showed my memo round, amused by such brazen behaviour in a young female employee, but I never met him.

In September 1955 Nick and I married. He was now working for the *Daily Express*. We found a two-room flat on Primrose Hill and spent a week's honeymoon in his aunt's cottage in Suffolk. Soon I was pregnant; we planned to have six children. I worked through most of my pregnancy, and translated a book in the evenings to improve our finances. Translating and nausea have gone together in my mind ever since, because I translated two more books during my next two pregnancies. There was no maternity leave. But I was invited to return to Heinemann. 'Only you'll have more children, I suppose,' said the director, who spoke to me gloomily, and I agreed that I would.

My second daughter was born less than eighteen months after my first, and by then I was working at home as a reader. Nick's career as a journalist was going well, and Lord Beaverbrook sent him to New York. He instructed him to go alone, taking the view that a wife and children were an encumbrance to a young reporter, but Nick insisted on my joining him with Josephine and Susanna. He flew out, I followed with the babies on a listing French liner. The next year was the only one of my adult life in which I have not worked. I saw little enough of Nick, but I was happily absorbed in the children.

We arrived back in 1959. London was preparing to swing. I was pregnant again, and at once found work reading for several publishers. My career, such as it was, took second place to the demands of husband and children. I no longer wrote poetry, and it still did not occur to me to try my hand at journalism. But one day Katharine Whitehorn, who had been at my college just before me and whose column in the *Observer* made her one of the most admired journalists of the time, held out a friendly hand and asked me to write a couple of pieces for the *Observer*. I was surprised – no one had invented the idea of an old girls' network then – and I'm still grateful. All I remember of the articles is that one was about baby clothes; perhaps they both were. I managed to irritate older women in the family with my confident pronouncements, which seemed a good thing at the time. Katharine then got me a column in a magazine called the *Motor*. I was 'Woman at the Wheel', and wrote a monthly piece on topics such as how to keep children amused in the car, how to avoid creasing your evening dress when driving to a dance (you sit on tissue paper) and so on. Since I could barely drive at the time, I didn't last very long on the *Motor*. My next patron was a male Cambridge contemporary, Ronald Bryden, who offered me children's books to review for the *Spectator*. My daughters were precocious readers, and they appreciated them even more than I did. In one fat batch of books came Ted Hughes's *Meet My Folks!*: they loved the poems, I declared it a classic.

By the time I was twenty-eight I had had four children. The work I was doing was precious to me because it gave me something to exercise my mind while allowing me to stay at home. You can breastfeed and read at the same time, and write reports and reviews when the children are asleep. But it was the lower end of Grub Street. What changed things for me was disaster and sorrow. My third child, a boy, was born with many things wrong. He never came home from hospital, but died when he was a month old. I wrote something about that experience, and began to think I might write more. I also determined to have another baby at once, and my third daughter, Emily, was born on her missing brother's first birthday. But as that sorrow passed, another came. Nick – my charming and successful husband – became a bolter. He fell for the office vamp, and that started him on a series of affairs. I learnt not to be surprised if he did not come home at night. One day he would insist that our marriage had been a mistake, and that a divorce would be the best solution. A few weeks later he would change his mind, bombard me with flowers, rings and letters insisting that he was really happy in the marriage, and wanted more children. For a while all would be well, until another irresistible girl appeared. So it went on. Looking at an old diary reminds me what a heap of dejection I let myself be reduced to.

A friend's mother said to me, 'You didn't go to Cambridge to spend your life crying. Find yourself proper work.' A tough woman, she did not think reading for publishers was proper work. Her husband was a BBC executive, and an interview was arranged. Before I went, she warned me, 'Don't *mention* the fact that you have children when you go for the interview. Pretend you haven't any, or you won't even be considered for a job.'

In fact the first job I was offered outside publishing was on the *Evening Standard*. Charles Wintour took a risk in giving it me, and it was a crucial step, that move from the sedate world of the reader into the alarms and excursions of newspaper life. This was in October 1967. Suddenly I was doing things I had never imagined I could do, talking to politicians on the telephone from the deafening din of the newsroom, running after Jennifer Jenkins round Ladbroke Square for a comment, scribbling copy in a taxi and dictating it from a call box. Routine to journalists, frightening for a beginner, but when I realized I could do it, just about, I almost began to enjoy it. I stopped being a heap of misery, and found a life and friends of my own. With this things changed between Nick and me; but our marriage remained precarious.

I was now reviewing novels for Ian Hamilton at *The Times Literary Supplement* and for the *Observer*, where Terence Kilmartin became my mentor and friend. His touch was light, his speech hesitant. 'Oh, and by the way . . .' he would start, and pause. You waited happily, pleased to be asked to write anything at all for him. I began with shorter notices, my highest ambition to review novels. That seems unbelievable now, since reviewing novels in batches is the worst paid and least rewarding critical job there is. Still, it was more bearable doing it for Terry than for anyone else. He teased me and criticized my work, and sometimes my behaviour, without ever giving offence. He was never solemn, but he believed that literary pages have an educational aspect, and that the odd difficult word that sends readers to the dictionary is part of the process. He'd grown up in Ireland, gone to be a tutor in a French family in his teens, acquiring perfect French and a wide knowledge and appreciation of literature, music and painting in the process. He was in the Special Operations Executive during the war; at the end of his life he was translating Proust. Brave and loyal, he remains for me the model of a literary editor and a much missed friend.

About this time another friend from Cambridge, Julian Jebb, then working for the BBC, invited me to take part in a books quiz programme on television. He used some celebrated figures – Cyril Connolly, Lord David Cecil, Mary McCarthy – alongside unknowns like me. I was in several programmes, and my confidence grew. When the job of assistant to the literary editor of the *New Statesman*, Anthony Thwaite, came up, I put in for it and was appointed.

Three days a week at Great Turnstile, between Holborn and Lincoln's Inn Fields, seemed ideal. My daughters were at school, and I had four days at home. This was just as well, because even as I was due to start, in April 1968, Nick made one of his more spectacular bolts, disappearing abroad for several months with a new love. But also that summer, Anthony Thwaite went on holiday, leaving me in sole charge of the back half of the *Statesman* for four whole weeks. It was the most generous gift he could have given me. For a month I had a headache, and for a month I was the happiest person in the world. *My* pages, *my* writers, *my* decisions.

The *Statesman*, like Heinemann, was lodged in tall, narrow premises, with the back half of the paper – books and arts – at the top. Critics and book reviewers came at their various speeds up the stone stairs to the big room in which the presiding genius was Melaan Bunting, a secretary of the old kind, meaning she could well have run the back half of the paper herself. She sat surrounded by reference books and poetry collections, she knew the quirks of all the contributors, she could sub copy and had an eagle eye for a literal. We laughed a lot together. Her parents were Australian – English-born mother, Chinese-born father – and her son was John Williams, the guitarist. I've never known anyone quite like Melaan, and I admired her greatly, and mourned her when she died too young of emphysema.

For the first time I began to review books I selected for myself – this is when the pieces collected in this volume start. *The Journals of Claire Clairmont*, published in 1968 in the American scholar Marion Kingston Stocking's beautiful edition, sparked my interest in the Shelley circle, which had been off limits at Cambridge. Ida Baker's memoir of Katherine Mansfield started me thinking about that extraordinary life which I was later to write, and make into a play. I picked out volumes of Virginia Woolf's letters, and feminist books by Mary Ellmann and Eva Figes. There were Byron's letters, and lives of Dorothy Parker, Zelda Fitzgerald, Horatia Nelson. I read, I wrote, I subbed. One afternoon, working through a deep pile of poems submitted to us, I came on some so good I burst into Anthony's office saying, 'Here's a real poet!' They were Douglas Dunn's, and became his *Terry Street*.

I learnt from the *Statesman*'s regular contributors. V. S. Pritchett's copy, typed by his wife Dorothy, then worked over again by him in minute inky scratches, rendered up, when you'd struggled with it half the afternoon, language that seemed as natural as breathing, yet always surprising too. Then there was David Cairns on music, Charles Fox on jazz and Philip French on theatre, all passionate for their subjects. Our art critic, Robert Melville, first made me look properly at Bonnard and Balthus. He was rumoured to have Picassos stacked up in his flat in Gower Street Mews, although I never saw them; and he was a gentle and humorous presence in the office. One day a contributor came in with his copy, blustering, 'Not a single word is to be cut or changed.' Robert, the old pro, sitting quietly by with his impeccable script in his hand, murmured, 'You can change anything you like in *my* copy, Claire.'

It was a busy, complicated time. In 1969 Nick again decided he wanted to live with me and the children, and, although I was doubtful about the prospect, I agreed. I had kept a dream of family life. We started again. There were still times when we delighted one another. We decided we would have another child. Nick was now on the *Sunday Times*, and away a great deal on foreign assignments. In effect, I ran the house and the family, while he pursued his brave and dazzling career; he was a skilful and brilliant journalist, winning awards and admired by his peers.

Dick Crossman became editor of the *NS* in June 1970. He said I could have maternity leave – my baby was due in September – and come back when it felt right. James Fenton took over as assistant literary editor, and the plan was that I would go on writing for the paper during my leave. My son Tom was born in August, and found to have spina bifida. It meant that he would be paralysed from the chest down, and suffer many other problems. He might need a valve in his head to combat hydrocephalus. For months – well, for years – there were hospital visits, consultations, decisions to be made; my diary is full of notes about his progress. He became a beautiful, lively baby with a large head, who 'crawled' by pulling himself around on his arms. I fell in love with my child, as you do, and knew I could not go back to work yet.

I was still writing for the *Statesman*, and in May 1971 I produced an article in a series we called 'Reappraisal', about Mary Wollstonecraft's love letters, which had bowled me over when I came across them in the London Library. The day after the piece appeared I had letters from several publishers and literary agents, urging me to write a biography of Wollstonecraft. Nick, who had just published a book himself, was generous and helpful, telling me I had to decide whether I would return to the *Statesman* job – Crossman still kept the possibility open for me – or try to write a book. He took paper and pencil and made a list of pros and cons. We discussed them, then he said, 'I think you should write the book.' I agreed, and Deborah Rogers became my agent. She asked me to prepare a synopsis, which I managed over the next two months. I found a young American woman as a part-time helper with Tom, and made forays to the British Library, the Bodleian and the GLC archives, and a quick visit to the archives in Paris; but mostly I worked at home, using the resources of the London Library, with Tom beside me in his basket.

In the summer of 1972 Theresa McGinley came from Shropshire to be Tom's Nanny, and quickly seemed more like a fourth daughter in the family. I worked through that year and most of the next and finished writing the book in August 1973, just before Tom's third birthday. In September we all went to Brittany for a seaside holiday. Tom had a red trolley in which he wheeled himself about, our hotel was on the beach, Nick sailed, the sun shone and we swam and ate enormous French dinners, platters of prawns, steaks, salads, fruit, ice-cream. One day we had a picnic inland; we found a secluded meadow, and in the heat we all stripped off our tops. I have a vivid memory of thinking what an idyll it was, Nick with his little son, surrounded by bare-breasted wife, nanny and three lovely daughters.

A month later, Nick was killed by a heat-guided Syrian missile on the Golan Heights, where he was reporting on the Yom Kippur War. He was not quite forty-two. For his children and his parents the loss was irreparable. For his many friends and contemporaries it was a black moment, made worse when our fellow journalist Francis Hope died very soon afterwards in an air crash. Two of the brightest lights of our generation had been put out, reminding us all of our mortality. I grieved for Nick and still mourn his terrible death. I wish he were alive now, fulfilling his promise, lighting up the lives of so many who loved him. I should like him as a friend, even though our marriage, begun with such expectations, had gone so wrong. But if it hadn't, I might not have been pushed into finding the work I enjoyed; and without his encouragement I might not have written my first book.

The pieces on the next few pages are all taken from the period after I joined the *New Statesman* in 1968.

# Scott and Zelda

*Save Me the Waltz* by Zelda Fitzgerald

No publisher would have reprinted *Save Me the Waltz* if it were not the work of Scott Fitzgerald's wife, and can be read as a gloss on his marvellous novel of the same period, *Tender is the Night*. Her book appeared in 1932, his was planned earlier and published two years later. Neither was a success at the time.

Who wanted to read about the twenties during the Depression? 'A rather irritating type of chic' is what the *New Statesman* critic found in Scott's novel, which he had laboured at from 1925 to 1934, and continued to work on years later. *Tender is the Night* is, for all its flaws and carelessness, something like a great book, showing us very clearly the power of the artist to change particular personal experience into something utterly different; in the book, he is fair to all the characters and situations, as he couldn't be in life.

He himself was well aware of the fact and the cost of such artistry: he'd said to Zelda, when she began to train as a ballet dancer: 'I hope you realize that the biggest difference in the world is between the amateur and the professional in the arts,' and he showed some understandable bitterness when she sent Maxwell Perkins her novel without letting him see it first. Perkins was his editor, and *Save Me the Waltz* covered much of the same ground as what was already written and planned of his novel, which she'd seen. He wrote to Perkins: 'The mixture of fact and fiction is calculated to ruin us both, or what is left of us, and I can't let it stand.' It was indeed revised, more perhaps with an eye to content than to style. A year later, in 1933, Scott told a psychiatrist that Zelda believed anything was possible, and used his material like a mischievous little boy drawing on an artist's canvas, with no awareness of 'the enormous moral business that goes on in the mind of anyone who writes anything worth writing'.

What strikes one forcibly about *Save Me the Waltz* is that most of the best passages are not concerned with the life she lived with her husband. David Knight, the character who represents him – Scott made her change the name from Amory Blaine, hero of his *This Side of Paradise* – is indeed a nonentity, as Scott complained, adding that *he* had made Zelda a legend. But he continued for the rest of his life to contribute to that legend, portraying her with a passionate regret for the love they had once shared; the generosity is his, as she acknowledged after his death.

*Save Me the Waltz*, written in six weeks during a schizophrenic breakdown, is in form a fairly conventionally shaped story about a Southern girl, Alabama, youngest daughter of Judge Beggs, a rigid, old-fashioned and domineering father. Here is the South, the period (First World War), the excitable sensibility of a young girl with nothing to do but shock her small-town world, and with all the means when a thousand young men in uniform arrive to amuse her. She falls in love with a youthful painter, marries in New York, dances, plays pranks; they're famous, and c-r-a-z-y about each other. There are terrible bits of purple writing, but we see what Zelda wants us to see. Later, on board ship for Europe and describing the Riviera and Paris world, the book sags: there is a baby, there are flirtations, love sours. Alabama takes up ballet, drives herself beyond all normal limits in her frenzy to succeed; she falls ill, and returns to the States for the death of her father. On his deathbed she frantically questions him about the pain of life; it is too late, he cannot answer. 'Ask me something easy,' he murmurs, uncharacteristically.

It could be claimed that the theme of the book is the presence of Judge Beggs in his daughter's life; her dreams of escape, her revolt against his authority and traditions, the failure of her husband to provide an equivalent moral presence: all relate to him. Alabama suffered cruelly as one of a generation of girls uneducated for anything but marriage, precipitated into a world their parents could not have foreseen. Her turning to ballet, which consumed time and energy and even her body with its physical demands – she was too old to start, too proud not to go at it like a tigress – expresses perhaps a belated respect for her father's belief in hard work, integrity and moral imperatives.

In plot, *Save Me the Waltz* (the title refers not to romantic memories of Scott but to her ambitions in the ballet) is almost entirely autobiographical, and it is part of the evidence of her ability and arresting personality. That she was jealous of Scott's fame and talent she acknowledged; that she wrote the book partly out of that jealousy, partly (as she took up painting and dancing) out of loneliness caused less by his work than by his compulsive gregarious-ness and drinking – and partly to give *her* version – this is true.

She was, after all, still the same Zelda Sayre who had spent her last night in Alabama before her New York wedding lying awake and plotting with a friend ways to attract attention in New York, such as sliding down the banisters of the Biltmore; the same Zelda who'd inspired one of Scott's friends to write in his diary on first meeting her: 'Temperamental small town Southern belle. Chews gum – shows knees.' Exactly a year later he was writing: 'She is without doubt the most brilliant and most beautiful young woman I've ever known.'

She was both, but she became incurably (though not all the time) insane, and she and Scott drove one another to self-destruction. In her mad bouts she dwelt on his drinking, so that the doctors asked him to give it up as part of her cure, but he would not or could not; a fact Hemingway might have pondered before writing his malicious letter to Mizener in 1949 in which he suggested that Zelda drove Scott to drink out of jealousy of his work. But then Zelda had called Hemingway 'bogus'.

In *Tender is the Night* she appears as Nicole, also beautiful, mad and spoilt; curiously, Scott makes her experience literally the classic Freudian fantasy of rape by her fictional father. (Judge Sayre, it's worth noting, did not approve of Scott, calling him 'fella' with fine Southern scorn.) He attributes to a minor character, in a notable scene, the dreadful attack of eczema that was one of Zelda's symp-toms; and at the end, of course, he delivers Nicole, healed, to another man who embodies some of the qualities Fitzgerald himself would have liked to have had in relation to her, had he not been a writer.

Her book is a furious, brave and typical gesture, like a flawed piece of glass thrown glittering up into the air; his book is in no sense an attempt to work out his personal problems, but a marvellous using of those problems, his and hers. I'm very glad to have read *Save Me the Waltz*, but there's no doubt that it is in his art that she endures. 'Zelda and I were everything to each other – all human relationships. We were sister and brother, mother and son, father and daughter, husband and wife,' he said; he might have added, 'and Muse and artist'. As everyone knows, he died of drink; and she was burned to death later in a lunatic asylum.

*New Statesman*, 1969

# Newfoundland

*Words for a Deaf Daughter* by Paul West

A child with brain damage is one of the most intolerable gifts life can offer; to write a book celebrating such a child is a triumph of man's power not merely to accept and endure but to find order and beauty in whatever is. For this Paul West deserves all our thanks, since most of his readers must be potentially like the people who turn reprovingly away from his daughter Mandy in the street: 'they don't like a universe that's absurd'.

Confusion reigns in our minds; some mothers are chided by the authorities for failing to love and care for their subnormal children, others for morbid attachment to them. Some doctors persuade families to sacrifice one defective child to the 'good' of the rest by putting him in an institution. The Nazis killed them with a zeal that is not found altogether shocking by those who speak of the harsh demands of evolution. Rudolf Steiner schools, and projects such as the Camphill Village Communities for mentally handicapped adults, tell us that there are also people other than parents who are willing to devote their lives to scaling environment to these vulnerable members of the human race. Undoubtedly this is a test of civilization; but it is a hard test.

West and his wife began by loving their child, unaware of her handicaps and proud of her beauty; and they have continued to love her with what one guesses is a different kind of love from that given to her elder sister, who progresses into life away from them, but which has nothing sickly about it. 'We steal your condition (steal *into* it) by means of risky analogies, like the mystic borrowing the lover's terms.' 'Until I knew I had to bring the world to you, I don't think I knew or saw the world at all,' he says, allowing on the same page a tribute to his wife's role in ceaseless bottom-wiping and blotting up of pools. Mandy converts the entire house into her own 'pleasuredrome', strung with balloons, paper monsters dangling on drying Scotch tape, umbrellas – the paraphernalia we briefly allow our first two-year-old; and he watches her rather as those whose love for animals is both intense and intelligent watch and learn wisdom from them.

'Attentiveness for its own sake could well be what the mentally handicapped person has as his own special gift'; he mimics Mandy's with his own poet's attentiveness, and sees (and offers us) this different, surreal world. The absorption is of the kind new mothers and new lovers show; but, in Mandy's case, it must be unremitting. Special school relieves the parents and distracts her; but, as he sees, for her school is play; if she is to learn, it will be at home. She is his kingdom, safeliest when by one man mann'd.

He ponders her future, since the book is a letter addressed to her and not to us, for the day she may be able to read it. He speaks of the 'indefatigable effort' of teaching her words, but clearly he is brilliantly equipped to make the effort, such a parent as an absurd universe does well to offer such a child. He has written a hymn of hope, but he knows the dangers of her state: 'I want you to be anything but passive, but I also want you to survive'; 'you are living in a dark through which others shepherd you.'

Whether Mandy herself will ever progress from ecstatic listener while her father chants words from French bottle labels to reading this book remains in doubt. But he must for many of us succeed in enlarging our categories of what is bearable to dwell on, show us how some understanding and much love can grow from pain. He has made more things seem possible, and that is the true work of the poet.

*New Statesman, 1969*

# A Fallen Woman

Reappraisal: *Letters to Imlay* by Mary Wollstonecraft

Two o'clock – My dear love, after making my arrangements for our snug dinner today, I have been taken by storm, and obliged to promise to dine, at an early hour, with the Miss —s, the *only* day they had intended to pass here. I shall however leave the key in the door, and hope to find you at my fireside when I return, about eight o'clock. Will you not wait for poor Joan? – whom you will find better, and till then think very affectionately of her.

How many novels start as well as this? It is a love letter, written in a city in revolution, from an eminent bluestocking lady of thirty-four to a captain in the American army. The date is 1793, the town Paris, the woman Mary Wollstonecraft; for all her professed allegiance to Reason, her letters speak of spontaneity, warmth, clinging affection and a sensibility that make Marianne Dashwood seem a model of prudence and steadiness in comparison. As someone who has 'always been half in love' with J. J. Rousseau, Mary gives free rein to her feelings and her expression of them.

The letters are extraordinary; they describe, directly and fluently, the sensations and emotions of love and longing, and of pregnancy and motherhood, with a frankness not equalled again in England till the twentieth century. Mary possessed a melancholy temperament and her love affair was mostly a matter of separations and disappointments (hence the abundance of letters); but she could be spirited and happy, especially when talking of her baby or imagining good days ahead. Here and there she adopts a highflown manner, usually when she begins to preach to her errant lover; much more often she writes, as the best letter writers do, with the appearance of being off her guard: 'when my heart is warm, pop come the expressions of my childhood into my head'; 'I do not want to be loved like a goddess; but I wish to be necessary to you'; 'If you do not return soon . . . I will throw your slippers out at window, and be off –

nobody knows where.' Missing him, she 'makes the most of the comfort of the pillow', turning to the side of the bed where he lay. She meets friends who observe she is with child: 'let them stare! . . . all the world may know it for aught I care! – Yet I wish to avoid —'s coarse jokes.' She feels the 'little twitcher' move inside her, speculates whether it sleeps or wakes, grows anxious when it is still: 'I sat down in an agony till I felt those said twitches again.'

The letters tell their own story, but it is as well to fill in the background. Mary, fresh from the success of her *Vindication of the Rights of Woman*, but suffering from an unreciprocated passion for the artist Fuseli, decided to visit Paris in December 1792. The French admired her and at first she admired the revolution. Her circle included Tom Paine and the Helen Maria Williams to whom Wordsworth addressed a sonnet. In the spring of 1793 she met, at the house of an English friend, Gilbert Imlay, a native American who had fought in the War of Independence, written a still readable book on the topography of Kentucky and Ohio as well as an overblown novel, *The Emigrants*, aimed at reforming English divorce law and proclaiming the idyllic possibilities of life in the American wilderness. Imlay has been roughly handled by Mary's biographers for his treatment of her, but I find it impossible not to have some sympathy for him; clearly he got himself into a false position; he had neither the nature to settle into matrimony nor the strength of mind to break off the affair which seemed so sacred and binding to her. Probably he was bowled over by her fame, her charm and her unusual sexual forwardness; the wooing was very swift. An early meeting place was at the Neuilly toll-gate, known to them as the 'barrier' (*la barrière*); the child, conceived there, was often referred to as the 'barrier-girl' and Imlay's good moods as his 'barrier-face'.

They went through no marriage ceremony, but Mary registered herself with the American ambassador under the name Imlay (probably as a protection against imprisonment, to which English subjects became liable when war was declared). Both lovers at times referred to her as a wife, but Mary spoke cheerfully about not having 'clogged' her soul by promising obedience; their arrangement was of that semi-formal variety most difficult to manage smoothly. In spite of a grumble or two, she was delighted with her pregnancy, having strong theoretical views about maternity; but already Imlay was called away on business, the first of many separations that indicate the rapid cooling of his attachment.

At least they provided us with Mary's letters: her love, her reproaches, her self-chastisement for doubting him, her joy in the child. She followed Imlay to Le Havre, where Fanny was born in May 1794, under the care of an admiring midwife. 'Nothing could be more natural or easy than my labour,' she wrote to a woman friend. She was out walking eight days after the birth, and suckled her child: 'My little Girl begins to suck so Manfully that her father reckons saucily on her writing the second part of the R - - - ts of Woman.'

Soon Imlay was off again, and the story grows sadder and sadder as she travels with the baby to Paris, London, and then, on Imlay's business, to Scandinavia. His infidelities drove her to desperation and she twice projected suicide, the second time saturating her clothes before walking into the Thames (Mirah's method in *Daniel Deronda*; Charles Kegan Paul suggested that George Eliot was inspired by Mary). She was rescued by friends and Imlay tried to behave 'kindly' towards her; but kindness, when one looks for love, is the worst torture:

> I never wanted but your heart – That gone, you have nothing more to give. Had I only poverty to fear, I should not shrink from life. – Forgive me then, if I say, that I shall consider any direct or indirect attempt to supply my necessities, as an insult which I have not merited.
>
> I have been hurt by indirect inquiries, which appear to me not to be dictated by any tenderness to me. – You ask 'If I am well or tranquil' – They who think me so, must want a heart to estimate my feelings by.

But Mary's behaviour could be trying; on one occasion she rushed into a room where Imlay was sitting with some friends and thrust the two-year-old Fanny on to his lap. This was typical of one aspect of her – the impulsive, dramatizing side – but equally she knew how to pull herself together again. The most important and affecting aspect of the letters is their picture of a woman refusing to accept that she is 'ruined', a resourceless victim of seduction and abandonment; she goes down into the depths of misery again and again, but repeatedly determines to be rational and independent, to learn to cope with her situation both emotionally and financially and to give up her lover, in the end, without bitterness or demands. It was not easy for her, jealous, passionate, agonized for her child: 'my little darling is calling papa, and adding her parrot word – Come, come!' There is something heroic in her final words to Imlay: 'I part with you in peace.'

The story of the publication of the letters provides a tragi-comic epilogue. Few love letters survive, and those that do generally remain unpublished for decades; but Imlay preserved these and returned them at Mary's request. In 1797 she married William Godwin and died within a few months in childbirth; whereupon this odd man, as an act of devoted homage, published her impassioned letters to her former lover. Deeply mistrustful of violent emotion at first hand, he seems to have been fascinated by the evidence of it at one remove; at any rate, though he tried to calm the Wollstonecraft temperament in Mary and later her daughters (Fanny and Mary, who married Shelley), he greatly admired it in her words to another man. Perhaps he felt safer thus. His preface begins: 'The following letters may possibly be found to contain the finest examples of the language of sentiment and passion ever presented to the world.'

Godwin's action in publishing them called down the satirical contempt of his opponents. Even Mary's supporters thought he had done her a disservice; an anonymous defender writing in 1803 attacked Godwin for his failure to protect her reputation by silence about her personal life. He was probably right; the eclipse of Mary Wollstonecraft in the nineteenth century can be partly attributed to Godwin's revelations, which shocked middle and upper classes alike: a revolutionary thinker and unchaste to boot!

Godwin expunged Imlay's name from his edition, but it was generally known; he was ill regarded and disappeared from the scene, never (as far as we know) taking any interest in Fanny; he is thought to have died in Jersey in 1828. Fanny was kindly brought up by Godwin; her stepsisters Mary and Claire Clairmont were lively girls, but she was melancholic and committed suicide, alone in a Swansea inn to which she had travelled for the purpose, in October 1816; a sadly effective repetition of her mother's efforts.

Mary's letters were reprinted in 1879 by Charles Kegan Paul and again in 1908 by Roger Ingpen. Both editors felt obliged to explain away and apologize for some of her behaviour and freedom of speech, and Ingpen quaintly dismissed Imlay as a 'typical American', always dashing about on business. The only good modern biography is a long and meticulously scholarly one by another American, Ralph Wardle. Mary Wollstonecraft is not much known in this age when we are able to be more understanding of her behaviour and also of her lover's. Perhaps it is time for a new edition of her letters.

*New Statesman*, 1971

# The Wife's Story

## Katherine Mansfield: The Memories of LM

> All manuscripts notebooks papers letters I leave to John M. Murry likewise I should like him to publish as little as possible and tear up and burn as much as possible he will understand that I desire to leave as few traces of my camping ground as possible.

In spite of this morsel of Katherine Mansfield's will, John Middleton Murry published every scrap he could find, and her tigerish desire for privacy was sacrificed to please a public avid to sift through her secrets. But who can blame him? She was a genius, of the kind who provokes both worthy and unworthy curiosity, both the prurient wish to hear of the ill health and sexual practices of the mighty, and the abiding and educative human craving to try to enter into the minds of those we admire, to become them for a space (and I suspect the two kinds of curiosity are inextricably blended). What fury fills us when we think of the pious executors and grandchildren who burn letters and memoirs to protect the good name of the dead.

Ida Constance Baker (otherwise known as LM, Leslie, the Mountain or Jones) who, at the age of eighty-three, has written a full account of her long friendship with Katherine Mansfield, confesses that she was very angry with Murry at one time for publishing all KM's private, personal papers. But now she has forgiven him; her own relationship is described quietly, her own treasured letters – those Katherine had not made her burn – printed at last.

We must be very grateful to her. Here is a valuable supplement to the two biographies (Mantz, 1933 and Alpers, 1954) and to the journal and letters. As well as many hitherto unpublished letters, it contains extra information about the early years in London between 1908 – the time of her second arrival in Europe – and 1912, when she met Murry. This was the period of hectic and impoverished *vie de bohème*, and Katherine destroyed her own journal recording her love affairs, first marriage, pregnancies and abortions; on this last topic she was silent even to LM. Another particular source of interest is the multitude of glimpses into the daily domestic routines that were crucial to her health and work later, and in which Miss Baker played so important and generous a part.

Early in their friendship, which started at Queen's College, Harley Street, in 1903, LM dedicated herself to the service of Katherine, perceiving, although there was never much intellectual rapport, that she was an exceptional person and soon realizing that she needed the sort of help that could come only from a friend who put no value on her own affairs or time. Throughout Katherine's life LM came when she was summoned and disappeared again (sometimes reluctantly) when dismissed, gave up her jobs, took on domestic work that was totally uncongenial and endured scoldings and ridicule. She was mocked to her face and cruelly dealt with in letters, the journal and even stories. Why did she endure it?

Obviously she loved Katherine passionately, and the relationship was more complex than a simple served and serving one; KM felt that LM was too emotionally dependent on her, hence the 'incubus' accusation; but she was dependent too, and could be jealous: 'I only love you when you're blind to everybody but us.' To say that it was a lesbian attachment does not explain much; LM points out that Katherine's first husband considered that this was the cause of the break-up of the marriage, and mentions that she did not even know what lesbianism was at that time. K's mother thought the friendship 'unwise' too, in a euphemism familiar to anyone who has been at a girls' school; in fact Katherine was pregnant by another man when she married. Katherine herself certainly knew what lesbianism was, as her journal makes clear, and was capable of flirting with either sex, but she was never in love with LM in the way she was with Murry or Francis Carco; only she enjoyed her power of attracting and enslaving, and then felt guilty and irritated by the humble, fussy adoration.

Ida Baker ascribes most of Katherine's bad temper to illness, and understandably stresses the positive aspect of the friendship, which emerges in her letters rather than in the journal. These letters, inconsistent, bossy, sweet, furious or cajoling, shine with the light of Katherine's sensibility; outside the letters, the narrative sometimes creates the impression of a Katherine reverently shrouded in a butter muslin of conventional phrases. It is an all-passion-spent exercise, taking no account of passages in the journal that described hostilities or extremities of emotion between the two women, referred to as toothache by Katherine. There was for instance a scene in March 1914 when Katherine, coming out of Murry's room, found LM with her 'poor face all stained and patched with crying' beside the fire, and tucked her up and kissed her with 'quick loving kisses such as one delights to give a tired child'. '"Oh," she breathed, when I asked her if she was comfortable. "This is Paradise, beloved."' A paragraph later, Katherine is lamenting her inability to enchant Murry.

This pendulum swinging between the elusive Murry who could not look after Katherine and the utterly devoted LM continued till the last few weeks of K's life, when she withdrew from both. Until then the situation was this: Murry was quite incapable of nursing Katherine, making practical arrangements for her comfort – she was usually in pain and always weak – or even of loving her enough. LM alone would nurse and love and dust and light fires and shop and sew on buttons and bring the breakfast tray and the lunch tray and run after her with jackets that K childishly flung down. There is no doubt that she, with her genius and her illness, needed a 'wife' as well as a husband. And LM was that wife as truly as Murry was her husband; a wife whose protective instincts often maddened K into rage, but to whom she wrote in June 1922: 'try and believe and keep on believing without signs from me that I do love you and want you for my wife'. Without her Katherine Mansfield would not have been able to write even what she did.

Koteliansky called LM Katherine's 'sole and only friend'; in a sense she allowed Katherine to live the two lives – though both were brief – that a woman who burns with a desire to work and to love needs. In allowing us to trace the course of this extraordinary friendship from adolescent enthusiasm through many trials and quarrels to the final mutual acceptance, Ida Baker has continued her service to her friend.

*New Statesman*, 1971

# La Belle Dame Sans Merci

*You Might as Well Live: The Life and Times of*
*Dorothy Parker* by John Keats
*A Month of Saturdays* by Dorothy Parker
introduced by Lillian Hellman

How do you like your Dorothy Parker? Straight from the page, all staccato typewriter jokes, or in a biographical mausoleum encrusted with psychological interpretation and two large photographs of the big, beautiful, brown, short-sighted eyes? Students of the macabre will go unerringly for John Keats's *You Might as Well Live*. Many of her words are entombed within, but her spirit puts in more appearances in *A Month of Saturdays*, a collection of her *New Yorker* reviews of the twenties and thirties, with an introduction by Lillian Hellman and Al Hirschfeld's perfect drawing on the jacket. There she sits with her drink and rueful smile, meditating some piece of character assassination, probably on herself. In fourteen pages Lillian Hellman tells us about the self-contempt, the bad taste in men, the deterioration when drink made her dull and repetitive, the entirely theoretical socialism, the habit of embracing and denouncing, the crazy way with money, and of course the delicate, clear wit which 'usually came after a silence, and started in the middle'.

Style and wit are rare and precious, and very difficult to bring alive in biography. Turn to the reviews: although there are traces of self-indulgent padding and repetition (her spoken jokes she never repeated, surely a unique piece of restraint), the level of both humour and judgement is high indeed. She puts across the agony of sitting at the typewriter with this dreadful book to review, the desperation that makes the reviewer clown and pun; and conducts imaginary exchanges with those friends who share her tastes and standards and expect her to be ruthless in adhering to them.

Nearly all the books she had to review were terrible, but that is the lot of reviewers; perhaps she commanded more choice than most. She deserved to: *Appendicitis* by Thew Wright AB, MD,

FACS, elicited what was for her a long piece: 'when I saw that it started "Let us divide the abdominal cavity into four parts by means of four imaginary lines," I could only murmur, "Ah, let's don't."' Her favourite illustration was 'Vertical section of the Peritoneum' – 'It has strength, simplicity, delicacy, pity, and irony.' And the reproduction of bacteria inspires her to:

> Think of it – no quarrels, no lies, no importunate telegrams, no unanswered letters ... and, at the end of twenty-four hours, 16,772,216 children to comfort them in their old age ... I wish, I wish I were a poisonous bacterium.

Another time she apologizes for having fallen into reviewer's superlatives. She had been praising Hemingway in phrases such as 'the greatest living writer of short stories', and a kindly reader wrote to draw her attention to the still living Max Beerbohm and Rudyard Kipling. Parker climbed down with infinite grace, ending with the whispered emendation: 'Ernest Hemingway is, to me, a good writer' – a phrase we reviewers might well hang in pokerwork above our desks.

Equally memorable is her encounter with Emily Post over the matter of etiquette, culminating in her flat refusal to adopt the safe conversational topics recommended in the guide:

> I may not dispute with Mrs Post. If she says that is the way you should talk, then, indubitably, that is the way you should talk. But though it be at the cost of future social success I am counting on, there is no force great enough ever to make me say, 'I'm thinking of buying a radio.'

Social success was not a problem for Dorothy Parker, at any time in her life till the last years, when, according to Keats, her few living friends grew understandably apprehensive about calling on her in her hotel room where she might be found crouching on a rug littered with bottles and dog faeces, muttering 'You're Jew-Fascists. Get out of here.' Those who spend their emotional capital faster than the common rate often make sordid ends: Beau Brummell, Wilde, Scott

Fitzgerald. Keats gives us the good years too, when she was queen of the Algonquin wits (sometimes known as the Vicious Circle), an intellectual meritocracy who asked no questions about backgrounds, enjoyed the courting of the rich, drank and whored, and held no morning-after post-mortems; but on the whole his book reads like every mother's nightmare about what you don't want to happen to your daughter.

Keats has worked very hard, asked a lot of questions and compiled a long list of facts about Dorothy Parker; probably more industry has gone into the making of his book than its subject put into her entire *œuvre* (her husband Alan Campbell once left her to work for an afternoon and placed a hair on the typewriter keys; when he returned it was still there). No pains are spared. We are given the intellectual background:

> Darwin's theory of evolution had been brought to public attention, leading some people to question the authority of the Bible and even the existence of God. Such talk would have been both exciting and comforting to young Dorothy . . .

and the medical background:

> . . . as the *Merck Manual of Diagnosis and Therapy* says: 'Modern studies indicate that, with few exceptions, only individuals with serious personality maladjustments become chronic alcoholics.'

And Montaigne is called in for comment on whether her personality was changed by the abortion and miscarriage episodes.

And yes, a picture does emerge, of a little woman shaped like a beehive with appalling taste in clothes and interior decoration, who liked knitting and wouldn't wear glasses, accepted money and foreign trips from men she despised; whose ambivalent feelings towards her Jewish father and Christian stepmother warped her nature into a ferocious distrust of her own affections and achievements; who tried to live like one of the boys and celebrated her partial success in verses that read like A. E. Housman with wisecracks; who earned and spent a fortune in Hollywood during the Depression and joined in some curious parlour pink antics; and who was rather improbably married (on and off) for nearly thirty years to a much younger and probably bisexual man. We are indebted to Keats for his labours, and for anyone interested in the cultural history of the period his book is obligatory reading. But it's a mercy Dorothy Parker is not alive to review it, because he has succeeded in what one would have thought impossible: he has very nearly turned her into a bore.

*New Statesman*, 1971

# PART TWO

# LITERARY EDITOR

At the *New Statesman*, Tony Howard had taken over as editor from Crossman in 1972. John Gross was his literary editor but he was about to move on to edit *The Times Literary Supplement*, and before the end of 1973 Tony and John approached me with the suggestion that I might follow him as literary editor. Tony, with characteristic kindness, insisted that it would be altogether better for me to have a demanding job than to stay at home. John, over coffee at the Holborn Kardomah, gave me a powerful account of the satisfactions to be found from editing: not the same as writing a book, perhaps, but serious and even exciting work, competing each week to make your pages the best. I didn't need much persuading.

Tom was due to have an operation at Great Ormond Street early in the year. Jo, my eldest daughter, had just won a scholarship to Cambridge to read mathematics, and her sisters were both doing well at school. Theresa generously assured me that she would stay with us until Tom was five. Nick's mother came to help care for Tom while he was in plaster after his operation, and Great Ormond Street was blessedly close to Great Turnstile.

So I took the job at the *Statesman* and started work in January. Years later, Jo told me this was the time I became recognizably the person I am now. I had to appear confident, at any rate, and the pace of work was such that I was carried on too fast to worry much. I was happy to inherit the best established contributors, but I wanted to make something new, and I looked for younger writers. Paul Theroux wrote in my first issue and Clive James gave me a fine Byronic 'Epistle to John Fuller' as its lead. Other early contributors were Shiva Naipaul, Jonathan Raban, Alison Lurie, Alan Ryan, Julian Mitchell, Hilary Spurling, Neal Ascherson, Marina Warner and Victoria Glendinning. Timothy Mo was my deputy for a while; he left to write full time, becoming deservedly successful as a novelist. Craig Raine reminded me recently that I told him, 'I'm going to make you famous,' and burst into peals of laughter. What was that about? Craig was a serious reviewer, I was serious about making good pages, but I had to joke about it too. It was like crossing your fingers for luck; and I knew he didn't need me to make him famous.

I wanted the book pages to have a critical edge, to be sharp without being portentous. The back half of the *Statesman* was traditionally apolitical, and I took it that my job was to engage as seriously with literature as the front of the paper did with politics. Best to be witty while you were about it if you could, but it was not a frivolous activity, being a reviewer. One critic who asked to review a particular book turned in a piece which proved he had not read it through, and I never gave him work again.

Being able to print poetry was one of the best parts of the job. I wrote to poets I admired for their work – Larkin, D. J. Enright, Derek Mahon, Gavin Ewart, Hugo Williams were some of them. John Fuller's 'Wild Raspberries' is a poem I remember admiring when it came in; seeing it again in his *Collected Poems* recently, it struck me again how good it is. In 1974 there was a *New Statesman* Prize I judged with Victor Pritchett, which we gave unhesitatingly to Derek Walcott for his long narrative poem *Another Life*.

Martin Amis was a contributor and then my assistant. His first novel made me laugh with pleasure at its high spirits, and because he had that rare thing, a voice of his own, not borrowed from anyone else. His speech was unmistakable too, the deep smoker's voice coming as a surprise from his slight frame. He had the presence of a star already. Sure of himself and sure of his taste, he was rude about what he didn't admire, as assured as the most arrogant young Oxbridge don. He could have taught English at Oxford too, if he hadn't been a writer, and found his territory and subject in the rich mix of London.

I'd never seen anyone's hands shake in the morning as Martin's did. He rolled his own cigarettes out of a neat tin. He also turned in his reviews scrupulously finished on time. And he was an acute sub of other people's copy. Run it once more through the typewriter, he would say, if he didn't quite like what he read. We still used typewriters then, the kind you had to hit hard. Martin was unfailingly good humoured, and, if he was not the smoothest or wittiest of that circle, I had no doubt he was the cleverest person I could hope to work with. And the most competitive. They could be a fierce bunch, Clive James, Ian Hamilton, Craig Raine, Martin Amis, James Fenton, Chris Hitchens, and I sometimes felt I was surrounded by a band of pugnacious younger brothers, charming, extraordinary, intellectual elbows out. They were intent on success, as novelists, poets, critics, political journalists or television performers. They glittered with ambition. I've enjoyed watching them all shine ever since.

Soon Julian Barnes joined this formidable nursery, every bit as clever, a shade less fierce in manner. When he turned up to be interviewed for a job with the *NS* he announced he liked the sound of the idle life we lived, up late, three-hour lunches, off early to the wine bar, he'd heard. His cool humour made him into one of the paper's star writers, with an adoring following.

I made friends with other writers. One was Jim Farrell, who won the 1973 Booker Prize for his odd, marvellous novel, *The Siege of Krishnapur*. He told me he'd been born a rugger player and trans-formed into a writer by polio, and he was full of contradictions, half worldly, with his flat in Egerton Gardens where we perched on piles of books to drink exquisite wine, and half innocent. He cherished a dream of a pastoral life and regretted that I was not a shepherdess rather than a literary editor. But none of his many devoted friends was in the least bucolic; we were all sorrowful when he retreated to Ireland, and grief-stricken when he died a cruel death there, falling from rocks while fishing.

Jim and I were both friends of Alison Lurie, who arrived every June from the States, armed with needle-sharp curiosity about the way we lived in London, and as kind in person as she was astringent in her novels. Then there was Paul Theroux, with whom I sometimes rambled round London, while he told me about his ambitions – he called me his boastee – taking in everything with his insatiable writer's eye as we talked. One day, boating on Regent's Park lake, he asked me to name the different species of ducks, and was shocked that I couldn't. In my own country, he said, I should know them all. I think he learnt them then and there, and could probably still give their names.

While I was at the *Statesman* my book on Mary Wollstonecraft was published. It caught the feminist wave, attracted a lot of reviews and attention, and won a prize; even the film rights were sold. I found myself broadcasting, judging prizes, serving on committees, writing a script about Virginia Woolf for German television, travelling as a cultural delegate to the Soviet Union, and altogether in danger of taking on so much 'literary' activity that it left no time to get on with writing more books.

So I left the *Statesman* in 1977, intending to concentrate wholly on writing. It was a bad decision. I was very happy on the paper, working with people I admired and liked; the bustle of office life was congenial to me, and I especially enjoyed being able to try out new talents. Once I had left, I realized what a mistake I had made. And within two years, in which I managed to finish a short book on Shelley, researched and set aside another on Katherine Mansfield, gave up a project on 'Mark Rutherford', and had an anthology turned down as too gloomy, I put in for the job of literary editor at *The Times*. After an interview I was summoned to the *Sunday Times* by Harold Evans and offered the job there instead. It was an amazing moment for me.

The drawback to the literary editorship at the *Sunday Times* was that the paper was going through industrial troubles, and I started work in the autumn of 1979 in an extremely confused situation. At home things were also difficult, and worse than difficult. One of my daughters was struck by an illness which ran a grim course for a year and led to her death. Work became my refuge. Work and death are at opposite ends of the spectrum, and working as an editor puts constant demands that fill the mind; you have to plan ahead, argue with colleagues, make decisions. I found something consoling in the perpetual batches of books coming into the office to be sorted, sent out, discarded. I worked late every day at the *Sunday Times*, bicycling to and from the office through the Camden and Bloomsbury streets, pleased to be alone and inaccessible to everyone, the traffic like a rough sea to be breasted. I would get home and go straight into the kitchen to make dinner for my schoolboy son and his current helper. The girls went, Jo to teach in Mozambique, Emily to read engineering at Warwick and then to work as an engineer. My mother was descending into dementia, and I had to make hard choices and arrangements for her. The next years were full of the deaths of old and young.

But work went on. At the *Sunday Times* the balance between the cultural part of the paper and the rest was very different from the *New Statesman*'s half politics, half books and arts. Culture was a small enclave in a very large product which went out to millions; the *Statesman* sold only in the ten thousands. Yet the *Sunday Times* had always taken critics from the *Statesman*. Raymond Mortimer and Desmond Shawe-Taylor were still writing for the *Sunday Times* when I joined, John Carey had been spotted in the pages of the *Statesman* by Harold Evans and put under contract, Julian Barnes came to the paper as my assistant, and I signed up Paul Theroux, Ian Hamilton, Marina Warner and Victoria Glendinning to write regularly. This was good. At the same time the relative standing of the books pages within the paper was much lower than in the *Statesman*. I was told by one colleague that I was not a 'proper journalist' but a dilettante. The proper journalists were inclined to see us as peripheral, and too keen on filling our columns with long grey paragraphs of *words*. I became fierce in defence of words, critics and intellectual values during my years in the Gray's Inn Road.

There were few problems of this kind as long as Harry Evans was there. Working under him was like being at the court of Louis XIV. When he beamed his attention fully on any one of us, we were all, men and women, a little in love with him. 'Let's make these headlines a bit sexier,' he would say, coming into the literary department on Thursday afternoon and putting his arms round us. We wanted to please him. If he liked a review, he took the trouble to write to the contributor, and to make him feel as if he were part of the family. Not many editors do this. Harry was loved, even if we sometimes swore at him when his attention was distracted or his favours divided.

I had no fights with Harry, who upheld my view that the book pages should represent the best in critical judgement. I got on with Frank Giles too, who followed him as editor. I remember only one argument with him, after I had asked John Carey to review the three election manifestos in 1982. Frank objected strongly on the grounds that the book pages should not be political. I wanted the manifestos judged for their literary quality, I explained. Hugo Young supported me in conference, and Frank allowed me to go ahead. Carey judged the Conservative manifesto the best written, not too surprisingly, since it was the work of Ferdinand Mount.

I planned issues as far ahead as I could, aiming to have at least one review to catch readers who normally ignored book pages. There was a short golden period when John Carey and the historian John Vincent alternated in the lead from week to week. Both were natural journalists with lethal powers of attack. They did not go for the kill every week – in fact they probably praised more often – but they were renowned for their savagery. From them I learnt the appeal of blood sports. I used to whoop with joy over their copy.

With Andrew Neil's arrival as editor in 1983 things did not improve in the literary department. He wanted to sack John Mortimer (too left wing) and Marina Warner (too highbrow). At the same time he was obsessed with the idea that books should be reviewed by famous names, cabinet ministers and celebrities. There *are* politicians who write well – Jenkins, Foot, Powell among them – but they are few. One minister wished on me did not understand the difference between reviewing and handing out the party line. Another politician sent in copy written by his secretary. Celebrities understandably think their name is what matters, not how they write. Neil and I battled over this throughout my time with him. I said the *Sunday Times* could *make* names famous by using good writers and showing we were proud of them; but I could never persuade him to feature book page names at the front of the paper, or in advertisements, as the *Observer* did.

Neil suggested I should try to get Anthony Burgess to write for the *Sunday Times*. I said I admired his reviews in the *Observer*: presumably we would be offering him more money than our rival paper? No, no, I was told, we couldn't afford to pay more. Why didn't I just fly to the south of France, take Burgess out to dinner, and persuade him to write for us? As a plan, it seemed to lack something, and I let it fade away. Conversely, I failed in my attempt to sack Woodrow Wyatt, who was under contract when I joined the paper. He arrived at what was meant to be the fatal lunch looking woebegone, and when I told him I wanted to end his contract, he became pathetic. Could he not stay on and write just the occasional piece? Then he launched into an account of his early days in the Labour Party and in India. On these topics he was entertaining. I found myself agreeing he might continue. Although I gave him very little work, I came to like him, and I realized he could have tried to intimidate me by telling me he was a close friend of Murdoch. But he hadn't said a word.

I cherish the memory of another lunch, with Charles Monteith of Faber & Faber. Literary editors were invited regularly by the heads of major publishing firms to these ritual treats. The procedure was to concentrate on food and wine until about halfway through the main course, when the publisher would draw out his new catalogue and take you through it. Some praised every book, the more sophistic-ated passed over a few, saving their best effects for favourite titles. On this occasion Charles turned the pages slowly and thoughtfully. Fiction, general, biography, poetry passed by as I sat poised to listen, sole half consumed in front of me. At last he spoke, more memorably than any publisher I have ever lunched with. 'I'm afraid . . . I don't think there's *anything* interesting at all in our spring list, Claire.' I wanted to hug him.

Neil regularly spoke of book publishing as a sunset industry. I argued that books fuelled and nourished other industries, films and television. Another row we had was about the best-seller lists. One day I was formally instructed that they must be printed right across the top of the book pages. I said I was not prepared to do this. The book pages did not serve the best-seller list, they put forward an alternative view of what might interest our readers. The deputy editor, Ivan Fallon, was sent to make me comply. We were locked in battle when Victoria Glendinning came in to the office with her review. I turned to her and asked her how she would respond to book pages laid out as suggested, with the reviews appearing below the best-seller lists. For one second she hesitated, then, 'Ridiculous', she said. Ivan Fallon turned tail before these two Furies, and the idea was not raised again.

Neil and I had another fight over a review by Hugh Brogan of a book critical of US policy in Guatemala. As editor, he had every right to order out a review, but I fought him on this too, and it appeared with only a few words changed. Neil became so suspicious of my way of doing things – reviewing the wrong books, sending books to the wrong reviewers, giving space to books he did not approve of, overlooking ones he did – that he announced he was going to have a computer print-out of all book titles as they came in. He and Fallon would go through them and send down instructions. I agreed cheerfully, because I suspected he had no idea of how many books came through our department every week. I did ask him if he had thought of consulting the *Bookseller* or the publishers' lists, but he insisted it must be the computer. The system was put into action at once. A young woman came to our department each week to list the hundreds of titles by hand; she then transferred them to a computer and finally produced print-outs. It was a very large task, even though by the time she got to the shelves most of the important books had already been sent out to reviewers. A forest's worth of paper was churned out, but no instructions based on the print-out ever came down from the editor or his deputy, and after a while the system lapsed.

One day Rupert Murdoch appeared on the stone with Neil, who was heard complaining about the highbrow tendency of the book pages. 'Leave the book pages alone,' said Murdoch. 'Nobody reads them anyway.' I decided I would take this as an expression of support from our proprietor.

I stayed with the *Sunday Times* until 1986, but I never enjoyed it as much as the *Statesman*. I cherished my contributors, Anita Brookner, John Keegan, David Lodge, Peter Ackroyd, George Melly, Adam Mars-Jones, Jonathan Raban, Anthony Storr and Christopher Ricks among others. When Julian left, John Ryle came as my assistant. Neil's suspicion of another highbrow – John came from the *TLS* – was allayed when he learnt that he was ghosting Mick Jagger's memoirs. Here at last was someone on the books pages who lived in the real world. And when the real world beckoned John away in 1984, Sean French, who was already contributing and advising us on young writers, took over. My view was that it was best to have a deputy cleverer than you are, and I kept up the tradition to the end.

\*

As literary editor, I had to cover the Booker Prize each year, and in my first year at the *Sunday Times* I was a judge. Margaret Forster, Ronald Blythe and Brian Wenham were my fellow judges, David Daiches our chairman. I was determined that Alice Munro's *The Beggar Maid* should be on the short-list. I didn't expect it to win, but I knew it should be there. So I dug in my heels, and after some hard bargaining it went on. (Fifteen years later she won the W. H. Smith Prize, to my joy.) But the big contenders for the Booker in 1980 were, by general consent, Anthony Burgess's *Earthly Powers*, a huge, ungainly, careless book full of life and energy; and William Golding's *Rites of Passage*, a finely constructed work by an established master, but with something slightly stale about it – I even wondered whether he had written it some years earlier and left it in a drawer. The night before our final meeting I lay awake telling myself I must decide between these two. But in the morning Daiches began by dismissing the Burgess book as one that needed no further consideration – it simply wouldn't do. I then made a pitch for it, for its range and vitality, for the way Burgess applied his imagination to the world we were living in, for his heroic powers to entertain. At the end of my speech I saw that not one of my fellow judges agreed with me. Seeing that Burgess was out, knowing that the other judges had only just consented to Munro being on the short list, I gave my vote to Golding.

While we were talking, we were brought a message from Burgess to say he would come to the dinner only if he had won. I felt sympathy for him. There is something brutal in making writers into circus performers for the media. Better for short-listed writers to be told in advance, whatever the public's appetite for watching humiliation, disappointment or triumph. When the announcement was made that year, I saw a tear on Golding's cheek. It should have been a private tear.

While I was at the *Sunday Times* the job of editor of the *TLS* came up. Once again, John Gross was leaving, to go to the *New York Times*. I was encouraged to apply for the editorship, and was short-listed. But I was in two minds about it. It would have been a great thing to be the first woman editor of the *TLS*, and I thought I could do the job. What made me hesitate was the knowledge that if I took it on, the commitment would be so big and the work so demanding that I would have no time or energy left to give my son. He was already fatherless, and still a small boy. I had thought it better for him to have a working mother than one perpetually absorbed in him and his problems, but there was a difference between being a literary editor and editing the *TLS*. I judged it would take me two years to feel on top of that job, and I hesitated.

Any crack in your ambition will be apparent when you are interviewed for a job. There were in any case other excellent candidates – Jeremy Treglown, who got it, was admirably qualified – but I think my own uncertainty about whether I really wanted it helped to rule me out. When I was told, I felt relief, but also guilt, because I had not pursued the prize with all flags flying, full steam ahead. And I had lost it for my sex as well as for myself. I still can't decide whether I was right or wrong.

# Out of Africa

### *The Black House* by Paul Theroux

It takes courage for a writer to abandon a tone of voice which he has mastered and to attempt something completely different; but it is the sort of courage a serious writer needs. Paul Theroux started publishing novels in 1967 and has produced a series of brilliant and much praised books each of which, though more than funny, was without doubt very funny indeed. *The Black House* marks a departure from this series: any jokes lurking in the narrative are of a depressed and bitter kind, jokes involving disappointment, betrayal of friends, disgust with the way things are. This may be partly because the hero is neither a young man nor even – as Theroux's last hero, 'Saint Jack', was – a middle-aged man able to comfort himself with fantasy. Sickness, sourness and despair afflict Alfred Munday, an anthropologist forced into early retirement away from a sunny African location and 'his' people, the Bwamba, into the damp Dorset village his wife Emma has hankered after.

In part, then, it is a novel about the expatriate condition, a condition Theroux is in a good position to explicate; he has lived and set novels in Africa and Singapore since leaving his native America, and is now himself settled in England. He has to an unusual degree the qualities a travelling writer needs if he is to be more than a travel writer: he can soak up atmosphere as quickly and thoroughly as a sponge, and he does not intrude his own personality. His English village, its flora and fauna, topography and moods, indoor and out, are here as sharply outlined as any of his earlier exotic settings. Anyone who has been an interloper in an English village – and it's the commonest way of experiencing country life today – will recognize the accuracy of the descriptions. Pleasure has to be found in cold, rain and early darkness ('it never gets this dark in London', as one baffled visitor points out); there is a good deal of slyness, social unease, bonhomie that cracks quickly. Munday's views on Africa, delivered at the village hall, do not help him along any more than his bad temper when he is baited at the pub by the villagers or condescended to by the squire over sherry.

Two episodes touch on expatriate torments with particular acuteness. In one, Munday takes the umbilical train to London for the day and meets first with an old tea-planter friend who cannot disguise the misery of his present life, reduced to incompetent English whores, macaroni cheese in pubs, bus-catching and evenings of television in Ealing – he, who had once bossed hundreds. Later on in the same day Munday takes tea with an old flame whose only asset now is her pretty daughter; left alone over the fruitcake with this schoolgirl for a moment, Munday politely asks her how she likes London, and the child answers laconically, 'Mummy fucks my friends.' He is shocked, as we are. Mummy returns to assure him that marriages are broken by the strain of English life after the ease of post-colonial society.

Munday and Emma, however, have the innocent mutual dependence of certain childless couples. They don't feel that strain consciously. In parental mood, they invite down a Bwamba friend Munday had helped (and studied) from his boyhood; Emma is maternal, but Munday finds himself no longer able to like the younger man, aware of the villagers' suspicions of a black and unable to tolerate him outside his natural setting. One of the best things in the book is the cross-country walk on which Munday cruelly drags his friend in his thin shoes.

'I sometimes feel I could have discovered all I needed to know about isolation and perhaps even tribalism right here . . . and witchcraft of a sort,' says Munday at one point; the parallel between the African village community and the English one is never far from his mind. And in fact he is caught up in some English witchcraft, a haunting providing the other strand to the plot. Sinister and erotic, this is the most technically adventurous part of the narrative, and it put me in mind of a Henry James ghost story; only there the sexual element is never allowed to surface, whereas here it is not only explicit but insistent.

There is a tremor of uncertainty at the end of the book. Munday reaches some resolution whose value is not quite made clear; and he himself grows shadowy, more possessed by his ghost than in possession of himself. But then the book is about a man panicked by doubts about just where he and other creatures do belong. The degree of skill with which Theroux handles these various themes and the level mastery of his writing have produced a novel of unusual scope and promise still more for the future.

*New Statesman,* 1974

# Anger and Accommodation

*Seduction and Betrayal* by Elizabeth Hardwick
*Reader, I Married Him* by Patricia Beer

There is a scene early in *Tess of the D'Urbervilles* when Tess's mother chides her for having failed to hold out for marriage with Alec D'Urberville. Tess cries out: 'O mother, my mother! . . . How could I be expected to know? . . . Ladies know what to fend hands against, because they read novels that tell them of these tricks; but I never had the chance of learning that way.'

Tess herself could scarcely have known about the novels read by ladies and the lessons learnt from them; the remark is really Hardy's own, and he puts it here to point the difference between the innocent, untutored heroine of his tragedy and the type of woman he perhaps expected to be reading her story: a woman who had learnt, partly through novels, the importance of accommodating her instincts to the smooth running of society. For nineteenth-century women readers certainly did look to fiction for models and warnings and patterns of behaviour, and few writers failed to apply themselves with particular care to the problem of the feminine model. It was known to be in a state of crisis. Questions of innocence and anger, of sexual guilt, of frustration and adjustment to the existing social framework, are raised regularly from Fanny Burney and Jane Austen on. It is especially interesting to see that, whereas the nineteenth century opened with a deliberate, careful and successful suppressal of the doubts and demands of the feminists of the 1790s, it came to a close with a crop of works in which women figure either as pitiful victims or as hysterics and killers. All the piety, fear, invocations of duty and renunciation as the supreme female virtues, all the swallowing back of bile, culminated in some fine womanly anger. Gwendolen Harleth, the heroine of *Daniel Deronda*, George Eliot's last book, which appeared in 1876, is a hysteric and a killer by instinct. She quite ruthlessly determines to push out another woman and her children in order to secure for herself a husband, though she fears him and finds him disgusting, rather than face the only alternative open to her – that of becoming a governess. To be reduced to the condition of governess seemed almost as horrible to a middle-class girl in nineteenth-century fiction as for a working girl to lose her virtue: both meant an almost ritual outcasting.

Gwendolen's later murderous inclinations mark her quite clearly as a forerunner of Ibsen's fierce women. In *Hedda Gabler*, written in 1890, and in the character of Rebecca West in *Rosmersholm*, which came out four years earlier, frustration and hysteria are brought to a terrible climax. The plight of Hedda and Rebecca West was aggravated, no doubt, by the isolation of Norway, but they were recognized, hailed and assimilated in England: Dame Rebecca West is, in fact, our living reminder of the response they found amongst intelligent English girls.

Two books that touch on this subject of anger, suppressed and explosive, have just been published. One is by the American writer Elizabeth Hardwick: it has an arresting title, *Seduction and Betrayal*, and a rather less arresting subtitle, 'Women and Literature'. It consists of a series of essays linked – perhaps a little loosely – by the fact that each essay considers in one way or another 'the arrangements women make with men', both within the framework of fiction and in their actual lives. It is a broad sweep, and the author has chosen to alight here and there only; but where she does she always has something illuminating and to the point to say.

The other book is by the British poet Patricia Beer: a study of four nineteenth-century women novelists and their view of what George Eliot referred to as the 'woman question'. The four she considers are Jane Austen, Charlotte Brontë, Elizabeth Gaskell and George Eliot. It too has an arresting title: *Reader, I Married Him*. These words are, of course, taken from Charlotte Brontë, and I imagine Patricia Beer chose them partly because they underline her theme of the close interdependence between her authors' living conditions and the tone of their books. Both she and Elizabeth Hardwick respond with warmth to the appeal for sisterly understanding implicit in those words of Charlotte Brontë's; and both discuss her life and work at some length.

Of course, she has to be a central figure in any study of women writers of her century; and it is not too fanciful to suggest that, for her, life itself was something of a betrayal, though she was careful not to say so. Her underlying sense of desperation, her latent anger and her attempts to deny that anger, have an emblematic force.

Elizabeth Hardwick says: 'The worries that afflicted genteel, impoverished women in the nineteenth century can scarcely be exaggerated. It was Charlotte's goal to represent the plight of the plain, poor, high-minded young woman. Sometimes she gave them more rectitude than we can easily endure, but she knew their vulnerability, the neglect they expected and received, the spiritual and psychological scars inflicted upon them, the way their frantic efforts were scarcely noticed, much less admired or condoned.' And Patricia Beer reminds us of the tyranny of old Brontë and the automatic assumption within the family that the girls should make sacrifices for their infinitely less talented brother. Mrs Gaskell, in her great biography of Charlotte, worries a little at this fact, but does not question the appointed role of the son. Her attitude can perhaps be assimilated to her own inconsolable grief upon the death of her only son, little Willy: much as she loved her four daughters, they were a perpetual source of anxiety to her – would they marry, would they marry suitably, what would they do if they did not marry? – whereas the son, had he lived, would have been her reward, one feels: her release, even.

There was nothing strange, then, for Charlotte or her sisters in making sacrifices for Branwell. But there was much more to swallow than that. Patricia Beer quotes from a letter Robert Southey wrote to Charlotte in 1837, when she had ventured to ask him for advice on a literary career:

> Literature cannot be the business of a woman's life, and it ought not to be. The more she is engaged in her proper duties, the less leisure will she have for it, even as an accomplishment and a recreation. To those duties you have not yet been called, and when you are you will be less eager for celebrity.

To this Charlotte replied:

In the evenings, I confess, I do think, but I never trouble anyone else with my thoughts. I carefully avoid any appearance of preoccupation and eccentricity, which might lead those I live amongst to suspect the nature of my pursuits. Following my father's advice – who from my childhood has counselled me just in the wise and friendly tone of your letter – I have endeavoured not only attentively to observe all the duties a woman ought to fulfil, but to feel deeply interested in them. I don't always succeed, for sometimes when I'm teaching or sewing I would rather be reading or writing; but I try to deny myself; and my father's approbation amply rewarded me for the privation.

The sense of outrage with which one reads both these passages is increased when one recalls the fervent admiration Southey had expressed as a young man, forty years earlier, for the author of *A Vindication of the Rights of Woman*. But it is not really surprising that he did not send copies of the works of Mary Wollstonecraft to Haworth Parsonage. A wall had gone up, the cordon sanitaire Jane Austen's generation set between the doubts, hopes and demands of the 1790s and the Victorian era. Mary Wollstonecraft's ideas had been almost totally rejected; and even worse than her ideas was the spontaneity of her life, which offered a model for disgrace and tragedy to all young women after her.

Jane Austen's remark about a Mr Pickford she met in Bath in 1801 – 'as raffish in his appearance as I would wish every Disciple of Godwin to be' – tells us, with her customary succinctness, what her view of Mary Wollstonecraft's husband was. She did not make direct attacks; there were others to do that, from Hannah More to Harriet Martineau. But the general insistence throughout Jane Austen's novels on the necessity of accommodating oneself to society as it is, whatever its defects, for fear of something worse, owes more than is usually acknowledged to the events of the 1790s. This is a period from which very few of her letters survive, but she was already adult, able to follow the political controversies of the day and certainly apprised of the case of Mrs Godwin. There was, in fact, a family link with one of Mary's patrons, since the Reverend Austen taught his son.

*Sense and Sensibility*, drafted and then revised for the first time in the 1790s, contains a portrait of a girl who allows her feelings to strip off the protection afforded by decorum. Marianne Dashwood risks seduction (her predecessor in Willoughby's attentions actually gives birth to his child) and the pain she endures by being publicly jilted is as agonizing as any betrayal could be. Jane Austen was fascinated by the character of Marianne: she gives her more physical presence than any of her heroines, with her transparent brown skin, black curly hair and frequent blushes betokening rage or pleasure as often as modesty. (When betrayed, she covers her face with her handkerchief and 'almost screams with agony'.) She is endowed with superabundant energy (energy was the quality Godwin considered most valuable), with honesty and with an inability to suppress her instinctual reactions to whatever she encounters. The logic of the book, and some inner determination of Jane Austen's, demand that she be tamed. In his introduction to the Penguin edition of *Sense and Sensibility*, Tony Tanner has said: 'One can feel that there is something punitive in the taming of Marianne and all she embodies, indeed one might think that something is being vengefully stamped out. It is as though Jane Austen had gone out of her way to show that romantic feelings are utterly non-viable in society.' What Marianne embodies is precisely the spontaneous side of Mary Wollstonecraft, her rejection of prudence and decorum, her scorn for the forms of society. To Jane Austen, this had come to seem exceedingly dangerous; as D. W. Harding said of her, she 'genuinely valued the achievements of the civilization she lived within and never lost sight of the fact that there might be something vastly worse'. Might be! She knew there was something worse: the anarchy of the French Revolution, the disorder and despair of the woman who sought to make her own rules as she went along.

Marianne is not permitted to lose her chastity; she has to remain accessible to the reader, and for most nineteenth-century writers unchastity was enough to disqualify a woman from being written about in fully human terms. Such women tended to appear as stereotypes, denied development. Mrs Gaskell, for instance, despite her courage in attempting the portraits of several fallen women, regarded them as irredeemable except through prolonged punishment ending in death. She seems to concur in society's punishment and, in Patricia Beer's excellent words, 'regards sexual intercourse outside marriage as a kind of disease with after-effects. It may not have been the heroine's fault that she caught it, or she may have been guilty of little worse than imprudence, but it cannot possibly be annulled and the results are automatic and inescapable.' The idea that she might *want* sexual experience is not to be entertained.

It is not surprising to find the following comment on Charlotte Brontë's engagement in a letter of Mrs Gaskell's: 'I am sure Miss Brontë could have never borne not to be well ruled and ordered. I mean that she would never have been happy but with an exacting, rigid, law-giving, passionate man.' We may feel that the last epithet is in contradiction to the other three, which is perhaps in itself a commentary on the erotic ideas of women in the middle of the century.

Patricia Beer points out that Charlotte Brontë, although in *Shirley* she put in a strong formal plea for education and work opportunities for women, simply did not inhabit a world in which ideas of women's rights could take root. She could not escape the emotional conviction that marriage, meaning the subjection of the wife, was the only fate to be desired. Her heroines often dream of escape from physical confinement, but they are always running in the direction of a masterful embrace.

Elizabeth Hardwick has something particularly fine to say about Charlotte's struggles:

> How to live without love, without security? Hardly any other Victorian woman had thought as much about this as Charlotte Brontë. The large, gaping flaws in the construction of the stories – mad wives in the attic, strange apparitions in Belgium – are representations of the life she could not face; these Gothic subterfuges represent the mind at breaking point, frantic to find a way out. If the flaws are only to be attributed to the practice of popular fiction of the time, we cannot then explain the large amount of genuine feeling that goes into them. They stand for the hidden wishes of an intolerable life.

'The hidden wishes of an intolerable life': it is a memorable phrase, and can stand for a good deal that puzzles us in nineteenth-century fiction. Men were not unaware of these hidden, gothic horrors. Thackeray could not let Becky Sharp be simply on the make; she had to be turned into an evil, snake-like presence. Dickens's women (as John Carey has recently pointed out) wield their needles and scissors, those very tokens of subjection to domesticity, with murderous darts and jabs when they are roused. And even George Eliot, who took upon herself the mantle of male wisdom, and seems almost to have enjoyed frustrating her heroines' aspirations, shows others than Gwendolen with murderous impulses. Lydgate's remark in *Middlemarch* about his lovely Rosamond seems to fit in here: 'He once called her his basil-plant, and when asked for an explanation said that the basil was a plant which had flourished wonderfully on a murdered man's brains.'

George Eliot's approach to the 'woman question' is the more surprising when one reflects on her friendship with women who were actively engaged in the struggle for education, employment and the vote. Patricia Beer praises her for having a mind 'too subtle and reflective to take the plain straightforward view', and quotes her remark on the unlikelihood of finding a perfect plan for educating women, since none had yet been found for men. But this is, of course, the sort of argument that blocks all political action, and does her little credit.

I would like to end on quite a different note, with a story of my own. The year before George Eliot's death, a Manchester girl of twenty-one, named Emmeline Goulden, proposed to her much older fiancé – he had been a friend of John Stuart Mill – that they should enter into a free union rather than going through a marriage ceremony. He pointed out that the precedents were unfortunate – citing Mary Wollstonecraft – and she agreed reluctantly to a church wedding. Thereby, she became Mrs Pankhurst. But the whirligigs of time acted strangely for her. In 1927, long after the vote had been won, at the cost of much anger, her daughter Sylvia gave birth to a child conceived outside wedlock. Mrs Pankhurst's horror was so great that she refused ever to see Sylvia again, and died soon after. Now Sylvia had been neither seduced nor betrayed; she had planned her action cheerfully and deliberately; yet her mother felt that she had exposed the family to unendurable mockery and condemnation. Anger remains a complicated emotion.

Radio 3 review, printed in the *Listener*, 1974

# Criminal Conversation

*The Letters of Caroline Norton to Lord Melbourne*
edited by James O. Hoge and Clarke Olney

Honour is due to Caroline Norton for her considerable part in changing the English law relating to the custody of infants (until 1839 the mother had no claim at all) and matrimonial status (until 1857 a married woman could not inherit or bequeath property, nor could a deserted wife protect her own earnings from her husband). She was active in these matters because they affected her personally; she disclaimed any interest in 'equal rights' and, characteristically looking back into the eighteenth century, said she had no wish to be taken for 'something between a barn-actress and a Mary Wollstonecraft'. Some may think she has deserved her fate, which has been to be remembered as a society beauty who became involved in scandals and raised a clamorous voice against her sufferings: and it is this Caroline who appears in these hitherto unpublished letters. They remained in the possession of the Lamb family until 1953, when they were deposited in the Hertford County Record Office; the late Clarke Olney and James Hoge worked from microfilm – the English have not been quick to explore their own treasure-trove.

The granddaughter of Sheridan, Caroline was black-eyed, high-spirited and witty. Sydney Smith called her a 'superb lump of flesh' with just that note of equivocation she has so often drawn. Her grandfather's remark on seeing her led in, a tiny girl, was that she was not a child he would care to meet in a dark wood. George Norton, who became her husband, fell determinedly in love with her when she was still of school age but, growing maddened by her indifference and independence once they were married, turned to blows and then legal bullying. Mary Shelley, becoming her friend, wrote to Trelawny in 1835:

> Had I been a man I should certainly have fallen in love with her; as a woman, ten years ago, I should have been spellbound, and had

she taken the trouble, she might have wound me round her finger
... Now do not, in your usual silly way, show her what I say. She
is, despite all her talent and sweetness, a London lady. She would
guy me – not, perhaps, to you (well do I know the London *ton*!)
but to everyone else – in her prettiest way.

A London lady she was, with her small blue drawing-room
in Westminster, her late arrivals at dinners, her quarrels with
George and her radical enthusiasms. Needing money to live as
she chose, she wrote poetry, plays and novels and edited ladies'
magazines, undeterred by pregnancies; and spiritedly she sent off
a letter to the Whig Home Secretary, Lord Melbourne, soliciting a
place for her husband, though he was a Tory. Lord Melbourne
arrived in the blue drawing-room in person in 1830, and for the next
six years (during which he became Prime Minister) he saw her
almost daily.

He was nearly thirty years her senior; his wife (Caroline Lamb)
had lately died; and he was a man peculiarly susceptible to the
delights of a quasi-paternal relationship. Caroline Norton offered
him beauty, charm, a sharp interest in everything that interested
him and something like an eighteenth-century sense of fun; more, she
idealized him for his urbanity, his power, wealth and well-preserved
good looks. 'Dearest Lord,' she wrote when they were apart; or 'Will
of the Wisp', when his expected letter failed; 'Pet Lamb', she told
him, was her sister's name for him. And he wrote to her, 'I have
been in despair today at not seeing you ...'

Crisis came in 1836 when the petty but violent quarrels between
Mr and Mrs Norton – unconnected with Lord M – became too
much for either of them to bear, and she left home. George removed
her three sons and, probably egged on by Tory advisers, brought a
suit against the Prime Minister for criminal conversation (i.e., adultery) with Caroline. She found herself deprived of her children,
whom she loved passionately, and equally deprived of Lord M, who,
from the moment scandal threatened, withdrew, advising her (by
post for the most part) to return to her husband, terrified lest she
should try to compromise him.

The most interesting of these letters relate to this period. It is clear from them that she was as deeply wounded by Melbourne's pusillanimous withdrawal as by the loss of her children. 'Well! I beg pardon. I don't want to torment you – all I say is, *worse* women have been better *stood by*,' is followed up by:

> I have your note. You need not fear my writing to you if you think it *commits you*. I *struggle* to think over all the fortuitous circumstances which make *your* position seem of more consequence than *mine*. I will not deny that among all the bitterness of this hour, what sinks me *most* is the thought of *you* – of the expression of your eye the day I told it you at Dng St – the *shrinking* from me & my burdensome & embarassing [sic] distress.
>
> God forgive you, for I do believe no one, young or old, ever loved another better than I have loved you . . . I will do nothing foolish or indiscreet – depend on it – either way it is all a blank to *me. I* dont much care *how* it ends . . . I have always the memory of how you *received me that day*, and I have the conviction that I have no further power than he *allows* me, over my boys. *You & they* were my interests in life. No *future* can ever wipe out *the past* – nor *renew* it.

Later, pathetically, she says, 'The fault is in *me* – I do not attach people'; still later there are very bitter outbursts against his behaviour, against the past, against other women friends of his; and she has a '*paid-off, cast-off* feeling'.

The court found Caroline and Melbourne innocent; George himself later admitted he had not really suspected them, and Melbourne left a note at his death reiterating innocence. In her novels Caroline persistently condemns adultery, and in real life she cooled an eager peer who burst into her bedroom with the words 'adultery is a crime, not a recreation'. The present editors are nevertheless inclined to think these letters change the picture. I cannot agree with them. It seems more likely that she was so disappointed and disgusted with her experience of sex within marriage as to lack any wish at all to embark on extra-marital ventures of that kind. In a sense she and Lord M were the perfect couple; her tragedy was that she could not quite cope with George, and that later Lord M found himself a far more fascinating and safer 'daughter' to dote upon, in the shape of Queen Victoria.

He told his royal mistress that all the Sheridans were a little vulgar. Even after her death in 1877 Caroline has kept that taint of vulgarity about her. Lord David Cecil, understandably taking Lord M's position more seriously than hers in his urbane biography (*Lord M*, 1954), presents her as a liability, stresses his kindness and says nothing of her pain at the severance of the relationship. Caroline's biographers, Jane Perkins (1909) and Alice Acland (1948), although more sympathetic, still underplay what it must have meant to her. No doubt Philip Ziegler, who is working on a new life of Melbourne, will set the record straight. Meredith, in his deplorable *Diana of the Crossways* (1885), made a fictional version of Caroline which attributes immoral behaviour of another kind to her – she sells political information to a journalist to spite a lover – but leaves out most of the real miseries of her story.

People have not liked her clamorousness. She knew this, and made one of her fictional heroines complain that she is always accused of behaving like an actress. But she had serious wrongs to clamour against, not only the defection of her beloved but the loss of her children (the youngest was dying before she was sent for, dead when she arrived) and many years of persecution by her husband. These letters, on the whole scrupulously and informatively edited, should raise her stock a little by filling in the portrait. There is no faked emotion in this, written in June 1837:

> I hear nothing of you as I used to do, and feel much the same dreariness of heart that one does when watching by a sick bed: – every thing very cold, very dim, & very silent, & the clock ticking very loud.

And she had a genuinely good heart: seven years later she was writing comfortingly to the old man who had broken her heart and was now himself a prey to depression: 'Dearest Old Boy . . .'

*New Statesman*, 1975

# Maggie Tulliver's Little Sisters

## Essay on William Hale White, or 'Mark Rutherford'

Just to the east of Waterloo Bridge, in the Strand, there is a row of tall houses, deep and solid to match their height. No. 142 has a restaurant in the basement today, and a wine bar at ground level; if you climb the stairs, you find offices on all the upper floors. I trespassed into them a few weeks ago, explaining that I was thinking about George Eliot, who once lived there. 'George Eliot? Who's he?' asked a well-dressed young man in one of the offices.

You expect writers who take false names to leave some eddies of confusion for posterity – even ones as well known as George Eliot. An obscurer friend of hers, who lodged at No. 142 at the same time as her, in the early 1850s, also adopted a pseudonym: he wrote under the name 'Mark Rutherford'. She knew him as William Hale White. He is not much remembered by either name today, which is a pity, because he wrote some remarkable books. They draw directly on a private store of memories and emotions, and you sense quite strongly that he took up a mask in order to be nakedly confessional in a way he could not otherwise have managed. He concealed his authorship even from his family. If you like his books, as I do, you cannot help growing interested in his life; and the episode of his early friendship with George Eliot is a curious story in its own right.

In 1852, when he was twenty-one, he was expelled from a theological college for questioning the divine inspiration of the Bible. He had to find a job. A friend in Hampstead put him up, and he walked down the hill, day after day, with the idea of persuading some publisher to employ him. He was a nice-looking boy, with a high forehead, curly brown hair and even features; but he was shy and agitated by his situation, and he was turned down more than once. Presently, he arrived at No. 142 the Strand, where John Chapman, the publisher of free-thinking books, conducted his business. Chapman was then thirty-one years old. He had just bought the *Westminster Review*, and had perpetual money troubles.

To help with the rent for his enormous house, he made his wife, Susanna, organize it for lodgers. She was fourteen years older than him, and, to assist her with the housekeeping and the care of two children, he appointed a Miss Elizabeth Tilley, closer to him in age, who was also his mistress. A third woman living under his roof at this time was Marian Evans, not yet transformed into George Eliot: she was thirty-three. She had been in love with Chapman for a while, but her feelings had calmed after various scenes with her two rivals, and Chapman's tactlessness in dwelling on what he termed 'the incomprehensible mystery and witchery of beauty' (which, in his view, she lacked). In his diary, he noted: 'My words jarred upon her and put an end to her enjoyment. Was it from a consciousness of her own want of beauty? She wept bitterly.'

But Marian Evans was a pragmatist, and she cooled as she wept; by 1852 the relationship was fairly strictly professional. In fact, it was she who effectively did much of the editorial work on the *Westminster Review*. None of this was known to Hale White when he came to the Strand seeking a job, of course. His first meeting with Chapman went like this:

> I was received, if not with cordiality, at least with an interest which surprised me. He took me into a little back shop, and after hearing patiently what I wanted, he asked me somewhat abruptly what I thought of the miracles in the Bible.

Hale White's cautious answer that he did not believe literally, but considered the miracles a statement of divine truth, contented Chapman.

> The result was that he asked me if I would help him in his business. In order to do this it would be more economical if I would live in his house, which was too big for him. He promised to give me £40 a year, in addition to board and lodging. I joyously assented, and the bargain was struck.

Chapman and his new assistant were, in fact, ill assorted. But Chapman's lodger, Miss Evans, did see something particular in the nervous young man who, like her, had come from a provincial backwater to London; like her, had undergone a crisis of religious faith; like her, felt an intense need for human affection, without knowing how to go comfortably about giving or receiving it. She was kind to him from the start.

Hale White was the son of a Bedford bookseller with a radical turn of mind. The family were Dissenters, and Hale White had agreed to prepare for the ministry at his mother's insistence and for lack of a practicable alternative: he had dreamt of becoming an artist, or going to Oxford. In his three years at theological college, he said later, he learnt nothing and made no friends. But he began to read Wordsworth and Carlyle, and formed some fixed ideas of what he did not like – in particular, the cant of English Dissent that had lost touch with all spiritual and political enthusiasm. After his expulsion from college, there was no question of returning to Bedford to join his father's trade – it was doing badly. He had to make his own way. At first he arranged to go to Stoke Newington as a schoolmaster, but, after one night in an attic above the empty schoolroom, he packed his bags and fled. When he arrived at the Strand, then, the little experience he had had of adult life had shaken his nerve. 'I was a mere youth . . . awkward and shy,' he wrote later, recalling the day on which he came to No. 142 and had lunch there:

> Miss Evans sat opposite me . . . She was then almost unknown to the world, but I had sensed enough to discern she was a remarkable creature. I was grateful to her because she replied even with eagerness to a trifling remark I happened to make, and gave it some importance . . . She was attractive personally. Her hair was particularly beautiful, and in her grey eyes there was a curiously shifting light, generally soft and tender, but convertible into the keenest flash . . .

This quotation comes from a factual account Hale White wrote after George Eliot's death. At this time she was on a pinnacle of fame, and her widower had published a biography presenting her as a wholly saintly figure. Hale White protested against this version of the woman he had known, and rejected Leslie Stephen's description of her as 'eminently respectable'. He also suggested that 'one of the reasons why she and Chapman did not agree was that she did not like his somewhat disorderly ways'.

I think Hale White himself must have nourished some ambivalent feelings about the disorderly ways at the Strand. He had been brought up in the most rigidly puritanical tradition where sexual matters were concerned. The Chapman ménage undoubtedly gave him a few shocks. In his fictionalized account of his youth, *The Autobiography of Mark Rutherford*, his first book, he omitted any reference to Mrs Chapman or Miss Tilley, and turned Marian Evans into Chapman's niece.

During the months in which Hale White and Marian Evans were both living at No. 142 – from the early summer of 1852 until October 1853, when she moved away – she was going through a period of acute crisis. In the summer of 1852 she was in love with Herbert Spencer – the violence of her feeling is quite clear from a letter lately opened at the British Museum and soon to be published – and when he, like Chapman, rejected her on the grounds of her want of beauty, it must have been hard to bear. It was something, perhaps, to be worshipped by young Hale White at that point. Whether the following scene was true or imagined – and it is not possible to tell – it is at least an indication of the way in which the real Hale White was affected by the real Marian Evans. Chapman is called 'Wollaston', Marian 'Theresa'.

After breakfast some proofs came from the printer of a pamphlet which Wollaston had in hand. Without unfastening them, he gave them to me, and said that as he had no time to read them himself, I must go upstairs to Theresa's study and read them off with her. Accordingly I went and began to read. She took the manuscript and I took the proof. She read about a page, and then she suddenly stopped. 'O Mr Rutherford,' she said, 'what have you done? I heard my uncle distinctly tell you to mark on the manuscript, when it went to the printer, that it was to be printed in demy octavo, and you have marked it twelvemo.' I had had little sleep that night, I was exhausted with my early walk, and suddenly the room seemed to fade from me and I fainted.

When I came to myself, I found that Theresa had not sought for any help; she had done all that ought to be done. She had unfastened my collar and had sponged my face with cold water ... With a storm of tears, I laid open all my heart. I told her how nothing I had ever attempted had succeeded; that I had never even been able to attain that degree of satisfaction with myself and my own conclusions, without which a man cannot live; and that now I found I was useless, even to the best friends I had ever known, and that the meanest clerk in the city would serve them better than I did. I was beside myself, and I threw myself on my knees, burying my face in Theresa's lap and sobbing convulsively. She did not repel me, but she gently passed her fingers through my hair ... She gently lifted me up, and as I rose I saw her eyes too were wet. 'My poor friend,' she said, 'I cannot talk to you now. You are not strong enough, and for that matter, nor am I, but let me say this to you, that you are altogether mistaken about yourself. The meanest clerk in the city could not take your place here.' There was just a slight emphasis I thought upon the word 'here'. 'Now,' she said, 'you had better go. I will see about the pamphlet.'

When I went back to my work I worshipped Theresa, and was entirely overcome with unhesitating absorbing love for her. I saw nothing more of her that day nor the next day. Her uncle told me that she had gone into the country, and that probably she would not return for some time, as she had purposed paying a lengthened visit to a friend.

We know – and Hale White must have learnt at some point – that Marian Evans moved away in order to be with George Henry Lewes, the married man who replaced Spencer in her love and reciprocated it. Hale White never advanced an opinion on this: in general he kept to a rigid view about the obligations of spouses. But later he expressed his regret at losing touch with her, and put it down to diffidence on his own part. He wrote a story called 'Confessions of a Self-Tormentor' in which she appears as a young widow who does her best to be kind to a gauche boy, while he gracelessly rejects her affection.

I think that she remained in his mind as a model of the sort of woman he found desirable and a little frightening and felt – perhaps

– he had denied himself. Certainly, in his own last novel, he drew a wholly admiring portrait of a young woman who deliberately transgresses against the sexual and social code, as Miss Evans did in 1854.

Hale White too left the Strand in February 1854, in spite of an offer of a 'partnership' from Chapman. It is hard to see it as anything but a retreat. He went to lodge with a pious family friend whose half-sister, Harriet, he later married, and his father found him a job. It was a deadly dull clerkship at Somerset House, where he was surrounded by brutish and silly colleagues. It was torture to him.

Harriet, sweet but intellectually null, bore some children, but was soon struck down by multiple sclerosis; it paralysed her progressively, but did not kill her until 1891. Hale White worked at his civil service job and political journalism to eke out his income and pay a house-keeper. He became hypochondriacal, insomniac and depressive.

Marian Evans lived another thirty years in the city where he worked but they never met again. In 1876 Hale White wrote to her, asking her intercession with a publisher to find work for an old friend from the Chapman days. She was busy and low, writing *Daniel Deronda*, and asked Lewes to speak for the man and answer Hale White's letter, which he did politely. Hale White then wrote again, and sent her a picture. He must have been pressing for a personal response. But Lewes was again deputed to reply, this time a shade more formally, and with the desired effect. Hale White did not try again: she would not respond; probably she wanted no reminders of the Chapman era.

She died in 1880, on Hale White's forty-ninth birthday, a fact that moved him greatly. It was only after this that he began to write and publish his own books, first the two autobiographical fictions, *The Autobiography of Mark Rutherford* and *Mark Rutherford's Deliverance*, then a historical novel, *The Revolution in Tanner's Lane*. The next three are studies of young women, all published in the early nineties, *Miriam's Schooling*, *Catharine Furze* and *Clara Hopgood*. Each takes the formative years of a girl from the English provinces and shows her struggling to find something more than the narrow birthright offered by small-town life. Maggie Tulliver's little sisters, you could say.

Well, it is true that Hale White read and admired George Eliot's books, and noticeable that he sets these three of his in the 1840s, when she had been a young woman (and he a child). And there are obvious parallels in the subjects and tone: comic provincials, small-town dramas, awkward intrusions of precept and irony. The characters of the heroines would all, I think, have interested George Eliot herself: clearly they embody some of Hale White's own frustrations and yearnings. They are also tributes to her moral vision. Miriam, most Eliotish of the heroines, is an uneducated but independent-minded beauty:

> She was a big girl . . . with black hair and dark eyes, limbs loosely set, with a tendency to sprawl, large feet and hands. She had a handsome, regular face, a little freckled; but the mouth, although it was beautifully curved, was a trifle too long, and except when she was in a passion, was not sufficiently under the control of her muscles, so that her words escaped her not properly formed . . .

That is well observed, particularly the last phrase. And the account of Miriam's escape from the provinces to London with her weakling brother, who takes to drink in a butcher's shop, and her passion and torment in grimy lodgings when she falls in love with a clergyman's son turned music-hall singer, is finely and sharply drawn. Hale White's book is a miniature beside George Eliot's canvas; but it is delicately put together, and its moments of intensity are as telling as any of hers.

*Catharine Furze* is a study of another spirited country-town girl. She takes on her mother's prejudices successfully, but is destroyed by falling in love with a married clergyman. The book suffers from a determination to make a tale of spiritual victory out of a story that really spells out loss, waste and defeat – not because Catharine needed adultery in itself, but because there was nothing else for her to turn to:

> The pattern of her existence was henceforth settled, and she was to live not only without that which is sweetest for woman, but with no definite object before her. The force in woman is so great that

something with which it can grapple, on which it can expend itself, is a necessity, and Catharine felt that her strength would have to occupy itself in twisting straws. It is really this which is the root of many a poor girl's suffering.

The final novel is the most surprising, containing in one of its two heroines, Madge Hopgood, a creature as bold as Marian Evans in real life, and bolder than any she drew. Madge first seduces her fiancé and then rejects him because she realizes her feeling for him is only physical, and goes on to bear his child as an unmarried woman. The portrait of Madge herself; the account of the effect of her behaviour on her mother and sister; the picture of the way in which the girls shift into a new class of penniless London intellectuals with links amongst foreigners and the working class – this is subtly, neatly and memorably done.

Hale White wrote no more novels after this one, which was roughly handled by critics for its immoral theme. He did go on, however, to produce a handful of excellent and unusual short stories which touch on some bitter truths about Victorian life. He never strove for the grand manner. His writing, unlike George Eliot's, is constrained. But then his subject too was constraint, the sense of constraint that dominated the lives of most of his contemporaries. I think he got it down pretty accurately, because he himself had felt it so close to the nerve and unrelieved. He had never been able to leap sideways as Marian Evans did; he hadn't the power. But he did manage to write small, vigorous masterpieces of the puritan conscience trying to beat out a narrow path for itself. He deserves to be more widely read today. It is sad that Marian Evans never knew what her young man achieved. She would surely have approved.

Radio 3 review, printed in the *Listener*, 1975

# Oink

## Ottoline: The Life of Lady Ottoline Morrell
by Sandra Jobson Darroch

The story of Circe is a warning to all hostesses. The more invitations are looked for and parties flocked to, the more swine are likely to be grunting and rooting about in the mud later. John, Lamb, Huxley, Lawrence, Russell, Murry, Strachey, Woolf: Lady Ottoline captured them (and many more) one after another, first in her grey and yellow Bedford Square salon with the silk cushions, and later at Garsington, where décor and generosity were both memorable. Most rendered thanks with grunts, if not snorts. In the Bedford Square days Henry James advised her: 'Look at them, dear lady, over the banisters. But don't go down amongst them.' But to go down amongst them was exactly what she wanted to do.

Born in 1873, she had that sense of exclusion from intellectual and artistic life that went with an English aristocratic background and upbringing. She had lost her father early, her pious and conventional mother became an invalid and died when Ottoline was only twenty, her brothers were embarrassed by her: so tall, so intense, such a nose – would she enter a convent? So, to a very considerable extent, Ottoline made herself in her own image. There was her extravagant style in dress (although her insouciance about doing up a dropped suspender in full view of anyone was no doubt the superbness of her class). Her marriage to Philip Morrell was a step down socially: she sent for him and gave him permission to propose; thereafter she supported him loyally in his brave but unfortunate career as a Liberal politician. Motherhood did not come easily to her; after the birth of twins, of whom the boy died, she had no more children; instead, she pursued a course of unusual sexual freedom and useful patronage of the arts.

'The head of a Medusa; but she is very simple and innocent in spite of it, and worships the arts,' wrote Virginia Stephen at the beginning of their long relationship. Ottoline had enjoyed some educational opportunities denied to her friend, but had merely picked at them; a term at St Andrew's allowed her to discover that logic was too dry; a few months at Oxford, where she bicycled about with a pile of books strapped to her back, led to headaches and retreat to London. From early days she found her cultural enthusiasms arriving in the shape of men: a tour of Italy culminated in some passionate indiscretions with Axel Munthe; religious fervour led to warm exchanges with an elderly archbishop:

> Dearest Ottoline, Alas! The Queen has fixed Tuesday next for receiving the Bishops of the Lambeth Conference at Windsor, and my attendance there is absolutely necessary. What can be done about my address to your friends? . . . Would there be any chance of my seeing you Sunday if I were to call?

Asquith was another persistent, and sometimes sulky, admirer.

Later, it was her love of Russell's mind ('the beauty and transcendence of his thoughts' was her phrase) that led her to overlook the fact that she could 'hardly bear the lack of physical attraction'. It was an unusual basis, one imagines, on which to embark on a precipitate and long-drawn-out adulterous affair with a man who specifically said 'no woman's intellect is really good enough to give me pleasure as intellect'. But it seems as likely that it was a sign of her true generosity of spirit as that she simply could not resist acquiring the scalp of England's most famous philosopher.

Sandra Jobson Darroch, who writes with sympathy for her subject and has toiled lengthily and admirably to bring her out of the corners of other people's lives and stand her in the centre here, makes it quite clear that Ottoline did enjoy collecting scalps; that she sometimes lied to one lover about another; and that she applied slightly different standards to her own behaviour and to that of (say) her husband. Her infidelities were much forgiven; the discovery of his led both husband and wife into breakdowns and hospitalization. Still, Ottoline emerges with advantage in comparison with most of those she gathered about herself. Of course Strachey being malicious is more amusing than Ottoline being silly, but what a detestable man he was in his dealings with her.

Lawrence understood her better than most, with his suggestion that she suffered from 'a lack of robust self'; that 'she had no natural sufficiency, there was a terrible void, a lack, a deficiency of being within her. And she wanted someone to close up this deficiency.' Darroch points out that Ottoline complains of precisely this 'deficiency of being' in her own memoirs; and was never able to close it up, although until the end she gathered the young and artistically aspiring about her. She died of the ministrations of quack doctors. Her widower, lonely survivor into the years of the Second World War, took to bridge (a game not heard of at Garsington) and Darroch records the sad words of his deathbed: 'Partner, we can't make it. We haven't enough hearts.' Often puzzled, almost always generous and good in their lifetimes, the Morrells earned the right to this careful and gentle biography after so much swinishness.

*New Statesman*, 1976

# Three Essays on Virginia Woolf

## 1. Frontstage Wife

*The Letters of Virginia Woolf. Volume II: 1912–1922*
edited by Nigel Nicolson and Joanne Trautmann

Letters can have their sinister side; Virginia Woolf knew that. This is what she wrote in *Jacob's Room*:

> Let us consider letters – how they come at breakfast, and at night, with their yellow stamps and their green stamps, immortalized by the postmark – for to see one's own envelope on another's table is to realize how soon deeds sever and become alien. Then at last the power of the mind to quit the body is manifest, and perhaps we fear or hate or wish annihilated this phantom of ourselves, lying on the table.

Anyone who commits pen to paper must wish, sometimes, to snatch back the phantom self. But Virginia's ghost has special claims on us – and to some aspects of her nature this volume would certainly have ministered. She cared deeply for praise, approval, fame, for the ascendancy of Mrs Woolf as a literary eminence over any possible rivals, whether Lytton Strachey or Katherine Mansfield. Then she was herself enjoyably sensitive to the revelations of idiosyncrasy, period detail and quirk of character filtering through volumes of memoirs or letters: some of her finest reviews deal with such things.

She was not a secretive person. On the whole, it's true, she talked to herself (in her diaries) better than she talked on paper to other people; alone, she can coax and tease with no sense of strain, no desire to impress even the elderly Virginia aged fifty she imagines as reader; and she can outline her plans for work with the certainty that she is addressing an intellectual equal. But still these are the fluent and confidently penned words of a woman who knew her friendship was always a prize, never an imposition. Not many of her recipients threw away her letters – a subject to which I shall return.

When Leonard Woolf published *A Writer's Diary* (his selection from the twenty-six volumes of her diaries) in 1954, he felt obliged to justify his action in a preface stating his belief in her standing as a 'serious artist'. Perhaps he thought her neglected or under attack; hindsight sees also a gesture shielding her from the exaggerated interest in her private life and circle of friends which has grown up since. Do the letters feed the appetite for gossip merely, or do they relate to an assessment of her artistry? It seems to me that they do connect valuably with some of the strengths of the novels and criticism: a sense of comedy and a gift for catching the heartbeat of a house or a roomful of people, for conjuring up weather or mood in phrases of miraculous lightness and speed. Her sentences are never heavy or shabby. We may guess at strain in her at times, but what she writes retains its composure and grace. She is neither pompous nor dishevelled. And perhaps the strongest and most consistent impression she gives is not that of the greatly praised tremulous sensibility at work, but of unyielding intelligence, the intelligence of the Miss Stephen who expected much of herself in the way of work, discipline and proper attention to the matter in hand.

The letters are likely to find a specially attentive audience amongst those who will scan them for evidence of the woman writer's particular pattern of struggle. But it will be seen quite clearly that, while their author understood and discussed elsewhere the plight of the generality of her sex, she herself was very largely saved from it, by her own determination, by the social structure of the day, still working in favour of her class, and (chiefly) by a wise husband. If her times of madness and threatened madness, and her eventual suicide, give her an emblematic force as one more female victim of her own genius, it must be said that without Leonard's protection she would not have lived to write *A Room of One's Own*.

But she drew good fortune to herself alongside the ill, attracting the friends who fly about and perch on these pages, as well as the husband who used the larger part of his own strength and wits in her service. The early love notes to Leonard give rare instances of Mrs Woolf taking pleasure in her own person –

... the great variegated creature. She wishes me to inform you delicately that her flanks and rump are now in finest plumage, and invites you to an exhibition. Kisses on your dear little pate. Darling Mongoose. Mandril

(Interesting too to see how she thought of herself as the large Brute, of him as the little creature, the little beast, the 'little ribby body'.) For the most part, later, she suffers from her lack of children and, very largely, from a sense of deficiency in herself. There is vicarious pride in the love affairs and childbearing of her friends and above all of her elder sister Vanessa, who, in Virginia's view, combined painting, marriage, adulterous love and mothering to perfection. The editors describe Vanessa as having her personality reflected in the letters 'as the sun is by a shield', but I am not sure that this description is quite apt; Vanessa remains enigmatic and just out of focus, a formalized, semi-mythical figure, in spite of many chats with her on the subject of servants, of aunts, of the naming of children and other issues.

Servants are indeed an absorbing running theme of this volume. After an illness, in January 1919, Virginia wrote in her diary that she felt so reduced that 'even the muscles of my right hand feel as I imagine a servant's hand to feel': a curious and telling phrase, with its assumption that servants are necessarily worked to a condition of painful fatigue. The Woolfs normally had two young women to work for them, and many pages here are devoted to discussions, usually with Vanessa, of the moods, shortcomings, charms, sudden notices and withdrawals of notice of Nelly Boxall, the cook, and Lottie Hope, her friend, who was given to waking the Woolfs in the middle of the night to announce her own imminent death from unnamed, lightning disease. A note describes Lottie as a 'foundling'; she was given to shouting when she felt imposed upon; and her mysterious illnesses did, in fact, culminate in a necessary operation, performed at the Homoeopathic Hospital in Great Ormond Street. The last mention of her in this volume is of her convalescing 'at home' (whatever a foundling's home may be) and sending Virginia ('We drag on with Chars') long letters, 'from friend to friend'. It would be good to see both sides of this exchange, but Lottie and Virginia were evidently equally careless here.

There's another, more glaring gap in the correspondence. The years covered by this volume also encompass the six years in which Virginia Woolf knew Katherine Mansfield (who died in fact eleven days after the last letter was written, on 9 January 1923); but the strength of the link between the two women is not much in evidence here. Only one short letter is printed, and there is mention of the existence of one other. That there were more is certain, from references in Katherine Mansfield's letters to Ida Baker and John Middleton Murry and from her own surviving part of the correspondence, in which she thanks Virginia for gifts of flowers and cigarettes, and writes with a blend of archness and intensity that is, characteristically, both touching and irritating:

> Virginia dear, I shall love to come and dine on Wednesday night with you alone: I can't manage Friday. Ever since I read your letter I have been writing to you and a bit 'haunted' by you: I long to see you again . . . My God, I love to think of you, Virginia, as my friend. Don't cry me an ardent creature or say, with your head a little on one side, smiling as though you knew some enchanting secret: 'Well, Katherine, we shall see' . . .
>
> But pray consider how rare it is to find someone with the same passion for writing that you have, who desires to be scrupulously truthful with you – and to give you the freedom of the city without any reserves at all.

Leonard Woolf's account of the relationship is that his wife at first disliked Katherine Mansfield's cheap scent and cheap sentimentality, whereas he found her very amusing and liked her, despite a feeling that she disliked him. 'By nature, I think, she was gay, cynical, amoral, ribald, witty,' he wrote, adding that it was her husband Murry's Pecksniffian character he could not abide; and he felt it spoiled her too.

To Virginia she was the friend and the enemy. Elizabeth Bowen reported that, even many years after Katherine's death, Virginia could not speak of her without jealousy. And in the immediacy of her death she wrote in her diary: 'I was jealous of her writing – the only writing I have ever been jealous of . . .' – and went on – 'Probably we had something in common which I shall never find again in anyone else. (This I say in so many words in 1919 again and again.)' It is presumably to unpublished passages of her 1919 diary that Quentin Bell refers in his biography, where we find, in his discussion of Virginia's relations with Vita Sackville-West, the assertion that 'since her marriage, no one save Katherine Mansfield had touched her heart at all, and Katherine but slightly' and on the next page, still more positively:

> Virginia felt as a lover feels – she desponded when she fancied herself neglected, despaired when Vita was away, waiting anxiously for letters, needed Vita's company and lived in that strange mixture of elation and despair which lovers – and one would have supposed only lovers – can experience. All this she had done and felt for Katherine, but she never writes of her as she does of Vita.

The bare bones in the letters are a first mention in July 1916:

> Katherine Mansfield has dogged my steps for three years – I'm always on the point of meeting her, or of reading her stories, and I have never managed to do either . . . Do arrange a meeting . . .

– this to Lytton Strachey, who had met Katherine Mansfield at Garsington and reported her enthusiasm for Virginia's first novel, *The Voyage Out*.

In February 1917 Virginia is telling Vanessa that she has had 'a slight rapprochement with Katherine Mansfield; who seems to me an unpleasant but forcible and utterly unscrupulous character, in whom I think you might find a "companion"' (this a compliment of sorts, of course). In April, Virginia is going to see Katherine 'to get a story from her, perhaps'. By the summer the two writers are on close terms (this is probably the time of the letter from Katherine to Virginia quoted above), and by November the Woolfs' have starting printing Katherine's story 'Prelude', which is actually published in the autumn of 1918. Virginia told Violet Dickinson that 'Prelude' had been turned down by another publisher, and she defended it from what was clearly a blast of contempt from Clive

Bell – 'I only maintain that KM's story has a certain quality as a work of art besides the obvious cleverness, which made it worth printing, and a good deal better than most stories anyhow.' Otherwise she has little to say about it. Nor does Leonard give any estimate of its literary value, confining his comment in a note that it earned £7.11s.8d. for the Hogarth Press.

Things were never easy between the two women. Katherine wrote of Virginia, 'Ain't she a snob?' and privately described *Night and Day* as 'tahsome'. She was also a bit in awe of her, like many other people; an entry in her 1919 journal goes: 'If one wasn't so afraid – why should I be? this isn't going to be read by Bloomsbury *et Cie* . . .' They quarrelled when Virginia reported unkind remarks made by Bell and Desmond MacCarthy about Katherine to her – one of the tedious Bloomsbury gossip scandals, this. There was resentment over Katherine's review of *Night and Day* (she had earlier praised Virginia's not very good short story 'Kew Gardens' extravagantly). The *Night and Day* review reads rather well today: it commends the novel for its 'air of quiet perfection' within the Jane Austen tradition, but regrets that the author has not found some new form of expression. She remarks on 'her lack of any sign that she has made a perilous voyage – the absence of any scars. There she lies among the shipping – a tribute to civilization for our admiration and wonder . . . In the midst of our admiration it makes us feel old and chill: we had never thought to look upon its like again!'

Katherine's words were taken to heart, even if they were also resented. Virginia did not want to be Jane Austen all over again. And her next book, *Jacob's Room*, departs radically from the conventional structure of *Night and Day* and moves very much in the same direction as that on which Katherine was embarking in 'Prelude'. There is the same fragmentation, the same refusal to provide a structure around a graspable 'point' or series of points, the same delight in fluidity of character, the same insistence on the visual, the surface stir. Methods and form make the two writers at least cousinly at this moment. Virginia's voice in *Jacob's Room* is a finer, more piercing instrument than Katherine's in 'Prelude'; the empty space where Jacob exists is a subtler and more original device than anything yet done by Katherine. Still, the fact is that Virginia drew something from Katherine.

She also felt threatened by her ('The *Athenaeum* has . . . adopted Katherine as their writer of genius, which means, I'm afraid, that poor Mrs Woolf – but we writers are never jealous' she wrote to Vanessa early in 1920); and knew how to put her down, English lady to wild colonial girl. Then Katherine fuelled Virginia's hostility and superiority with 'Bliss', a story Virginia disliked with some justice for its shallowness: if *that* was the sort of success KM was going in for – . Murry made everything worse, and the tone of Virginia's posthumous essay on Katherine in the *New York Herald Tribune* ('A Terribly Sensitive Mind', 1927) obviously owes a good deal of its sharpness to Bloomsbury's detestation of the man and his cult of his dead wife. But if one returns to Katherine's last extant letter to Virginia, written from Menton, in which she recalls a visit to Asheham (the Woolfs' first Sussex house), it is impossible for us at any rate to resist its evidence of a nervous but true affection. Katherine is again giving the freedom of her city:

> Whenever I think of Asheham it is of clouds – big golden clouds, hazy, spinning slowly over the downs . . . Oh, how beautiful Life is – Virginia, it is marvellously beautiful. Were one to live for ever it would not be long enough . . . Farewell, dear friend (may I call you that)

What happened to Virginia's letters to Katherine? It is possible, I suppose, that Murry, in his pain and exasperation, chucked them out in 1923. The loss is the more to be regretted since Virginia's last references to the living Katherine appear so callous and beside the point. 'Perhaps we fear or hate or wish annihilated this phantom of ourselves': she may have thought so now. She refers to Katherine's 'complete recovery' a few months before her death and, during her last terrible visit to London, remarks to Lytton Strachey: 'What a joke that the Murry's have turned up again! I long to know further developments.'

The further development was announced 'sensationally' by Nelly the cook at breakfast not long afterwards: 'Mrs Murry's dead! It says so in the paper.'

But this is one strand only amongst the many other themes which could be traced through the 600-odd pages of these letters. Her literary judgements are quick, definite, very much her own. Reading *Ulysses* becomes a martyrdom; unshockable by the buggery of Bloomsbury, she is nevertheless shocked by Bloom, and sets her lines of demarcation against Joyce, in spite of Eliot's recommendation: 'a gallant approach', then 'smash and splinters'. But 'Tom Eliot's poem' pleases her at first reading, for sound if not for sense (it was *The Waste Land*). She chides Gerald Brenan for solitariness, his young man's habit of holding books up before his eyes – 'French literature falls like a blue tint over the landscape' – but rejoices herself in the tint of Proust, 'as if a miracle were being done before my eyes'. Clan loyalty makes her overpraise Lytton. She cares for Forster's good opinion, ventures none on his work. Perhaps the most arresting statement in the whole volume is her remark to him that her insanities have 'done instead of religion'.

*New York Review of Books*, 1977

# 2. Millionaire

*The Diary of Virginia Woolf. Volume I: 1915–1919*
edited by Anne Olivier Bell

Writers are not expected to be happy. The penalties of their attempts on fame are often taken to be emotional disorder, gloom, lassitude. The surprise of this first volume of Virginia Woolf's complete diary is that it brims with happiness; and it's not just that she had an archangel in the house to spread his protective wings about her – indeed, her few tiffs with Leonard are caused by his concern that she should not attend too many parties or give up her servants too readily to her sister. Her happiness in these years seems to run through and through the entire fabric of her life: 'But then I am happy ... every virtue should be natural to the happy, since they are the millionaires of the race.' The volume ends with the words, 'I daresay we're the happiest couple in England.' It does look as though the routine they established – retreats to Sussex, months in London, the round of visits from friends, gossip, the garden and enjoyment of the seasons, discreet praise of one another's work and then, more than anything, the work itself – contained almost every ingredient of happiness.

She was not a night diarist; 'casual half-hours after tea' were her time. The entries are irregular, following certain ebbs and flows of mood and moves from Asheham to Richmond and back, catching up after a Garsington weekend, consciously selecting weighty topics at times – such as what her cousin H. A. L. Fisher, in the government, had to say about the last stages of the war – or settling down to consider her friends as gravely as an anatomist; but more often sweeping up 'accidentally several stray matters which I should exclude if I hesitated, but which are the diamonds of the dustheap'. On occasion she grows querulous about a slight, or a fancied one; but beneath all there is a woman of force and self-confidence at work in these notebooks.

Philip Morrell told her she was 'heartless and terrifying'; some of her cruelties may arise from the very robust assertion of her own current state of health and achievement. She meditates a good deal on success and, although there are token remarks about her own lack of it, she knew her quality; it pleased her to be in demand as a reviewer and praised as a novelist. Success, she says, commenting coolly on the marital and professional failure of a friend, is 'an attitude of mind – the way one looks at life'. Noticing a dead horse on the pavement, she sees the pathos from a characteristic angle: 'to die in Oxford Street one hot afternoon, & *to have been only a van horse*'. In her enjoyment of her good fortune at not being a van horse, she sometimes sounds brutal: 'I'm a little doubtful, when I find a cheap ready made young woman out of an office in Oxford and lodging in Harrow, enthusiastic about Robinson Crusoe.' Seen through her own abundant leafiness, Katherine Mansfield and John Middleton Murry are 'leafless trees'. Most chilling is a remark made on passing a long line of imbeciles on the towpath at Kingston:

> The first was a very tall young man, just queer enough to look twice at, but no more; the second shuffled, & looked aside; & then one realized that every one in that long line was a miserable ineffective shuffling idiotic creature, with no forehead, or no chin, & an imbecile grin, or a wild suspicious stare. It was perfectly horrible. They should certainly be killed.

Brilliant, disquieting description; brave of the editor to leave this as it was written (though one would expect no less from an editor so exact and illuminating). Brave of Mrs Woolf too, to let the thought come, with the awareness of her own half-sister Laura shut up somewhere, as well as her own private affliction.

Yet Virginia Woolf's diary is not her 'friend', as Katherine Mansfield's journal was hers. Pressed by Ottoline Morrell, Virginia confessed to having no 'inner life'. She is not much given to self-complicity and layings-bare, more inclined to the brisk and comic. Indeed there are many scenes of pure, almost dramatic comedy: an over-conversational Desmond MacCarthy eased out of the house with an expedient fib about the cook's sister coming to stay; Beatrice Webb proposing a scheme whereby children's building blocks should be 'inscribed with the names of organizations so that in putting them together they would learn their civic duties' (but why, Virginia asks herself, is there this 'half carping half humorously cynical view which steals into one's description of the Webbs'?). Or there is Ottoline, wonderfully complaining that no one *really* falls in love nowadays – except Bertie, whose choice is so often unfortunate – while Virginia mildly protests that romantic love is not the only kind, and the sensible Newnham socialist, Molly Hamilton, interposes helpfully that *she* loves the Independent Labour Party.

Virginia can mock herself too, for her 'suburban' attitude in resenting unacknowledged letters and Christmas presents. She knows she is a snob, deplores her own malice when it produces a backlash, chides herself for pride in her own subtlety of mind. Only once or twice she seems blankly unaware of the absurdity of what she says: apropos Murry, 'I don't like couples where the husband admires the wife's work immensely', or her straightfaced account of Desmond MacCarthy and Leonard looking up the word f— together in the London Library and being 'saddened' to find the thumbprints of many earlier researchers on the page of the dictionary.

The diary, so much more direct and condensed, is more enjoyable even than the letters. There is little about her work (and most of these remarks were published long ago in Leonard Woolf's selection, *A Writer's Diary*), much about the outward state of her life, walks and weather – bad, like being inside a balloon, she said, good in the autumn when they went for mushrooms or blackberries under the downs, or in May ('teeming, amorous & creative' month) when they might eat out with fallen apple blossom under their feet. At Easter in 1919 she wrote modestly about her reasons for writing the diary: 'It loosens the ligaments.'

What sort of a diary should I like mine to be? Something loose knit, & yet not slovenly, so elastic that it will embrace any thing, solemn, slight or beautiful that comes into my mind. I should like it to resemble some deep old desk, or capacious hold-all, in which one flings a mass of odds & ends without looking them through. I should like to come back, after a year or two, & find that the collection had sorted itself & refined itself & coalesced, as such deposits so

78

mysteriously do, into a mould, transparent enough to reflect the light of our life, & yet steady, tranquil composed with the aloofness of a work of art.

Happy prediction from a millionaire of the race.

*New Statesman*, 1977

# 3: Introduction to *Mrs Dalloway* by Virginia Woolf

*Mrs Dalloway*, Virginia Woolf's fourth novel, offers the reader an impression of a single June day in London in 1923, culminating in an evening party given by the wife of a Conservative Member of Parliament in her Westminster house. The day is experienced through the eyes and the minds of diverse people, some but not all of them connected with the hostess's life, past and present; most are well born and comfortably off, and, where the poor and wretched make appearances, it is chiefly in symbolic roles. The book is constructed round the events of the passing hours of the day, though with many excursions into memory; the language is finely worked, now ironic, now lyrical, and the narrative is handed like a ribbon from one character to another, so that we see the world from several different perspectives. Yet Clarissa Dalloway herself remains the pivot, even to the extent that the distressed young madman Septimus Warren Smith, a victim of the war, whom she never meets but only hears about, appears to her as some sort of *alter ego*. Septimus's experience, and Clarissa's feeling of affinity with him, are responsible for the most powerful passages in the book, its account of psychosis, its attack on the medical profession, the description of suicide, and the meditation on the meaning of death – all, it might seem on the face of it, curious subjects to find woven into the celebration of a cloudless summer day in town and a formal evening party in Westminster.

Airy and haunting, it is a book that matches lightness with melancholy. Most of the strands that went into its composition can be clearly traced to their origins in Virginia Woolf's experience. She was forty when she began putting on paper the ideas that developed into *Mrs Dalloway*. This was in 1922. For her, the year had started in illness, a feared recurrence of her mental collapses of 1904 and 1913–15, and also a multitude of physical symptoms, including headaches and a persistent high temperature. Her husband Leonard told in his autobiography of accompanying her on a 'long odyssey through Harley Street and Wimpole Street' at this time; one specialist diagnosed diseased lungs, another inflammation of the heart, incurable and likely to prove fatal very shortly; a third discovered yet another incurable disease. The last Harley Street man they visited gave his three guineas' worth of advice as he shook her hand in farewell: 'Equanimity – equanimity – practise equanimity, Mrs Woolf.' It was, no doubt, excellent advice, said Leonard, 'and worth the three guineas, but, as the door closed behind us, I felt that he might just as usefully have said: "A normal temperature – ninety-eight point four – practise a normal temperature, Mrs Woolf."'

The Woolfs agreed to ignore Harley Street and follow the simple recommendations of their family doctor. She was to rest; and for three months Virginia did as she was told, with the result that both physical and mental collapse were avoided and her symptoms slowly cleared up. Her bed was moved into the sitting-room of Hogarth House, their Richmond home (they also owned Monk's House at Rodmell in the Sussex Downs). Hogarth House was shared with two faithful if temperamental maids, Nelly Boxall and Lottie Hope. It also housed the clutter and machinery of their own publishing firm, the Hogarth Press, for which Virginia normally did typesetting; but now she lay and read by the sitting-room fire, wrote a little and received visitors. A favoured one was her worldly brother-in-law Clive Bell, whose name-dropping and tales of intimate aristocratic luncheon parties provided the frivolous but absorbing entertainment she craved, and made their contribution to the book beginning to form itself in her mind.

In the spring she began to read Proust, whom she admired at once. Because she read him in French, she believed the foreign language shielded her from too direct an influence on her own writing; all the same, there is a Proustian glimmer about *Mrs Dalloway*. Her phrase for his style, 'as tough as catgut & as evanescent as a butterfly's bloom' (*Diary*, April 1925), could be applied as well to her own; though her scale is different, in *Mrs Dalloway* she sets her characters afloat on a glittering metropolitan social surface from which they plumb their deep separate pasts one after another. Proust's great work kept her company over the next few years.

At this same period the Woolf household was greatly preoccupied with politics as well as with publishing, for in 1920 Leonard had agreed to stand as Labour candidate for the Combined English University Constituency (seven universities other than Oxford and Cambridge at that time returned two Members of Parliament). Leonard's convictions put him on the left of the Labour Party, not as a revolutionary but what he called a 'heretical socialist', believing that society should be run for the benefit of consumers rather than for either capitalists or trade unions; he wrote a book to this effect, *Socialism and Co-operation*, and another, derived from his experiences as a colonial administrator in Ceylon, deeply critical of England's imperial policies. His declaration of political faith, put out for the election of November 1922, blames the old men and old methods of the two main political parties not only for the First World War, but also for the troubles of Ireland and the Empire and the disastrous economic condition of the country. He wanted the Treaty of Versailles revised to be fairer to Germany, with the hope of building a united Europe; he wanted disarmament and recognition of the Soviet Union, and he supported the League of Nations; at home he proposed an educational structure which would give real equality of opportunity up to university level. Finally, he called for a more equitable system of taxation with a 'specially graduated levy upon fortunes exceeding £5,000'. It is worth noting Leonard's political creed, because Virginia undoubtedly shared his main views; she sometimes travelled with him to political meetings – to Manchester, for instance, in 1921 – and she also helped to organize regular gatherings of the Women's Co-operative Guild at Hogarth House, and of the local Labour Party at Rodmell. She was, Leonard writes, not a thorough political animal certainly, but 'the last person who could ignore the political menaces under which we all lived'. In the early stages of planning *Mrs Dalloway*, 'the Prime Minister' was to be a leading character, to be contrasted with certain socially disruptive 'Scallywags'.

Leonard was no 'Scallywag', of course, but he took particular pleasure in standing against Virginia's cousin, Herbert Fisher, a Liberal of the type he most detested, who served as Lloyd George's Minister of Education, and whom the Woolfs knew socially. Virginia described Fisher as 'a thin-shredded thread paper of a man, whose brain has been harrowed in to sandy streaks like his hair'; when he spoke he used words that were 'cheerful' and 'colourless', 'slightly mannered & brushed up in conformity with some official standard of culture' (*Diary*, April 1921). Evidently she and Leonard were at one in despising his distinguished emptiness – characteristic of Westminster, and the rulers of the Empire, in their view. But, although she believed there was a good chance of Leonard getting into Parliament, he lost the election, the Conservative and Liberal candidates being returned once again; Virginia's views of such public men, only hinted at in the final version of *Mrs Dalloway*, were forcibly expressed much later in her pamphlet *Three Guineas*.

Another visitor to the Woolfs in 1922 was T. S. Eliot. He came to read his newly composed *Waste Land*, singing, chanting and impressing Virginia with 'its great beauty & force of phrase: symmetry; & tensity [sic]' (*Diary*, July 1922); and doubtless with its bleak images of dead men, some of which are mirrored in *Mrs Dalloway*. The two writers also discussed Joyce's *Ulysses*, which preceded *Mrs Dalloway* in taking a single day in June as its canvas. Eliot praised Joyce, Virginia disliked his work: a genius, she admitted, but pretentious, tricky and underbred, though she used the word 'immortal' of his final chapter, the famous interior monologue of Molly Bloom. Mrs Dalloway is a woman as different in style and experience as it is possible to be from Mrs Bloom; but it is hard not to think that, in giving expression to the flow of her thoughts, her creator showed she had learnt something from what she called Joyce's 'stunts'.

As Virginia recovered from her headaches and fever, she returned to her own half-written third novel, *Jacob's Room*. By the summer it was complete; the Hogarth Press published it in October, and it was immediately praised by Eliot, who told her it was 'a remarkable success', in which she had freed herself 'from any compromise between the traditional novel and your original gift'.* It was her first full-length modernist work (although she had written unconventional short stories like 'Kew Gardens' and 'The Mark on the Wall'),

* T. S. Eliot to Virginia Woolf, 4 December 1922 in Quentin Bell, *Virginia Woolf: A Biography* (London, Hogarth Press, 1972), Volume II, p. 88.

the first to take heed of the criticism and example of her closest and most admired colleague among contemporary women writers, Katherine Mansfield, whose stories were just achieving fame even as her health collapsed. Katherine never read *Jacob's Room* or *Mrs Dalloway* – she died in January 1923, in France – but she would surely have approved and admired. And now, during this summer of 1922, which was divided between Rodmell, Richmond and visits to friends, Virginia embarked on several stories around the figure of Clarissa Dalloway, who had already made a brief appearance with her husband, the well-meaning but largely vacuous Conservative Member of Parliament Richard Dalloway, in her first novel, *The Voyage Out*.

One of these stories, 'Mrs Dalloway in Bond Street', was completed and published in the *Dial*, an avant-garde American magazine, the following year. But the true *Mrs Dalloway* was not set in motion until the autumn, when the stories were abandoned in favour of a full-scale novel. At first there was no question of the madness and suicide themes. On 6 October she wrote two pages of notes as follows:

> Thoughts upon beginning a book to be called, perhaps, At Home; or At the Party.
>
> This is to be a short book consisting of six or seven chapters, each complete separately. In them must be some fusion. And all must converge upon the party at the end. My idea is to have some characters, like Mrs Dalloway, much in relief; then to have some interludes of thought or reflection, or moments of digression (which must be related, logically, to the next) all compact, yet not jerked.
>
> The chapters might be
>
> 1. Mrs Dalloway in Bond Street
> 2. The Prime Minister
> 3. Ancestors
> 4. A dialogue
> 5. The old ladies
> 6. County house?
> 7. Cut flowers
> 8. The party

One, roughly to be done in a month; but this plan is to consist of some very short intervals, not whole chapters. There should be fun.*

Of this plan, only the first and last chapters appear to have survived; and on the reverse side of the sheet are more notes, clearly relating to the proposed second section of the book on the Prime Minister:

P.M.

To give 2 points of view at once; authority and irresponsibility.
Authority prancing through the streets sending uneasiness to Gerard Street.
(diversion upon the respectable worldliness – from point of view of Scallywag who is looking at books.)
P.M. drives on.
Digression on china, French shops, Restaurants.
  Freedom-irresponsibility
    Contrast between thought and action
The guards changing
P.M. reaches Westminster
    (he has a card for the party)
The crowd assembled.†

The Scallywag who is looking at books will become Clarissa, pausing to look into Hatchards' window in Piccadilly, but the Scallywag himself will disappear; if there are traces of him in Peter Walsh and Sally Seton, they have both compromised too well with worldliness and authority to be thought of as threatening – he a colonial administrator, with a bad reputation where women are concerned, but still dining respectably in a Bloomsbury hotel; she the mother of five boys at Eton.

Two days after these notes were written, something happened which set Virginia's imagination working in an entirely new direction. She received the news of the death of an old family friend and

---

* Quoted from Jane Novak, *The Razor Edge of Balance: A Study of Virginia Woolf* (Miami, University Press, 1975).
  † Quoted from Novak, *The Razor Edge.*

society hostess, Mrs Kitty Maxse, a one-time protégée of Virginia's mother, regarded in the family as 'the paragon for wit, grace, charm and distinction'.* Virginia herself had disliked her, however, and thought her a snob. Mrs Maxse had been one of those who had tried to embark Virginia and her sister Vanessa, when they were girls, on a conventional social career, from which both had fled with great determination.

Her death was unexpected; she was only fifty-five, and had fallen down a flight of stairs. The possibility of suicide occurred at once to Virginia, although the idea seems to relate to her own cast of mind rather than to the facts of the matter. Mrs Maxse had merely fainted, slipped and been exceedingly unfortunate. But suicide was something Virginia thought about more than most. She had attempted it herself in 1913; and she kept the idea stored in her mind, to be taken out and examined from time to time, throughout her life.

She and Mrs Maxse had not met since 1908, and Virginia noted but did not attend the memorial service on 11 October. Her detested stepbrother George Duckworth was there, as an habitué of the dead woman's social world (he too makes an appearance, complete with sexual aggression, as Hugh Whitbread, in *Mrs Dalloway*). Three days later, Virginia's diary entry for 14 October shows her planning 'a study of insanity & suicide: the world seen by the sane & the insane side by side – something like that'. The same page of the diary introduces Septimus Smith for the first time: 'is that a good name?' she asked herself.

With the entry of Septimus Smith the early plans to make the Prime Minister a major character, rather than the mere dummy he becomes in the final version, were jettisoned. Just possibly Leonard's failure to be elected to Parliament in mid November tilted the book further away from politics; plus the substitution of first Bonar Law and then Baldwin for Lloyd George as Prime Minister. All the same, Virginia was still expressing her intention of criticizing the social

* Virginia Woolf, *Moments of Being: Unpublished Autobiographical Writings*, ed. Jeanne Schulkind (London, Chatto & Windus, for Sussex University Press, 1976).

system some months later. A diary entry for 19 June 1923 complains of 'almost too many ideas. I want to give life & death, sanity & insanity; I want to criticise the social system, & show it at work, at its most intense.'

There are further notes for 'A possible revision of this book':

Suppose it to be connected in this way.
Sanity and insanity.
Mrs D. is seeing the truth. Septimus seeing the insane truth.
The book is to have the intensity of a play; only in narrative.
Some revisions therefore needed.
At any rate, very careful composition.
The contrast must be arranged.
Therefore, how much detail and digression?
The pace to be given by a gradual increase of S.'s insanity on one side, by the approach of the party on the other.
The design is extremely complicated.
The balance must be very finely considered.
All to take place in one day?
There must be excitement to draw one on.
Also human.
The question is whether the inside of the mind in both Mrs D. and SS can be made luminous – that is to say the stuff of the book – Lights on it coming from external sources.*

These and other exploratory ideas and suggestions to herself (such as 'I want to think out Mrs Dalloway. I want to foresee this book better than the others, & get the utmost out of it' on 29 October 1922) may seem at odds with her own statement, made in the introduction to the American edition of *Mrs Dalloway* in 1928, that she had written the book 'as the oyster starts or the snail to secrete a house for itself . . . without any conscious direction'. But it is easy for an author to forget the precise history of a composition, and with hindsight the structure of a book can come to seem inevitable. The working notes may well have slipped from her mind,

---

* Quoted from Novak, *The Razor Edge*.

or may have seemed themselves no other than the secretions of her imagination.

In the middle of December, Virginia met for the first time the 'lovely gifted aristocratic' Vita Sackville West, 'florid, moustached, parakeet coloured . . . She is a grenadier; hard; handsome, manly', and she made Virginia feel 'virgin, shy & schoolgirlish' (*Diary*, December 1922). Almost at once Virginia heard of Vita's reputation for Sapphism, her word for lesbian love; which made her no less fascinating. During the course of the next two years the two women fell in love, though their physical affair did not begin until 1925. Vita is the only person known to have stirred Virginia to erotic feeling; it is a feeling that is partly given to Clarissa Dalloway in her reminiscences of her lovely, spontaneous girlhood friend Sally Seton. Clarissa states that she was more in love with Sally than with any man; Sally's mere presence under the same roof inspired Clarissa to rapture ('"if it were now to die 'twere now to be most happy" she thought'); Sally had taken her out in the moonlight and kissed her on the lips, giving her the 'most exquisite moment of her whole life'. All this Clarissa recalled exactly when both women were middle aged, married and mothers.

Virginia Woolf wrote this four years before Radclyffe Hall published her explicitly lesbian and, as it turned out, scandalous novel, *The Well of Loneliness*, which Woolf was to defend. Clarissa's musings may seem mild, but they are unequivocal, as she thinks how she 'could not resist sometimes yielding to the charm of a woman', and

> did undoubtedly then feel what men felt. Only for a moment; but it was enough. It was a sudden revelation, a tinge like a blush which one tried to check and then, as it spread, one yielded to its expansion, and rushed to the farthest verge and there quivered and felt the world come closer, swollen with some astonishing significance, some pressure of rapture, which split its thin skin and gushed and poured with an extraordinary alleviation over the cracks and sores!

This is a remarkable passage, whether it alludes to a sexual experience or is no more than an image. It is also linked by its context to

Clarissa's melancholy feelings about her celibate state, for it occurs as she is going to the single bed in which her husband insists she sleeps, undisturbed (and from which she hears him drop his hot-water bottle and swear in another room); it is associated with the 'virginity preserved through childbirth which clung to her like a sheet', and her sense that she had failed as a wife through her coldness.

Other men complain of her frigidity in the course of the book – her old admirer, Peter Walsh, who calls her icicle-cold, and the artist Sir Harry, who comes to her party and regrets her damnable over-refinement – but these passages in which Clarissa deplores her ethereal relations with her husband and nun-like, chaste existence are hard to read without reference to the known conditions of Virginia's and Leonard's marriage, which had the additional sorrow of childlessness (Clarissa is allowed one daughter, Elizabeth, though she is a markedly remote young woman). It was by Leonard's decree that Virginia had no children; he sought the backing of the medical profession, but only some doctors agreed with him, others advising quite the opposite. It was also Leonard's decision that there should be no sex, a resolve which may relate to his personal anxieties and repugnances as well as to his wish to care for his wife. Before his marriage, when he was a colonial administrator in Ceylon, Leonard had complained to his best friend Lytton Strachey that 'Most women naked . . . are extraordinarily ugly.'* When Lytton embarked on a postal campaign to persuade Leonard that he should marry Virginia – a campaign interspersed with flirtatious remarks of his own to Leonard ('Isn't it odd that I've never really been in love with you?') and, still more extraordinarily, an account of his own proposal to Virginia, which she accepted and he then hastily withdrew – Leonard responded with some theoretical initial enthusiasm, but it did not last and he appeared to have ended the subject by declaring in September 1909, 'Of course I know that the one thing to do would be to marry Virginia' but that 'the ghastly complications of virginity and marriage altogether appal me'. He predicted he would instead

---

* Leonard Woolf to Lytton Strachey, 25 November 1908, *Letters of Leonard Woolf*, ed. Frederic Spotts (London, Weidenfeld & Nicolson, 1989).

marry 'at forty a widow or ex-prostitute'. These are a young man's remarks to his Cambridge friend, of course; Leonard returned to England, things changed, he met Virginia (whom he scarcely knew except through Lytton's praises), did indeed fall in love with her, and soon persuaded her to marry him. They were, in some senses, an ideally happy couple, except sexually, and except for her mental instability, which manifested itself dramatically within months of the wedding. Yet it is odd that Leonard never referred to Lytton's letters when he came to write his autobiography. Some scholars, notably Roger Poole in his *The Unknown Virginia Woolf*, have argued that the experience of marriage was not wholly benign for Virginia, and that she suffered from the sense that Leonard controlled her too fiercely.

In her first diary entry for 1923 she has an outburst which bears on all this:

> I am in one of my moods, as the nurses used to call it, today. And what is it & why? A desire for children, I suppose . . . Let me have one confessional where I need not boast. Years & years ago, after the Lytton affair, I said to myself . . . never pretend that the things you haven't got are not worth having; good advice I think. At least it often comes back to me. Never pretend that children, for instance, can be replaced by other things.

And she goes on to describe Leonard telephoning her at the Bells' London house to express his displeasure at her for staying up too late:

> Late again. Very foolish. Your heart bad – & so *my self reliance being sapped, I had no courage to venture against his will*. Then I react. Of course its a difficult question. For undoubtedly I get headaches or the jump in my heart; & then this spoils his pleasure, & if one lives with a person, has one the right – So it goes on. (*Diary*, January 1923; my italics)

She acknowledged her reliance on him, her love and his perpetual goodness, but she was sometimes undoubtedly restless under his control, and resistant. In March she regretted his attitude to 'the social question', because he wanted to refuse invitations, whereas she loved 'the chatter and excitement of other peoples houses'. Again, in June, she complained about being 'imprisoned' in the suburbs by Leonard, 'too much of a Puritan, of a disciplinarian'.

Leonard's failure to arouse her sexual nature, followed by his complete denial of it, and his refusal to let her have children, were painful and troubling. So were the restraints he put on her social life. As she moved into her forties, she realized that she was losing the possibility of a child; on the other hand, she was beginning to be famous, and courted by hostesses; the world was at her feet, and here again Leonard wanted to spoil things. When Lytton Strachey read *Mrs Dalloway* he saw a discordancy in it, partly caused, he said, by the fact that Clarissa is only partly the character Virginia intended: 'I alternately laugh at her & cover her, very remarkably, with myself' (*Diary*, June 1925) is her report of his comment. It is an acute one, for the book is indeed disturbingly personal, the fiction in which she uncovers some of her own deepest wounds and allows her rage to speak.

In January 1923 she gave the manuscript a new name, *The Hours*. She worked at it only intermittently, for she was writing a volume of critical essays, *The Common Reader*, at the same time; and in the spring she and Leonard went to Spain for a month's holiday. In June she noted that 'the mad part tries me so much, makes my mind squint so badly that I can hardly face spending the next weeks at it'. It is not surprising that she found difficulty with this, since Septimus's experience of madness, through the effect of shell-shock, bears a close resemblance to what we know of Virginia's symptoms in her times of breakdown: hearing voices, self-disgust, loathing for the human race, terror of the way doctors forced their will on her. But she got through this triumphantly. Then, 'The design is so queer & so masterful. I'm always having to wrench my substance to fit it. The design is certainly original, & interests me hugely. I should like to write away & away at it, very quick and fierce. Needless to say, I cant. In three weeks from today I shall be dried up.' In August she wrote in her diary of digging out 'beautiful caves behind my characters', and in September she planned to study Lydia Lopokova, the ballerina who was to marry Maynard Keynes, as a 'type' for Lucrezia. In October she was 'in the thick of the mad scene in Regent's Park ... clinging as tight to fact as I can'. She worried about Clarissa, 'too stiff, too glittering & tinsely', but also 'I feel I can use up everything I've ever thought'.

The section on the doctors was written by the following spring (1924), when the Woolfs moved from Richmond to Tavistock Square, to Virginia's great pleasure. In May she noted in her diary:

> London is enchanting. I step out upon a tawny coloured magic carpet, it seems, & get carried into beauty without raising a finger. The nights are amazing, with all the white porticoes & broad silent avenues. And people pop in & out, lightly, divertingly like rabbits; & I look down Southampton Row, wet as a seal's back or red & yellow with sunshine, & watch the omnibus going & coming, & hear the old crazy organs. One of these days I will write about London, & how it takes up the private life & carries it on, without any effort. Faces passing lift up my mind; prevent it from settling, as it does in the stillness at Rodmell.
>
> But my mind is full of The Hours.

In July she made her first visit to Long Barn with Vita ('as a body hers is perfection'); in August she was depressed, fearing the book was 'sheer weak dribble'. Then she was writing the death of Septimus, and thinking of the end, the grand party, and Peter Walsh eating his dinner: 'I like going from one lighted room to another, such is my brain to me.' On 17 October *Mrs Dalloway* was finished.

She started revising at once, and in December

> I am now galloping over Mrs Dalloway, re-typing it entirely from the start, which is more or less what I did with the V.O. [*The Voyage Out*] a good method, I believe, as thus one works with a wet brush over the whole, & joins parts separately composed and gone dry. Really & honestly I think it the most satisfactory of my novels (but have not read it coldbloodedly yet). The reviewers will say that it is disjointed because of the mad scenes not connecting with the

Dalloway scenes. And I suppose there is some superficial glittery writing. But is it 'unreal'? Is it mere accomplishment? I think not. And as I think I said before, it seems to leave me plunged deep in the richest strata of my mind.

*Mrs Dalloway* was published on 14 May 1925. Technically and stylistically, it is among the most brilliant of Virginia's works. It has its thinnesses and weaknesses, one of which is the characterization of Elizabeth Dalloway's tutor, Miss Kilman, the unhappy young woman scholar detested by Clarissa and also apparently by her creator, who loads her with every vice, from being the possessor of an ugly mackintosh to greed at the tea-table of the Army and Navy Stores. Where Miss Kilman was drawn from, and why she gets this vicious treatment, remains mysterious, an uncomfortable blot on the book, and quite inessential to either of its two main themes.

One of these themes is that of London itself, Westminster, St James's, Bond Street, Piccadilly, Bloomsbury, Regent's Park, Tottenham Court Road, Fleet Street and the Strand: you can follow quite exactly the routes taken by Clarissa, Peter, Richard and Elizabeth, on foot or by bus. Virginia Woolf's enjoyment of the city and its pleasures breathes from the pages of the novel: its solid wealth, its motor cars and discreetly luxurious shops selling flowers and jewels to the rich; its stolid royal family, served by self-important courtiers; its luncheons, at which letters to *The Times* are drafted by majestic people of power, position and income; all buttressed by the Empire and mercantile Manchester. This London is full of past and also future, when Bond Street will be 'a grass-grown path and all those hurrying along the pavement this Wednesday morning are but bones with a few wedding rings mixed up in their dust and the gold stoppings of innumerable decayed teeth'. Its rich share with its poor the parks, notably Regent's Park, which provides the setting for the centre of the book; rich and poor also share the enjoyable novelty of an advertising slogan trailed across the sky by an aeroplane. The rich may even venture on to an omnibus to experience one of the pleasures of the poor, as Elizabeth Dalloway does. Servants, however, are likely to take their pleasure vicariously. Mrs Dalloway's maid Lucy is romantically thrilled by the loveliness of her mistress, and by the sight of Miss Elizabeth in her pink dress and the necklace Mr Dalloway has given her; Lucy 'couldn't take her eyes off her'. As for the very poor, like the street singer outside Marylebone station, she is entirely depersonalized; she has her dignity, but it is the dignity of a tree stump rather than a human being.

Similarly, the old nurse knitting on a bench in Regent's Park next to the sleeping Peter Walsh is transformed into something rich and strange:

> In her grey dress, moving her hands indefatigably yet quietly, she seemed like the champion of the rights of sleepers, like one of those spectral presences which rise in twilight in woods made of sky and branches. The solitary traveller, haunter of lanes, disturber of ferns, and devastator of great hemlock plants, looking up, suddenly sees the giant figure at the end of the ride . . .

> Such are the visions which proffer great cornucopias full of fruit to the solitary traveller, or murmur in his ear like sirens lolloping away on the green sea waves, or are dashed in his face like bunches of roses, or rise to the surface like pale faces which fishermen flounder through floods to embrace.

The cadences and imagery here take Woolf's prose very close to poetry. It happens again at another key moment in the book, as Peter Walsh prepares to set off for Clarissa's party:

> Everybody was going out. What with these doors being opened, and the descent and start, it seemed as if the whole of London were embarking in little boats moored to the bank, tossing on the waters, as if the whole place were floating off in carnival. And Whitehall was skated over, silver beaten as it was, skated over by spiders, and there was a sense of midges round the arc lamps; it was so hot that people stood about talking . . .
>
> And here a shindy of brawling women, drunken women; here only a policeman and looming houses, high houses, domed houses,

churches, parliaments, and the hoot of a steamer on the river, a
hollow misty cry.

This is the lyrical Woolf, steeped in her Shakespeare and Wordsworth
and William Dunbar, with his

> London, thou art the flour of cities all.
> Gemme of all joy, jaspre of jocunditie,
> Most myghty carbuncle of vertue and valour.*

The other central theme of the book is the posing of a simple
question: what is the connection between a fortunate, upper-class,
sociable, party-giving, middle-aged London lady on the one hand,
and an insignificant, mad and suicidal young man suffering from
self-hatred and alienation from the rest of the human race on the
other? Septimus is a clerk, meagrely educated but in love with English
literature, which he studied in the Waterloo Road after running
away from his parents' home in Gloucestershire. He volunteered for
the war early, eager to save the England of Shakespeare's plays. He
lost his best friend just before the Armistice, married Lucrezia, the
daughter of a Milanese innkeeper, brought her to London, opened
up his Shakespeare again, and went mad at the new message he
found there, hidden in the beauty of the words: the message that
'the secret signal which one generation passes, under disguise, to
the next is loathing, hatred, despair'.

Septimus knows he is going mad, because he hears his dead friend
speak to him, and because he can feel nothing. He suspects that the
world is without meaning, and that human beings in the mass 'have
neither kindness, nor faith, nor charity beyond what serves to increase
the pleasure of the moment'. He will not allow Lucrezia to have
children, and regards himself as a sinner for having married her
without love. She is simple, good, practical and protective, wishing
to shield him from the brutal interference of the doctors; but in
vain. And when one of the doctors comes to Clarissa's evening party
and announces the suicide of his patient, Clarissa shrinks from the

* William Dunbar, Scottish poet (d. 1513), 'London', l. 16.

doctor as evil, at once suspecting him of making life intolerable for Septimus. She withdraws from her party and considers his death. 'She felt glad that he had done it; thrown it away.' She sees it as a successful act of defiance:

> A thing there was that mattered; a thing, wreathed about with chatter, defaced, obscured in her own life, let drop every day in corruption, lies, chatter. This he had preserved. Death was defiance. Death was an attempt to communicate; people feeling the impossibility of reaching the centre which, mystically, evaded them; closeness drew apart; rapture faded, one was alone. There was an embrace in death.

For Clarissa too feels at times terror and 'overwhelming incapacity' in the face of the necessity of living her life to the end. Although she returns to her party, and is greeted with love, the reader has been made to feel that she and Septimus are indeed, however tenuously, linked, both by their response to beauty – the beauty of words, the beauty of London – and also by their terror of the controls and demands laid on them by others.

The great power of the book lies in this question as to how Septimus and Clarissa are connected with one another; and the question itself has become more compelling in the fifty years since Virginia Woolf's death, because we can see, as few of her early readers could, that it is being addressed by the author to herself, and that she is both the celebrant and the mourner, both the person who is driven mad and the beloved person at the party – both Clarissa Dalloway and Septimus Smith. There is something magnificent as well as touching about her achievement; as about the fact, noted in her diary with pride, that it was the first of her novels to be completed without the interruption of mental breakdown.

Oxford University Press, 1992

# Daily Bread

*English Bread and Yeast Cookery* by Elizabeth David

In my English grandmother's house the children knew exactly what to expect on the table by the day of the week, as the huge Sunday roast was put through its ritual reincarnations, cold, hashed, rissoled, etc., until the dubious relief of fish on Friday. This was not uncommon in lower-middle-class Edwardian households, I am told. At the same time, during the first decade of this century, my French grandmother was making her potages and ragouts and omelettes with a wood-burning stove. She continued to feed her family through two wars, and coal and gas and electricity, and helped her English daughters-in-law to become lively and comforting cooks in turn. My mother could and did make a *gratin savoyard* as well as a treacle pudding.

This was the old family way for kitchen customs and tastes to travel from region to region. Elizabeth David, rather like Boulestin before her, has given us all French and Italian grandmothers. But where Boulestin wrote for a public still supposed to employ cooks, Elizabeth David's influence has been as much in transforming our *batteries de cuisine*, the aspect and atmosphere of our kitchens and gardens, as in putting the flavours of the Périgord, of Lyons or Rome or the Veneto on to our plates. She has made us nostalgic -- and never more so than when John Minton embellished her words with his drawings in *French Country Cooking* (Penguin) in 1951 -- for worlds most of us could not possibly know.

For two and a half decades she has turned our faces away from England. We were a very willing generation to grow greedy and reject Anglo-Saxon culinary conditions. Our infancies had been ruled over by Truby King (of New Zealand), so that many of us were starved by his system of clock and bottle in our cradles. The war and rationing encouraged whole worlds of fantasies about food and travel to flourish in our heads. In the fifties standard English cookery books were still recommending the use of dried egg and margarine, with a pinch of sage as the most dashing herb on the shelf. Against such a background Elizabeth David appeared as liberating and delightful as Homer Lane to the young Auden. Our eclectic kitchens became the hearts of our houses.

Now we are being led to consider one of our native traditions again. Elizabeth David's occasion is partly her bafflement that what is sold in our shops as bread by the big bakery companies can be consumed willingly by anyone; it's also a sense that numbers of men and women are prepared to spend time baking their own bread but that we have lost our traditions here. So *English Bread and Yeast Cookery* has much more than the touch of history and topography that one finds in all good cookbooks. It is a work of devoted scholarship, using all manner of records of the past to re-establish its practices.

A good half of the text is given to a rigorous and carefully illustrated account of types of wheat and flour, milling processes, yeast, ovens and factories. There is a formidable amount of detail involved, and some readers will be impatient to reach Part II on p. 255, where the practical instructions begin. But even if you decide to start the book there, you will find yourself turning back for references and practical advice. For instance, the old belief that yeast needs sugar to feed on is scotched here. Or we are usefully told that there is an operative stone-mill off the Old Kent Road in London whose flour you can buy from the Ceres retail shop. Again, an account is given of the Chorleywood Bread Process, evolved in the sixties, whereby most of our factory bread is now made by an instant method – that is, with much larger quantities of yeast and no proving time at all.

For those who don't know, the 'proving' is the enlarging of the bread dough as the yeast works on it, 'like a lively white cushion, growing bigger and bigger' (so Alison Uttley described it). Mrs David's suggestion for home cooks that the dough be left to prove overnight or even longer under a polythene sheet, with a smaller amount of yeast, transforms breadmaking at once from a nervous and uncertain activity into pure satisfaction. While you sleep, or work, or go to the opera, your bread peacefully makes itself.

A mournful chapter on the present all-too-observable decline of traditional French bread offers a crumb of comfort: it is not traditionally French at all, but a Viennese import of the eighteenth century. With characteristic sense, Mrs David refuses to persuade us that we can hope to reproduce the classic *baguette* with our flour and domestic ovens. She is discouraging too about the combat fatigue induced by attempts to make croissants, but she gives again her marvellous *saucisson en brioche* recipe, and one for *petits pains au chocolat*, on which generations of impoverished Sorbonne students kept going.

Still straying from England, she restores the pizza that dare not give its name to an honourable state. But her emphasis remains English. Listen to the roll-call of our regional breads and cakes: lardy and saffron, wigs or wiggs, bockings, barleymeal bonnags, Mrs Tashis's little puddings, singing hinnies and Sussex plum heavies.

Elizabeth David dislikes uniformity, as all true cooks do. How right she is to blame the toaster that aspires to produce evenly brown slices. She uses instead a metal plate over the gas burner that makes every piece different, 'differently marked, irregularly chequered with the marks of the grill, charred here and there, flecked with brown and gold and black'. She also detests falsity. Here is the passage in which she describes a modern confidence trick whereby factory bakers install 'live' bakeries within their retail shops, the idea being to lure in customers with the smell of hot bread:

> Those who fall for the hot and crusty line regardless of the price soon perceive for themselves that while its aroma may be as heady as the scent of a beanfield in midsummer its taste is suspiciously like that of the supermarket loaf, its texture still that of boiled wool. For all that your bread shop may be decked out as a wholesome little old country bakery with smell to match, the dough has been made by methods very little different from the ones used in the great big shining factory. And it is a fact of life that *all* bread, home-made, factory-made, bakery-made, good, indifferent, and just plain awful, gives out a glorious smell while it's baking and for a few minutes after being drawn from the oven.

I find this exceedingly sad: the smell of baking bread, like the smell of freshly cut grass, has always spoken of innocence and virtue. Now we know it's no guarantee of anything.

*Sunday Times*, 1977

# Two Essays on Thomas Hardy

## 1. The Boy in the Grass

*The Collected Letters of Thomas Hardy. Volume I: 1840–1892*
edited by Richard Little Purdy and Michael Millgate
*An Essay on Hardy* by John Bayley
*The Older Hardy* and *Young Thomas Hardy* by Robert Gittings

When Thomas Hardy was a small boy he lay on his back one day, felt the sun's rays filtering through his straw hat, and decided he did not want to grow up. He 'did not want to be a man, or to possess things, but to remain as he was, on the same spot'. His mother was not pleased when he told her, but the idea that it might be better not to live life did not go away. It comes in a letter to Rider Haggard on the death of his child:

> Please give my kind regards to Mrs Haggard, & tell her how deeply our sympathy was with you both on your bereavement. Though, to be candid, I think the death of a child is never really to be regretted, when one reflects on what he has escaped.

Hardy was fifty-one, and childless; and a child to him is often himself as a child. He told Gosse, in one of his rare letters that approach intimacy, 'You would be quite shocked if I were to tell you how many weeks and months in byegone years I have gone to bed never wishing to see daylight again.' On his eighty-sixth birthday he was still claiming that 'He had never expected much' and that he was not one who loved life desperately. This degree of reluctance to embrace life, so odd in a man who studied its appearances so lovingly, is one of Hardy's most strongly marked characteristics. It's as though he had to keep perpetually on guard against being caught out and disappointed.

The letters indicate someone careful, efficient, closed; there is no flow of outgoing warmth. It is well known how tenacious he was of his privacy, how he dismissed and lied to would-be biographers and wrote misleading memoirs, intending to pass them off as his second wife's work. The biographer's problem with Hardy is how to relate this dry, defensive man to the diffident but super-responsive presence felt in the poems and novels, a presence so attractive, so aptly described by John Bayley as a 'tremulous tender fleeting entity'. Secrecy lies like a crust on his skin, suggesting something abnormally sensitive or damaged within.

Some of this crust was lifted by Robert Gittings in the first volume of his biography of Hardy, revealing enough to make it clear that he could not find him a likeable man. In the second volume, which is again exactly researched and well weighed in its judgements, he confronts the question of Hardy's adult personality more fully. He shows him torn between his Dorset peasant roots and success in the literary social world. He describes him as a perpetual adolescent, unable to escape from his obsessions, crushing first one wife and then the next.

Gittings reveals that Emma Hardy's terminal illness went almost unnoticed because of Hardy's passion for Florence Dugdale; and that Florence was no sooner his wife than she too receded into one on whom many burdens were coldly placed with no return of tenderness. Evidently Thomas was not a good husband, self-centred to the point of cruelty, self-concealing, touchy and mean, giving (in Emma's phrase) 'neither gratitude nor attention, love, or *justice*, nor anything you may set your heart on'.

At least Gittings has done Emma the justice she yearned for, in taking her character and unhappiness seriously. And he has performed the same service for the infinitely more pathetic Florence, the pretty, sickly Enfield schoolmistress Hardy managed to smuggle into the structure of his domestic life while Emma still lived and to whom Emma, in a moment of grim comedy, confided the thought that Hardy bore a close resemblance to Dr Crippen.

Later, in a ghastly parody of Emma's supposed madness, which consisted of keeping a bitter private diary called 'What I think of my husband', Florence took to writing hysterical letters to friends, especially young women who still caught the old eagle's eye. For Hardy was stirred by beauties to the end, like the milkman scolded in *The Hand of Ethelberta* for 'pouncing upon young flesh like carrion crow – 'tis a vile thing in an old man'. But he defends himself with ''Tis; and yet 'tis not, for 'tis a nateral taste.'

This natural wisdom was noted by Hardy when he was still under forty and not long married, in a novel about a woman struggling to lead a double life between her Dorset peasant family and her grand friends. Emma Hardy disliked it: 'too much about servants', she said. It also suggests a deeper source of distress in his life.

Gittings establishes with beautiful clarity the pattern of Hardy's repeated fallings in love after his marriage. Most of the ladies were literary women whom he was able to help in their careers, but in all these affairs they remained sexually inaccessible, whatever he may have hoped. They were of a class in which anything else was apparently unthinkable. Now, as Gittings points out, the women of Hardy's own family, all of whom he loved and admired almost without reservation, had been different. Not only his mother but both his grandmothers had conceived children outside wedlock. A good, if not clinching, factual case is made by Gittings for Tess herself being modelled on Hardy's paternal grandmother.

John Bayley also points out how Tess, Hardy's most vivid and intimate creation, the character towards whom he feels most possessive, 'My Tess', became 'both the girl of his youthful dreams and of his adult sense of a lost and unregarded past'. The women of the past offered an erotic fulfilment that the women of the present denied to Hardy.

It is hard to think of anything more withering and numbing than this exceptional responsiveness to the impressions of the world, including women, which made Hardy a great novelist and poet, occurring in such a way that it actually severed him from the fulfilment he sought in women. His ambition, good and pleasing to his mother and grandmothers, led him to a world in which no woman rewarded him as his mother and grandmothers had rewarded his forebears.

Bayley points to the sense of loss suffered by Hardy as creator, as well as by Angel Clare, at the end of *Tess*. And there is scarcely one of his love poems that is not washed through with this sense of loss. It is now a commonplace to say that Hardy was more interested in dead women than living; perhaps it was that by dying they seemed to take their places in the lost erotic world of his grandmothers.

Hardy scholars are already indebted to Gittings, and now doubly so, or perhaps not quite doubly, since it is the first half of a writer's long life that shapes his work most profoundly. Still, he is good on the notebooks, into which Hardy and Emma copied facts from books and periodicals and which on occasion were poured pell-mell into whatever Hardy was currently working on. Hardy's abandonment of novel writing is attributed to a wish for freedom to say what he liked both in intellectual and moral matters and in personal revelation. He thought, quite wrongly as it turns out, that snoopers would be less likely to try to track his indiscretions in verse. Gittings adds, with typical common sense, that he may have found novels physically tiring to write. Poems are lighter.

*The Older Hardy* is a book rich in observation, always careful in the use to which it is put and occasionally hitting off an inspired phrase, when for instance he talks of Hardy's life 'feeding on the failing vitality' of Florence's, as in a fairy-tale. The sudden warmth of the deathbed scene is good, with Hardy asking to have kettle-broth made at the bedroom fire as his mother made it; a dish of parsley, onions, soaked bread and bacon. And the horrors of the funeral arrangements, heart to Stinsford, body to the Abbey, tutted over by the pious and getting a shocked cackle from the rustics, are given just as Hardy would have relished them.

It is a hard truth that men of genius may have bad characters, as Gittings shows Hardy had. Fortunately most Hardy-lovers are not his wives and not obliged to live with the bad character. They can slide away to the 'silent man who forces himself to speak' of John Bayley's phrase. Bayley's loosely structured essay is continuously interesting on the poetry and the novels. He suggests that Hardy used the conventions of Victorian extrovert fiction for his own ends, remaining unobtrusive within, 'a deer in the thickets'. It's a perfect image for Hardy, recalling incidentally the boy in the grass with his hat over his face. And although his book is not strictly biographical, he does restore to us that vulnerable Hardy who has somehow disappeared from Gittings's account.

*Sunday Times, 1978*

# 2. Memory and Loss: On Hardy's Poetry

Thomas Hardy is the great exception to the rule that lyric poets lose their voices as they age. The best of Hardy's love poems were not written, like those of Keats and Donne, when he was in his twenties but in his seventies. In them he addressed the wife he had slighted and neglected for decades, restoring her to youth and happiness – a young woman with 'bright hair flapping free' as she rode her pony along the wild Cornish cliff-edges, with 'gray eyes, and rose-flush coming and going'. He summoned her up in her 'original air-blue gown', and offered passionate elegies to her ghost: 'Woman much missed, how you call to me, call to me . . .'

It was too late for poor Emma to enjoy the tribute, and the poems caused anguished jealousy to Hardy's second wife, Florence, long secretly loved but now herself relegated to the dusty indifference he accorded to accessible women. But the greatness of the poems was seen by critics and public alike, and Hardy has remained one of the most popular of English poets ever since. He went on writing until his death in 1928, and his collected verses cover nearly nine hundred pages, on every one of which there is something odd, powerful or poignant.

Hardy is the poet of memory, loss and regret, not only for women, but for a whole world centred on his native Dorset. His forebears were all countrymen and women. Although he cast them off and concealed their existence in the name of Victorian respectability, it was they who nourished his writing, their history and the changing features of their lives that filled both novels and poetry: the vanishing world of isolated villages, the culture of woodland and moor, the itinerant workers, shepherds, schoolteachers and tranters (carriers), the farm labourers and church musicians such as his father and grandfather had been.

His first known poem was inspired by his Dorset past, a remembrance written at the death of his grandmother of her telling him about his own birthplace when she first came to it:

> Our house stood quite alone, and those tall firs
> And beeches were not planted. Snakes and efts*
> Swarmed in the summer days, and nightly bats
> Would fly about our bedrooms. Heathcroppers
> Lived on the hills, and were our only friends;
> So wild it was when first we settled there.

And his first published poem told a village story of the girl forced to marry against her will and saved for her true love by a fire on her wedding night. When it appeared in the *Gentleman's Magazine* in 1875, the editor changed Hardy's 'her cold little buzzoms' to 'her cold little figure': sadly, the 'improvement' remains in the collected works to this day.

Hardy kept all his life a child's eye for detail and a wondering sense of the tricks played by time. A poem about landscape paintings at the Royal Academy broods on the fact that all the models for the greenery – leaves, blossom and grass – are now brown, withered and dead. Bird song, in another poem, prompts him to reflect that a year ago none of the singers yet existed, but were mere 'particles of grain,/And earth, and air, and rain'. Inanimate objects inspire similar thoughts: finding the metal skeleton of a sunshade under Swanage cliffs, he speculates how long ago it was abandoned there, and in what circumstances. Noticing how a woman smiles at a blank wall, he elicits the reason, that someone had once traced the shadow of her son upon it, and she keeps the memory of the faint drawing under the new whitewash.

On a summer walk, winged thistle seeds rise at the brush of a petticoat; on a winter walk, the drops on a gate bar look like a row of silver buttons. A city shopwoman, thinking of the family she hopes to have, imagines how her future children's 'shining heads would dot us round / Like mushroom balls on a grassy ground' – a characteristically awkward and delightful image.

At Christmas 1915, Hardy, now seventy-five, remembered how he was told as a child that the cattle knelt in their pens at midnight,

---

* Efts are small lizards.

and confessed that, if he were invited to look now, he would go, 'Hoping it might be so', despite his unbelief. The child who had played the accordion at four, and the fiddle soon after, kept the rhythms of village music and celebrated the traditions and secret stories of village life for eight decades. He said he never sought to present a 'view' of things, but relied on fugitive impressions; yet in his private movement from the land and the culture of speech and song to the town and the written word, he was part of the general cityward migration, and spoke for its aspirations and its regrets. His fugitive impressions have helped to form the images most of us still carry around, of a pastoral culture which was narrow and harsh, but with its own natural dignity and beauty; and which we join him in mourning, because we know it can never return.

*Country Living*, 1990

# Snapdragon

*For Love Alone* and *Letty Fox: Her Luck* by Christina Stead

Christina Stead was born in Sydney in 1902; she came to Europe in 1928, lived in America during the forties, left for Europe again during the McCarthy period and has now completed the circle back to Australia. Her best-known novel is *The Man Who Loved Children*, a mammoth study of the family as a battleground of monsters prepared to fight to the last claw. It's a book that has been much admired without becoming generally popular; her others are very little known in this country. But Lillian Hellman said last year that she ought to be given a Nobel Prize; other, younger critics have become interested in her work; and now Virago, with its usual excellent judgement, has put out two of her novels of the mid forties in paperback.

Paperback monsters – they are huge books, like catalogues or encyclopaedias of the female condition. Somebody should have made her leave out a lot; she is like an unappeasable hostess piling up the plate. It's all good, but it's too much; the reader flags. (This is not just reviewer's grouse.) But then one has to say that they are also magnificent books. They are cold and snappish, solid, very literary; with a great deal of digested reading of classic fiction behind them. Anyone who doubts whether there are still real books being produced should read one this summer.

They are classically conceived, too, in spite of the elephantiasis. *For Love Alone* – the wrong title, suggesting a soft-hearted book – is the story of an obsession and its breaking. Teresa (of *The Man Who Loved Children*) determines to break away from the remnants of her family and from Australia and finds her motive power in her love for Jonathan Crow, a young university teacher who sails for London ahead of her. Crow is a wretch; he uses women to buttress his own shaky confidence and whines about his poverty. But Teresa needs an idol and he is smart and quick and helps her to see there are possibilities apart from the horrors of Sydney. The first third of the book makes one's bones ache by its picture of the lives of those nice Australian women, spinsters, office and college girls, aunts and sisters all concentrated on trousseaux and prying into one another's prospects. To get away from this Teresa takes a factory job, pinches every penny, walks miles to work, rejects a decent suitor and half starves herself for several years till she has the passage money to Europe. Crow writes her occasionally flirtatious letters; she dreams of and adores him.

She arrives to find London grimy, dark and depressed; these are the thirties. Crow treats her with nonchalant cruelty. It becomes a tale of two city atmospheres, Sydney thick with genteel sweat, London poverty at the Gissing level, with Euston Road lodgings, rude landladies, and a cup of tea at Lyons a luxury. It also concerns itself with ugly cravings, since both Crow and Teresa are the victims of ideals of chastity and find no decent way of coming to terms with it. The good man who appears for her at the end is quite insubstantial, much less vivid than her last sight of the graceless Crow, luridly reflected in a cheap jeweller's window.

The patently autobiographical aspect may be responsible for the density of the atmosphere, the emotional charge of the book. Teresa is almost crushed, but the author is as near to being tenderly engaged on her behalf as one can imagine her being – whereas Letty, in *Letty Fox*, is a creature of tough, rubbery resilience and self-esteem who amuses her creator almost as much as Lorelei amused Anita Loos twenty years before. Letty is an American girl born about 1920. She quickly learns the lessons of her milieu: first, the necessity of trying to attach every male she meets to herself, by whatever means; second, the persistent extraction of money from men. Pleased with her successes and only briefly abashed by her failures, she narrates her own story without a trace of sentiment, as stoutly and straightforwardly as any young rogue bred to petty crime. The sexual act is nothing to her but a transaction; it's what you get in return that counts. You can see why, when the book was published in 1946, it shocked by its matter-of-factness, its claim to represent the experience of ordinary New York college girls.

Letty despises her mother, as all the women in the book do, because she has failed not only to keep her husband but – much worse – to extract any alimony from him. This is the essential, which everyone else manages much better. A wondering French observer remarks,

> What luck you have, you American women! Men who pay for everything and don't ask for accounts. Yes, it's Protestantism. The men believe they've done their wives insult and injury by sleeping with them. They must pay for ever! . . . And as for the women . . . they behave as if they are disabled for life as soon as they're married.

Letty's grandmothers and aunts and cousins are all in this business of selling and blackmailing on a sexual basis, producing children as reinforcements. One virtuoso aunt claims to have four who, although they are never seen, are used entirely effectively against her humorous but doglike husband until he commits despairing suicide.

Letty's reminiscences take her to England (a progressive school, smartly put down) and France; to her two grandmothers, one a rich hotel-owner; to college and New York office life, until she does finally enter the haven of marriage to a rich man. Her obsession with her looks, her clothes, her talents, her constant self-appraisal and awareness of her family's appraisal of her 'chances' have brought her to this necessary culmination.

A certain perspective is opened on to all this by Letty's father's mistress, always named in a whisper as *die Konkubine* by the other women and mysterious to them because she lives outside the rules of their game. She works; she refuses to bear children; she laughs and displays no jealousy, nor does she fret for money or marriage. So un-American is she indeed that she advises Letty, seriously considering psychoanalysis, to take the alternative: only 35 cents, she points out, for a fortune teller. The book is full of these sharp asides.

If Teresa's story is an *Education Sentimentale*, Letty's is a girl's *Tom Jones*. Both are real feats of imagination, their triumphs lying chiefly in the way they convey atmosphere and state of mind. Each concentrates on a single figure, one refusing the pressures of her environment, the other adapting all too perfectly. There is otherwise almost nothing by way of plot, and the many peripheral characters are presented flatly, often as grotesques. One doesn't credit them with inner lives. Instead, Mrs Stead's prejudices bristle about the place; and there is a good deal of grim humour. She's a formidable and entirely individual writer; I hope Virago will reprint more of her work.

*New Statesman*, 1978

# Patron Saint

*E. M. Forster: A Life. Volume II* by P. N. Furbank

Dorothy Parker, not much given to reverence, said in the 1950s she'd go on hands and knees to reach E. M. Forster. If she had it might have flustered him; but it was an improvement on earlier Americans who had been inclined to congratulate him on his Hornblower books. By now he had become a figure to be 'honoured for personal goodness and sanctity'. He was old – in his seventies – and he had lived through a period of amazing political upheavals and *volte-face* among intellectuals without shifting from his own consistently humane and temperate standpoint. P. N. Furbank suggests that the word 'holiness' had crept into some friends' views of him. An agnostic saint? Certainly his physical presence in Cambridge had its awe-inspiring aspect; he would appear in the front court of King's rather like an ancient, sacred tortoise who might decide to snap or draw in his head. One knew the wisdom was stored inside.

Lionel Trilling's wartime study praised Forster's work for going beyond the limitations of the liberal imagination, but put the emphasis squarely on his reliability: 'He is one of the thinking people who were never led by thought to suppose they could be more than human and who, in bad times, will not become less.' Without raising his voice (literally: he was wholly inaudible at a European writers' conference in 1935) or adopting a mandarin style, he had established his views on race, militarism, the Empire, the public schools, class, nationalism, business ethics, sexual orthodoxy and indeed most of the large issues of his time. He had taken on the burdens of the public man of letters, fighting with the BBC during one of its red-scare periods (1931), presiding over the National Council for Civil Liberties, signing joint letters protesting at book censorship, active for a while in the PEN club; but he had never grown what Coleridge, speaking of Wordsworth, called a 'moral film over the eye'.

Still, Furbank's Forster is not a secular saint. He is a tetchy, honourable, mostly endearing creature. One of the virtues of this book – and the second volume is still more enjoyable than the first – is the dry affection with which it is written. Furbank never deflates his subject; his personal feeling for the man is clear, though not obtrusive, and his own diary notes have been a valuable source. But he looks straight at the less pleasing aspects of Forster's personality: his misogyny, for instance, which led him to accuse women of wanting to destroy men's club life, while at the same time objecting to the idea of female homosexuality on the grounds that they shouldn't try to do without men. It also made him refuse Leonard Woolf's request that his wife should be allowed to read his homo-sexual novel *Maurice* and then complain that her critical estimate of his work was based on insufficient knowledge of it. Women were to him at best 'a sort of rich subsoil' in which to rest and grow – this was his phrase for his tyrannous old mother. At worst they might be labelled 'rubbishy little creature', as Evie was in *Howards End*.

A central theme of this book is inevitably Forster's experiences as a homosexual, which led him into some curious scrapes and guilty feelings as well as contentment. Like Isherwood (who was very frank about this in *Christopher and His Kind*) he was drawn only to young men of lower classes or different cultures; thus although there might be much friendliness between him and his loves, there was never equality. Nor was he ever able to enact what he imagined in his fiction, the setting up of a domestic life with a partner. He enjoyed being the benefactor and educator. No doubt he saw a great difference between paid encounters with male prostitutes arranged by sympath-etic friends and tender, long affairs. It is moving to read of his happiness when he met the policeman, Bob Buckingham, and believed himself loved, in his early fifties. But there was still a strong element of patronage, even though it came to include friendly patronage of Mrs Buckingham too. One can't help feeling distinctly uneasy about the account of this affair, partly because Buckingham himself – incredibly – denied that he was aware of Forster's homo-sexuality; and also because of the element of cruelty and exploitation which is clear in a letter from Sebastian Sprott to Forster in which he urges him to do everything he can to lure Buckingham away from his newly confined wife:

'She is so miserable when I am away.' And so on. Well then you have a nice line in counter-arguments, and among them FREEDOM, which is much thought of by any who want to appear modern.

It is clear that both Buckingham and his wife to a degree had their heads turned by being introduced into Forster's world; but the situation settled down into a fairly stable and happy one, with Forster godfather to their son and benefactor to the whole family.

Furbank picks his way through these difficult areas without being coy or sensational: a triumph of his own sense and good feeling. He is also deft and funny describing Forster's running battle with his aristocratic neighbours in Surrey over footpath rights, leases and a patch of woodland he cherished. But the two most absorbing sections of the book are probably the foreign ones. During the First World War, Forster, more or less a pacifist, got himself Red Cross voluntary work in Alexandria, visiting wounded British soldiers in hospital. Here he met Cavafy, studied Egyptian history, enjoyed his work and the sunshine but felt lonely until he fell in love, romantically, with a tram conductor called Mohammed, and saw through his eyes the horrors of colonialism. Furbank shows that *A Passage to India* owes something to Forster's Egyptian experiences as well as to India, where he went after the war to be secretary to the Maharaja of Dewas, taking part in the preposterous intrigues and rituals of the court. He returned to England deeply depressed and wrote apropos the half-finished novel:

> When I began the book I thought of it as a little bridge of sympathy between East and West, but this conception has had to go, my sense of truth forbids anything so comfortable. I think that most Indians, like most English people, are shits, and I am not interested whether they sympathize with one another or not. Not interested as an artist; of course the journalistic side of me still gets roused over these questions.

From this account it is Forster the journalist, not Forster the artist, who has been most acclaimed. Forty years later, when the book was dramatized, he again denied that he had written about the incompatibility of East and West, saying he was really concerned with the 'difficulty of living in the universe', as Furbank noted in his diary.

The implied verdict is that Forster himself managed it better than most. His lapses have rather the air of a spoilt only child's lapses, and did little damage. He was generous and loyal; he lived with what seemed a dangerous secret handicap in his generation, albeit an exciting one. Even though he stopped writing novels – nervous of his own success, suggests Furbank – his fame grew. And he never lost his descriptive powers. Nine years before his death he nearly died of a blood deficiency and wrote an account of the occasion:

Only weakness, and too weak to be aware of anything but weakness. 'I shan't be here if I get any weaker than this' was the nearest approach to a thought ... Bob's little finger pressed mine and pursued it when it shifted. This I shall never forget.

How well he observed the sensations; and when the real time came it was marked by the same calm and affection.

*New Statesman*, 1978

# Winter Words

*The View in Winter: Reflections on Old Age* by Ronald Blythe

Old age: are we lucky if we get there? Perhaps not, now that so many of us do. Ronald Blythe's panorama of the south coast of England lined with lightly tanned, well-dressed octogenarians gazing out to sea is distinctly eerie. What are they looking for? 'It is as though one needs a special strength to die,' he says; and the risk, if one lingers too long, is the loss of that most precious possession, the sense of individuality.

In the old days the Workhouse lay in wait. Now it is the geriatric ward or the Home (curiously named: the point about a Home is that it is not home). 'My friend went to one and she was bitterly lost. They just dumped her there . . . They lost my friend in a home,' comments one lady of ninety-one, aptly enough. For where a single Lear makes a tragedy, a large roomful must be an inferno.

One of the darkest themes of this remarkable book is the hatred that the middle aged can develop for their helpless, devouring parents, for the mother who has abdicated into childishness, the father grown mumbling and apologetic. Visiting time at the Home, according to an observant matron, brings guilt-ridden, middle-aged children who speak in hushed voices. Perhaps what they hate most is the view of their own futures.

But *The View in Winter* is not all gloom. Here is an extraordinary gallery of self-portraits, beings who expected never to be noticed again, who believed all their skills and pride and memories were about to disappear without trace; and Blythe saved them. Travelling about England over a period of several years, his gift was to hear them out, to perform the loving service of the listener. For him they were glad to spread their wings one last time; and he, like a man who has visited a beehive at the end of summer, came away with riches.

They speak of their childhoods, of the wars in which they fought, of babies lost, of mine disasters, of the Empire – source of much pride – and of their work which once seemed so important. One lady of eighty-six, newly bereaved of the friend who had shared her life, describes the grief which has swamped everything else: 'You must have memories . . . or it would not be the wonderful past which would be inside you but the dreadful now.' As one feared, age does not diminish this sort of pain.

A railway crossing-keeper's son starts to describe his wooing and soon his memory gives something more:

> I was a-courting her thirteen year. Thir . . . teen . . . year. I used to pull all the water up for her out o' that ol' well behind the pub where she lived with her aunty. I saw her brew and bake and do it all. She's the one, I thowt. Lovely, that well was but they condemned it. Ol' people thereabouts lived to be eighty and ninety a-side o' that well and niver took no harm from it. Soo that's the beginnin' o' the matter. I don't know where the end will be, do yew? I reckon we're comin' to it fast, but there it is.

His impression that the world is on the point of becoming not worth living in is shared by many of his contemporaries, whatever the hardships of their youth. Even the men who survived the horrors of the trenches in the Great War now speak lyrically of it as a supreme experience of comradeship; one darkly foretells that *now*, 'something awful must happen soon'.

The pace of change in this century contributes to this apocalyptic notion. Many learnt their skills from parents who had them in turn from a long line of ancestors, but have lived to see them become obsolete. The Montessori teacher, a brave New Woman who liberated herself and several generations of small children, sees today's little ones run out of her parties to watch *Dr Who*. The neurosurgeon and the engineer can hardly follow new developments in their fields, the farrier shut his father's and grandfather's forge one day and said flatly: 'It was the *time* to give up.'

The effect of these ancient voices, all between the covers of a single volume, is overpowering. Maybe this is why Ronald Blythe has diluted them with his own essays. They are well informed and wide-ranging in their literary allusions. But at the risk of sounding ungrateful about a book which has shaken me and which I intend to keep to hand, I'll say that even the most intelligent general commentary seems lacklustre when set against the truth in acute and particular shape. A last example: Lady Thelma, ninety, is now settled on a housing estate. She describes the mist of death coming towards her,

> Dear death, how I look forward to it . . . So weary, you know. This tiredness just falls on top of me like a dead weight. Such utter, utter weariness – you have no idea.

The next minute, with peals of laughter,

> Talking of the dead, I'd like some of the people I used to know to see me in my new bungalow. See their faces, you know. They'd look around and say, 'Thelma – *dear!*'

And how she lives, in Blythe's fine reporting, with her approaching death and her precious, individual laughter.

*Sunday Times*, 1979

# Rosa Mundi

*Burger's Daughter* by Nadine Gordimer

This is a big, unwieldy, even elephantine book, making little or no attempt to woo the reader, very difficult to get into, roughly and boldly constructed, with an ugly title: but I don't intend to be rude about Nadine Gordimer's new novel. To follow a writer as neat and crisp as she can be into a deliberately and monumentally awkward piece of fiction is more absorbing than to read most novelists going through well-oiled routines.

She has always been able to show us Africa, its flesh, earth and leaf, and this book even more than her earlier ones tells us how things look and feel, nails detail so that it speaks its own moral. The houses, gardens and pools of the South African bourgeoisie, the cityscapes, dreadful featureless townships, hot squares where typists eat their lunchtime sandwiches; the queue outside a prison, an empty flat, a leafy cottage doomed by a coming motorway. The visual record *is* the emotion here. A little boy drowned in his parents' swimming pool is remembered ever after by his sister for the pink flecks of his breakfast bacon vomited with the blue water as their mother tried in vain to revive him. Again, a character named Marisa Kgosana, whose husband is imprisoned on Robben Island, wears her splendid sexual beauty and her clear laughter throughout the book as though they were themselves banners for the cause of freedom: as indeed they become. Even more than in her earlier books, Gordimer has chosen here to describe so amply that comment is needless. It's an apt way of delineating a society in which everyone is officially prejudged on the basis of their skin colour.

This same intolerable condition made Lionel Burger, a successful doctor and father of the heroine, into a lifelong communist fighter against apartheid. He dies, still in his middle years, in prison. His daughter, named for Rosa Luxemburg, grows up to think of her parents' refusal to give up fighting apartheid as normal; prison visits, imprisonment and surveillance are her staples. Sometimes she even thinks of herself through the eyes of her surveillants. This may make her sound more accessible than she actually appears in the course of her story. For Rosa is drawn opaquely; and she is so distant from the norms we are accustomed to, so unresponsive to the usual promptings of the reader's imagination as it circles around the writer's, that I was often baffled.

Gordimer denies us any psychological analysis of Rosa. There is no dwelling on her intimate sense of herself, her feelings, her possibilities. It is important that she does not get on with men who might view her in that light; this is not the Portrait of a Lady; the traditional male approach to a young woman – what couldn't she do, what couldn't I rouse her to? – is nothing to her. She is already set on her own course; she knows what she can do, although we don't. She is without ambition and especially without erotic ambition. She is also quiet. Without the gestures of self-sacrifice and heroism she accepts that her path must lie through the prisons of South Africa. There is no mention of duty towards her parents' memory; she is curious about their past but not pious. Still, it was they who set off the little engine that works inside her. One would like to know more of its workings, although Gordimer implies that simple humanity is enough to explain it. But then what makes so many others deny the simple humanity of the Burgers? Is communism the only effective weapon against apartheid?

The climax of the book is brought about when Rosa visits Europe, having first worked skilfully and patiently to be allowed a passport. She goes to her father's first wife in a village on the Côte d'Azur among kindly, gossiping, sun-worshipping friends who live as though nothing had happened in the twentieth century. A meal on a terrace, flowers, wine, sun, love or the memory of love, these are their staples; and they cherish their own comforts carefully. Here Rosa for the first time becomes the mistress of a man she loves, a French schoolteacher away from his family to work on his thesis on the cultural effects of the colonial experience. The claims of private happiness, with all its romantic panoply, begin to be made. Rosa and her lover seem wholly congenial; he proposes that they should bind their lives together, adulterously but permanently, in Paris. Only, with this same lover she has looked at the paintings of Bonnard and he has remarked how they, like her Côte d'Azur friends, take no account of the experiences of the century, wars and camps and racial contempt; with him, if she accepts him, she will perhaps slide also into a way of life that is removed from public concerns. Can she do this, or even risk becoming a token expatriate South African liberal?

Gordimer endorses Rosa's determined rejection of the private world in favour of a return to South Africa and, inevitably, prison. She implies too that it is not really possible for the European mind to meet the South African experience, to encompass the nature of what is going on there. I accept her verdict; it seems to me that *Burger's Daughter* is written out of the moral commitment which makes charm and happiness look shabby if they are bought at the price of turning your back on atrocity.

Well, that's right. But also: I'm glad nobody made Bonnard feel guilty about painting what made him happy, a naked woman in the bathroom, a meal on the terrace.

Punch, 1979

# Girl with Scissors

*Christina Rossetti* by Georgina Battiscombe

Consider a girl of temper so violent that she 'ripped up' her own arm with a pair of scissors when rebuked by her mother. Consider the same girl at twenty-four writing this verse:

> It's a weary life, it is, she said:
> Doubly blank is a woman's lot:
> I wish, I wish I were a man:
> Or better than any being, were not:
>
> Were nothing at all in all the world,
> Not a body and not a soul:
> Not so much as a grain of dust
> Or drop of water from pole to pole.

The girl's father is an invalid, a scholar and exile who often expresses the wish that he were dead. In the family parlour hangs the portrait of her mother's favourite brother, John Polidori, once Byron's physician, later a suicide. Of the four children, two are called 'the calms': they are sensible like their mother; but Dante Gabriel and Christina Rossetti – she is the girl with the scissors – are 'the storms'.

Christina's life began in 1830 and was passed chiefly in north London; as Georgina Battiscombe tells us in her calm and sensible biography, it was outwardly uneventful. She lived at her mother's side until her mother died, and survived her by only eight years. Teaching, the only possible career then for a girl of her background, was unpleasant to her; she took up invalidism instead, like so many of her gifted female contemporaries (Elizabeth Barrett, Alice James). It is worth noting that her first mysterious breakdown came with adolescence, as if in protest against the unacceptable terms on which she was expected to live her life.

Two men would have liked to marry her, but she rejected both on religious grounds – one was a Catholic, the other a free-thinker, and Christina was a strict Anglican under her mother's influence; her sister Maria became an Anglican nun. For ten years Christina did voluntary work at the St Mary Magdalen Home for Fallen Women on Highgate Hill; she was deeply interested and horrified by their plight, and wrote several narrative poems around the theme. She was published and became well known, but remained awkwardly shy; and illness took her beauty. She made only two trips abroad. It is on record that she saw her first sunrise at the age of forty-seven. No wonder that she wrote of days

> when it seems . . . that our yoke is uneasy and our burden unbearable because our life is pared down and subdued and repressed to an intolerable level; and so in one moment every instinct of our whole self revolts against our lot, and we loathe this day of quietness and sitting still, and writhe under a sudden sense of all we have irrevocably forgone.

Only religion revived hope at such times, and throughout her life she celebrated its consolations and seemed to look forward eagerly to the experience of Paradise – a Paradise of rich fulfilment, of sunshine and music, sweet fruits and blooming flowers, the love of a heavenly bridegroom, 'heaped-up good pleasure', as she put it.

Battiscombe suggests that Christina, thwarted in her experience of *eros*, put her passion into her expression of *agape*: she rebukes both 'cheap' talk of sexual repression and any suggestion that there may have been an actual lover. Yet it is easy to see why other biographers – notably Lona Packer in her *Christina Rossetti* (Cambridge, 1963) – have wanted to find real sex somewhere. 'My heart is like a singing bird' demands something stronger than the pallid, sleepy Collinson or the tubby, absent-minded Cayley. Battiscombe is right, I think, to dismiss Lona Packer's theory of a love affair with the Rossetti brothers' friend William Scott; but there is a missing element in her own determinedly subdued and tasteful account of this anguished and surely enraged life that produced so much surpassingly painful and morbid as well as beautiful poetry.

Christina Rossetti's most famous poem is to this day 'Goblin

Market'. It has been read variously, as a straightforward fairy-story, as sexual fantasy, as a parable of temptation and redemption and, most recently (by Ellen Moers), as a memorial to the eroticism of the Victorian nursery, credited with many covert pinches and guilty tastings. This is a good point: 'Goblin Market' is both brilliant and embarrassing – embarrassing because it is a poem about innocence and experience by someone slightly over-insistent on the virtue of innocence, which she perhaps had deep doubts about.

Who was it, after all, who *did* taste all the forbidden fruit, who enacted everything his sisters had learnt from their mother and their church to deny? Christina's fellow 'storm' and favourite brother, Dante Gabriel. The more he lived his stormy life, surrounding himself with heaped-up pleasures, with beautiful models and mistresses, the more rigidly she retreated into the safety of absolute self-denial. No risk of hers could redeem him; she could only be Isabel to his Claudio. But she loved him to his death.

Another poem of hers, 'The Lowest Room', shows a young woman regretting the freedom of the pagan past, to which her sister replies that Christian virtues are better; this meek sister is rewarded with a husband, while her discontented elder is obliged to learn patience as 'year after tedious year' of her life goes by. The lesson is that it is bad to want experience, excitement and action, all those things enjoyed by men and free-thinkers. Christina, who could not dare to think of living like Dante Gabriel (except perhaps in Paradise), martyred herself and chronicled her martyrdom in deeply troubling poems.

If she was shy in life, as a poet her voice was confident:

> What are heavy? sea-sand and sorrow:
> What are brief? today and tomorrow:
> What are frail? Spring blossoms and youth:
> What are deep? the ocean and truth.

And if she repeatedly expressed a longing for death as an escape from the frustrations and weariness of this world, no one was more responsive to the scents and flowers and brightness of summer, and to the whole notion of ecstatic enjoyment. Battiscombe sees the tension between her Italian blood and her English upbringing as a source of pain and spur to genius; I suspect some deeper sense of outrage in her along the lines of the verses quoted at the start of the article: if she couldn't be Dante Gabriel, she would be 'doubly blank'.

Her life did become doubly blank. How painful it is to hear (from her affectionate brother William) of her 'oppressive gratitude' for insignificant favours, of her 'almost stereotyped smile'; how terrible the testimony of her last illness when, far from turning easily to long-desired death, she fell into mental as well as physical agony and, when left alone, screamed so loudly that her neighbour felt obliged to write a letter of protest to William. This is the girl with the scissors again. She was a magnificent poet; why is there no complete edition of her poems in print?

*Sunday Times*, 1981

# Darkness at Dawn

## *Vedi* by Ved Mehta

In 1919, the year that General Dyer massacred hundreds of unarmed Indians in a park in Amritsar – the scene so carefully reconstructed in the film *Gandhi* – Ved Mehta's father, Amolak Ram Mehta, was completing his studies at the King Edward Medical College, Lahore. Mehta jeopardized his whole future by helping to organize protest strikes; but he was an excellent student and in the event was able to take his finals. He set off for London to pursue further studies, and later won a Rockefeller fellowship to America. In India he became a public health official. His prosperity pleased but did not surprise his family, for his birth horoscope had predicted that he would ride upon an elephant, as only maharajas did, and sail the seas.

Amolak Ram Mehta was a remarkable man by any standards. His son Ved's achievements mirror his energy and success. One example: as a small boy Ved acquired a broken bicycle and set about mending it with the help of a servant. Then, secretly and with many tumbles, he taught himself to ride until one morning he was able to follow his three big sisters to school as they cycled through the early morning streets. The point about this story is that he was blind.

Ved went on, with his parents' support and his own unswerving determination, to wrest an education and career from the world. At fifteen he travelled alone to a blind school in Arkansas, and from then on America gave him most of his chances, including the funding of two years at Oxford. The *New Yorker* has published his writing regularly, and in 1975 he became an American citizen.

At the same time he has grown increasingly fascinated by his background and forebears. And the information he has collected patiently and tenderly through family documents and recollections is of interest as a microcosm of the colossal changes that have taken place in India during the past century.

*Daddyji* (1977) and *Mamaji* (1979) gave detailed accounts of the lives of his parents, up to the time when he was blinded by meningitis at the age of three. This new book describes Ved's own experience when he was sent away to a boarding school-cum-orphanage for blind children in the hope that it would make him independent. 'You are a man now' are the first words he remembers hearing, spoken by his father at the railway station where he saw him off for the 900-mile journey to school in Bombay, where no one spoke Vedi's native language. He was four.

The experience, which might have been fatal, proved useful. Vedi, cursed by blindness, was blessed with hugely compensating gifts: he was lovable, sociable and brilliantly quick and clever. 'A very jolly child' is how he was remembered by other pupils, though it's hard to imagine a four-year-old being jolly under the circumstances.

The Dadar School, founded by American missionaries to teach blind orphans a trade – mostly chair caning, which was thought an improvement on begging, and massage for the more adept – was run by an enthusiastic Bengali Christian, Ras Mohun, who had studied in America. Mr and Mrs Ras Mohun made much of the child of good family, but still he had to live amongst the rough big boys. In the dormitory Vedi was the only one to have a sprung bed and mosquito net, just as he was the only one with shoes, soft clothes of his own and special food. Surprisingly this did not make the others hate him; instead they admired his chubby cheeks and soft skin, and he became their pet.

By an outstanding feat of memory Mr Mehta has travelled back into the soul of the child he was, the child for whom time is unquantifiable, and each experience total. The Dadar School engulfs the reader as it did Vedi, with its boys' talk of ghosts, rats and snakes, not always imaginary; the horrible slippery floor of the bathroom and the great drain under the building; thrilling races and tugs of war devised by Ras Mohun, outings to the zoo and the sea. The partially sighted children described what they could to the blind. Braille reading and writing were quickly learnt by Vedi. Miss Mary, the fourteen-year-old pupil teacher, gave arithmetic lessons with a system of rotating pegs; the Cardswallah and the Chesswallah enthralled; but the 'Sighted Master' who slept in the dormitory seemed to all the boys part of a hostile and powerful world of the sighted. One night Vedi hid under his covers while the Sighted

Master did something to two boys who were brain damaged as well as blind. They were never heard of again.

Vedi came to love his friends, Christian Deodi, Muslim Abdul, Paran from the girls' dormitory, and to feel his allegiance lay more strongly to the Dadar School than to his distant home. Even so, he was often ill, and often felt he was living in a dream; and when he did return, he quickly readjusted again. His fear, and his father's, that he might become that tragic figure of the Indian scene, a blind beggar, had begun to be allayed.

A sad epilogue in which Mr Mehta revisits the school in search of old friends underlines how just that fear had been. Yet instead he is now the most illustrious member of the Mehta family, and has added this small classic of childhood to his other achievements. It is worth any number of nostalgic evocations of the Raj, and provides a touching epitaph for Abdul, Paran and the others to whom the gods gave no compensatory blessings.

*Sunday Times*, 1981

# PART THREE

# WRITER

I left the *Sunday Times* rather suddenly in 1986, when it was moved to Wapping. I didn't care for the way things were done. No doubt the print unions had to be brought under control, but the humiliation of the journalists by proprietor and editor made me unwilling to go on serving such masters. I was lucky enough to be in a position to walk out. That was the end of my brilliant career.

I became a writer. Slowly I adapted to the change: silence, hard slog, loneliness, old clothes. 'You've gone very quiet,' said Victoria Glendinning to me after I'd been out of journalism for a year. I still miss it sometimes, the feeling of perpetually renewed excitement, of belonging to a band of brothers and sisters who care passionately about the same things – books, reviews, journals, who's said what, who's writing where. Writing books is another life, mostly sweat and pain and panic, redeemed by moments of excitement during the research process, and a few of pure joy, when a paragraph or a sentence seems at last to express what you are trying to say.

In due course I married a writer, Michael Frayn. He is the hardest worker I know, and he tells me that writers don't retire, so perhaps I'll be able to make up for all the time I spent doing other things when I was young. Biography has become my province, and I have never attempted fiction, although I have come to think the gap between biography and fiction is not so great. Novelists and biographers are both excited and inspired by the patterns of human activity. They are both story-tellers. Both use the basic raw materials of life, birth and childhood, work and love, family structures, betrayal, woe and death. You need imagination even if you don't invent, and writers who invent very often depend on research too, their own or someone else's.

I am driven by curiosity, about the past and about human behaviour, and I enjoy all forms of research, from deciphering old papers to tramping in the footsteps of long-dead subjects. And I'm perpetually surprised by the oddity of what I stumble on, the weird and unpredictable histories that emerge when you turn back the covers over the past. Sometimes too the telling of one particular story, when a life has been carefully examined, will resonate in a larger area. When I explored the relationship between Ellen Ternan and Charles Dickens, it seemed to me I had stumbled on a story, fascinating in itself, that also illuminated a whole era and the assumptions made about relations between men and women of that era.

Writers are particularly prone to object to biography, seeing the biographer as a mere blunderer, piling up 'documented deeds and days and disappointments'. The phrase is John Updike's, and he also describes biography as trespassing on what he calls 'the human innocence that attends, in the perpetual present tense of living, the self that seems the real one'. Most of us cherish the idea of our essential innocence, though we should not be surprised if we appear less innocent to outside observers. It could be that writers are especially upset by the idea of biography because they know the power of the written word. But while some biographers wear hobnailed boots, biography is no more homogeneous as a form than fiction. I say more about this in my review of Janet Malcolm's book on p. 203.

I tell myself that older writers make better biographers because they have made a long journey themselves. Yet in attempting this condensed account of my own working life, I have not found it at all easy to understand what went on inside the head of the young woman I was. If she is a stranger to me now, what claims can I make for biography? This may be precisely the point, that we can't observe ourselves accurately – that it takes an outside observer to see what is going on in any life. I turn with some relief away from myself to other projects.

*    *    *

All the remaining reviews come from the years I have been working on my own. I particularly enjoyed writing for the newly founded *Independent*, where Sebastian Faulks was the first literary editor; and for Blake Morrison at the *Observer* and then the *Independent on Sunday*, and for his successor there, Jan Dalley. I have also appreciated being able to write longer reviews for the *TLS* under its editor Ferdinand Mount.

# Two Men and a Mask

*Oscar Wilde* by Richard Ellmann

Oscar Wilde lived his life as though planning to be the ideal subject for a biographer: the richly eccentric parents, the Oxford poses, the swift capture of social and literary success, the fatal passion, the trial scenes, the years in prison, the final degradation; and thrown over it all, the perpetually sparkling veil of wit.

He was always seeing and presenting himself. On his honeymoon, he begins an account of his first marital bedding to a male friend in the street. A visit from his beloved Bosie has to be described, even as it is in progress, in a letter to another friend. Mirrors enthralled Wilde, and any departure from style dismayed him: in *De Profundis* he complained of the prison *style*, and of how 'everything about my tragedy . . . is lacking in style'. Ellmann speculates that syphilis may have killed him; it seems quite as likely that it was the impossibility of keeping up his style that did it.

Richard Ellmann is deeply sympathetic to Wilde and pays him the tribute of a near-perfect biography. The witty subject has found a witty biographer who is also distinguished for his erudition and humanity. We may know, or think we know, all about Wilde already, but nothing in this long book seems superfluous. How good he is on Speranza (Lady Wilde) and the dreadful Willie, Oscar's brother, one of whose projects was to write 'improved' endings to Chopin's Preludes. How wonderful on Oxford, where, funny, absurd and triumphant, Wilde worked as a labourer for Ruskin's roadbuilding project, intoxicated himself on Pater's prose, flirted with Catholicism and Freemasonry, was rusticated for absenting himself in Greece and Rome ('I was sent down from Oxford for being the first under-graduate to visit Olympia'), and won the Newdigate and a Double First.

He shows Wilde becoming a star (a media star, as we say now) before he had written any notable work, made famous by Gilbert's satirical portrait of him in *Patience*, and on the strength of that fixed up by D'Oyly Carte with an American lecture tour on 'The Beautiful'. Wilde prepared carefully, packing a very fancy wardrobe but also letters of introduction to respectable and influential people. The American press adored the whole charade, which lasted for a year; Wilde also revelled in it, and the amazing thing is that he was then able to proceed to make himself into a good writer.

Ellmann is alert to the telling detail as well as the good anecdote both on the American tour and in Wilde's encounters with French culture. He recognized Verlaine's genius and was good to him in his disgrace, which preceded his own; he sought out Edmond de Goncourt, who labelled him '*au sexe douteux*'; the young Gide felt he had been spiritually seduced by Wilde.

*Salome* was written in French, and praised by Mallarmé and Maeterlinck (it was banned in England). Wilde took his English bride to Paris for the honeymoon; Ellmann thinks he was in love with Constance for a while, but she also brought some money. He edited a woman's magazine until he grew bored, and published *Dorian Gray* to scandalous success. He was happy, and began to write the plays that are his greatest achievement. He fathered his two sons and drifted towards danger.

Ellmann quotes Robert Ross's claim that he first introduced Wilde to homosexual acts, when Ross was an undergraduate at King's and Wilde was thirty-two. Ross was such an honest and honourable man that there seems no reason to doubt his word; but it is surprising.

Perhaps sex was not very important to Wilde. When he fell in love with the appalling Lord Alfred Douglas, their pleasure seems to have lain partly in tormenting one another and partly in hunting for boys together. Ellmann says Wilde began to think of himself as a criminal then, despite his belief in self-realization and his professed scorn for both moderation and hypocrisy.

The richness and thoroughness of the treatment of the terrible dénouement is such that one reads to the end and only then begins to question whether Wilde is quite deserving of the unqualified praise heaped upon him. The way in which he was treated by British law and society naturally disposes one in his favour; but there are some question marks over his character and his work, and the relation between the two.

Ellmann claims that Wilde was conducting an anatomy of his society, and a radical reconsideration of its ethics. He knew all the secrets and could expose all the pretence. Along with Blake and Nietzsche, he was proposing that good and evil are not what they seem, that moral tabs cannot cope with the complexity of behaviour.

But Blake was an innocent, and Wilde was an arch-sophisticate, delivering his wisdom in the guise of super-worldliness. His aphorisms, coming thick and fast, are one-liners that sometimes cancel one another out. And where Blake's and Nietzsche's attacks on received morality were wholehearted and passionate, Wilde's were often frivolous. Neither buying boys nor destroying himself by going for Lord Queensberry was a way of showing up the values of a corrupt society. Wilde (like Orton) was too implicated in what he attacked to be able to manoeuvre effectively, despite the noble courtroom defence of homosexuality.

Wilde is lovable, pitiable, brilliant and self-destructive, and there is a mystery about his self-destruction which Ellmann does not solve, or seek to solve. William Archer, who praised and defended Wilde, also made a telling attack (which Ellmann does not quote) when he suggested that there were two men behind the enigmatic mask presented to the public: Oscar, a cheap and facile mountebank, and Wilde, the true artist, whose work was to be esteemed and relished. This marvellous book tells you everything you need to know about Wilde, but perhaps a little less than the truth about Oscar.

*Independent*, 1987

# Time and Distance

*The Progress of Love* by Alice Munro

In the first story in Alice Munro's first collection – published in Canada nearly twenty years ago – a small girl goes out driving with her father, who has become a travelling salesman during the Depression. He takes her to an isolated farmhouse she has never visited before, where a good-looking woman living alone with her blind mother greets them warmly, teaches the little girl to dance and gives the father a whiskey. As they drive home, she realizes she will not talk about the visit to her mother, and feels her father's life

> darkening and turning strange, like a landscape that has an enchantment on it, making it kindly, ordinary and familiar while you are looking at it, but changing it, once your back is turned, into something you will never know, with all kinds of weathers, and distances you cannot imagine.

It's a perfect story, and a good point of departure for all Alice Munro's subsequent work, which has been an exploration of those weathers and distances, those landscapes that shift from the known to the almost unimaginable.

As she has grown older, her power to unravel a whole tangle of family history has grown stronger and surer, and this latest collection is her best yet. Munro is as much a regional writer as Walter Scott or Mauriac, which is to say she broods closely over her chosen territory, discovering richness in what many would be tempted to dismiss as dull and barren.

All her stories are set in Canada, and mostly in her native western Ontario, a wide landscape of farmlands and small lakeside towns where no great dramas have happened since the Indian wars, and where the people are traditionally narrow, conservative, religious and thrifty, many of them shaped in the mould of Scottish ancestors, although increasingly now feeling the breath of the affluent American culture to the south.

She has a tenderness for the strong, seasoned Canadian women who preserve their houses and their way of life as best they can against the inroads of new fashions in belief and behaviour. Yet she is not lamenting the passing of the old, or peddling nostalgia or folk wisdom. Time itself fascinates her and she will take a family through three generations of its history to demonstrate how impossible it is to draw a final line under any action.

In the title story, one woman's histrionic gesture, aimed at the conscience of a too easy-going husband, reaches its mark in an impressionable daughter; years later, grown up and married, the daughter commits a quite different act of destruction, intended, perhaps, to atone for whatever she imagines her mother's sufferings were. Another generation on, the effects are still reverberating, open to different interpretations. When critics call Munro Proustian (as they do) they may be pointing to this virtuoso grasp of a time-span as well as to her skill in deploying single physical details – a scrap of wallpaper, a blurred snapshot – as emblems of feeling.

One of the things that interests her especially is the way in which families normalize, or seek to normalize, what outsiders regard as abnormal. 'Monsieur les Deux Chapeaux' takes a few hours in the life of a family group: a small party is being given by the wife of Colin, a young schoolteacher. The pivot around which the story turns is Colin's brother Ross, noticed at the start clipping grass in front of the school with two hats rather than one on his handsome head. Everyone likes Ross; his mother keeps saying he is a mechanical genius – he does indeed tinker with car engines – and his sister-in-law flirts gently with him. But by the end of the story the atmosphere has been stained with fear and we see that Ross, the good-natured mother's boy, is a terrifying and inescapable burden on Colin's life. Nothing has happened, nothing has changed; only we have glimpsed the bad truth that has to be lived with.

Again, in 'A Queer Streak' a seriously eccentric farming family throws up one daughter clever and ambitious enough to escape to higher education in Ottawa, only to draw her back into its orbit through the unhinged behaviour of the next daughter. The eldest, trapped by her sense of responsibility, gives up her chances in order to look after her own people. But it is not a simple tale of abnegation. There are irrational forces at work in the sane sister as well as in the others, and her flight from Ottawa is a form of salvation as well as a sacrifice: she is not as tragic as she thinks she is.

These are not stories that set out to make neat moral points, they are not fables, and there are no narrative tricks in them. They are rooted in the sheer eccentricity of human beings and the places in which they perform: draughty boarding-house rooms, a deserted swimming pool, a rural skating rink with its scratchy gramophone waltzes. They reveal comfortable old Canada to us as exotic terrain.

Short stories still get short shrift. They are hard to review, hard to sell, not often awarded prizes. It seems absurd when you consider how firmly established the genre has been for a century, how various it is, and how much of our best modern fiction is embodied in it: think of Pritchett, Naipaul, Bellow, to name only three living masters whose short fiction equals their full-length work. For Alice Munro, it is clearly the natural medium. She is never going to write a blockbuster, thank goodness. Read not more than one of her stories a day, and allow them to work their spell slowly: they are made to last.

*Observer*, 1987

# Giant Crab

*The Memoirs of Ethel Smyth* abridged and
introduced by Ronald Crichton

'An old woman of seventy-one has fallen in love with me . . . It is
like being caught by a giant crab,' wrote Virginia Woolf early in 1930
when the composer Dame Ethel Smyth, who had just read *A Room
of One's Own*, sought her out. It was true that the objects of Ethel's
passion were sometimes in danger of being crushed, but Virginia
was flattered, amused, delighted. At once she settled down to reread
all the volumes of the Smyth autobiography, some of which she
had reviewed earlier, praising them for their courage, candour and
vitality. 'How did you learn to write like that?' she asked her new
friend. These are the memoirs that have been abridged into the
present volume. No wonder Virginia Woolf was held in thrall: Dame
Ethel is Ancient Mariner and Belle Dame Sans Merci rolled into
one, and her reminiscences are extraordinary. It is partly their range,
from Victorian upper-middle-class nursery to the Germany of the
late romantic composers; from the courts of reigning monarchs to
camel-riding in the desert; from the Paris of Proust to Holloway
Prison. It is also their revelation of a character in which spontaneous
emotion and driving ambition cut across every accepted view of
Victorian womanhood.

She did defy – or perhaps rather ignore – all the stereotypes of
her time, whether in matters of work, sex, class or even manners.
From the age of twelve she insisted on her vocation for musical
composition, an activity that no one in her milieu conceived possible
for a woman (and scarcely for a man). Before she was twenty she
had beaten her father – a general in the British army – into total
submission to her will by adopting the sort of tactics subsequently
used by the suffragettes. These included extracting credit from local
tradesmen ('put it down to the General') to finance illicit expeditions
to the London concert halls, where one of her amusements was to
watch G. H. Lewes beating out the rhythms on George Eliot's arm

(not always correctly, she observed). Ethel's next move was to depart for Leipzig, where she lived unchaperoned in lodgings and pursued her serious musical education. It was not an easy path. She tells the story of how Anton Rubinstein, asked to advise a beautiful young aspirant on her career, listened to her playing and then simply pointed to her fingers, her forehead and her heart in turn: '*Hier nix, hier nix, und hier nix!*' But Ethel was not *nix*. She was welcomed by the musical world, and even her family came to accept that music was her way of life and Germany her second home.

Over the next two decades she studied, composed and met most of the great figures of the day. Her love of Brahms's music did not prevent her from noting how he stared at pretty women 'as a greedy boy stares at jam tartlets'. She considered Mahler the finest conductor she ever knew, but found his personality resembled 'a bomb cased in razor-edges'.

Ethel's work did not stand in the way of her social activities, or her many passionate friendships. Throughout her life, she loved intensely, without regard to age or gender. She is quite candid about this, although there are some unexplained areas in the memoirs – a couple of nervous breakdowns, and a somewhat evasive handling of her love affair with Henry Brewster, an expatriate American aesthete with a wife. Even when the wife died, Ethel refused to marry him, although they worked together – he wrote librettos for her operas – and she nursed him when he was dying.

One's sympathy rather goes out to Brewster: on one occasion, having travelled across Europe to be with her for a few precious days in Scotland, he found her too absorbed in playing golf to spare him anything but the hours of darkness. An unkind woman friend remarked, 'Ethel not like idea old maid so trumped up little affair': characteristically, Ethel reports this, as she reports the detestation in which she was held by several eminent people, including Archbishop Benson, who was put off his sermon by even a glimpse of her through the windows of Lambeth Palace.

In one aspect she does resemble a baby bent on world conquest. Ethel's tweeds and tie, Ethel's voice, Ethel's emotions, were all larger than life. Each of her friends was perfect, each interest became obsessive; even her dogs were all canine prodigies. The heroic scale on which she lived allowed her to get on well with royalty, with whom she was always a favourite; neither the Kaiser nor Queen Victoria daunted her, and she was on intimate terms with the Empress Eugénie, whom she fondly saw as a great champion of women's rights.

In her fifties Ethel became a star suffragette. Her own struggles to get her music accepted in a male-dominated world made her naturally sympathetic, and a meeting with the elegant and queenly Mrs Pankhurst provided the *coup de foudre*. Ethel's attempt to teach Mrs P. to throw stones – they were practising for Downing Street – is one of her fine comic episodes; but it wasn't all comedy. Ethel bravely got herself arrested and imprisoned for the Cause.

One of the most endearing aspects of her memoirs is her awareness of her own comicality. Because she never stands on her dignity, she takes on true dignity and strength. And although the book is packed with wonderful anecdotes, it is also a record of an entirely serious professional pursuit. I do not know her music, a piece of shameful ignorance I shall now set out to remedy. Bruno Walter and Thomas Beecham were both admirers, which seems a sufficient commendation, and late German romanticism crossed with English traditional sounds – well, I shall find out. If it is anything like as good as her writing, it must be worth listening to.

[P. S. When I did listen to the music, I found it hard to distinguish from Brahms.]

*Observer*, 1987

# Never Bland

*A Woman of Passion: The Life of E. Nesbit 1858–1924* by Julia Briggs

We, and our daughters, and our nieces – and perhaps a few sons and nephews – have all read *The Railway Children, The Story of the Amulet, The Treasure Seekers, The Wouldbegoods, The Phoenix and the Carpet*. They were written at the turn of the century, were hugely popular with children and adults, admired by writers as various as Kipling and Wells, and have remained in print ever since. They have been televised and paperbacked; it's a rare household that cannot muster a battered Nesbit Puffin or two. Their recurring theme of lost and found fathers addresses itself to children's deep fears and hopes (and during two world wars it spoke to their common experience). Another theme, that of the wish granted that turns out to be awkward or frightening, goes similarly straight to the heart of the fantasies and semi-conscious terrors of many children. Subsequent writers have learnt from their triumphant mixture of the magical and the down-to-earth, which children take to so readily.

Despite her androgynous name, E. Nesbit's readers knew very well that she was a mother herself; she once wrote a letter to the *New Age* magazine, which had been running articles on the horrors of childbearing and brutal lack of consideration of husbands, insisting that most women are devoted to their husbands and adore having babies. The picture of a loving mother, drawing charmingly on her observations of her own large family for her stories, seemed to fit.

This comfortably maternal image was strongly established and important to her. As Julia Briggs writes, 'in her books, as in her correspondence with her admirers, [she] showed herself anxious to conform to their comforting picture of her'; and when Doris Langley Moore came to write a biography of the much loved author in 1933, she felt she simply could not make use of a great deal of the material she had gathered in the course of her extremely thorough research. Nesbit had died in 1924, but it would still have caused too much offence, not only to her surviving family but to her devoted readers.

Langley Moore's gift of her notebooks and research material to Julia Briggs, fully and warmly acknowledged by her, was indeed an act of generosity; it is also a rather singular occurrence in the annals of biography, this gift of material she herself felt obliged to set aside from one biographer into the hands of another. The results are to everyone's credit. This is a wonderfully solid, thorough and balanced book. The story it tells is consistently interesting and at moments extraordinary, and although some of the true facts of the Nesbit/ Bland household have been known since Langley Moore's revised *Life* of 1966, the picture presented by Julia Briggs is still fuller and franker.

Edith Nesbit – 'Daisy' to her family – was born in 1858 in Kennington, now part of the grey, undifferentiated mass of south London, but then still countryside, with flower-edged lanes and farms. She was the youngest, a fact Briggs thinks important, for she craved all her life the attention and petting that goes to the baby of a large family. There was a much older stepsister by her mother's first marriage, a sister and two brothers. The death of her father when she was four marked her imagination indelibly; but her twice-widowed mother was intelligent and resourceful, and gave her orphaned children an excellent upbringing. There were visits to the Crystal Palace with its dinosaur park, to the British Museum and Madame Tussaud's (both of which Edith continued to love in her adult years); there were schools, mostly hateful because they meant banishment from family life, but then restoration to the family when Mrs Nesbit decided to take them all to France. The chief reason for this was the tuberculosis from which Edith's sister Minnie was suffering, for which travel abroad was believed to be a palliative.

Apart from one terrifying experience when her sisters took her to see the catacombs of Bordeaux with their hideously preserved, hairy corpses (still very horrible, according to Briggs, who most conscientiously repeated the visit), France was idyllic, remembered and revisited with joy thereafter. It did not, however, cure Minnie. Leaving Edith at school in Dinan, Mrs Nesbit took her sick daughter back to London, where the doomed girl made friends with Christina Rossetti, and became engaged to a blind Pre-Raphaelite poet, Philip Marston, only to die a few months later. (The whole incident resembles a ghastly parody of Christina Rossetti's narrative poetry at its most morbid.)

By now Edith had become a poet too. She longed to be great, 'like Shakespeare, or Christina Rossetti', but she knew that in reality she wrote 'like other people'. She was, however, persistent and prolific, and soon began to be published in magazines. The Nesbits settled in Kent, in a big, rambling house, but during the 1870s they appear to have lost their money; they disappear and bob up again in Islington, where Edith met her future husband, Hubert Bland.

Bland is one of the minor enigmas of literary history in that everything reported of him makes him sound repellent, yet he was admired, even adored, by many intelligent men and women. A quick, clever Woolwich lad whose family was unable to buy him the commission he craved, he became, briefly, a bank clerk. While still living with his mother (he was also a spoilt youngest child) he invented aristocratic Yorkshire forebears, at the same time becoming a keen socialist for a while, and then a founding Fabian. He did not aspire to be consistent. He allowed his wife to support him with her pen for some years, but was always opposed to feminism:

> Woman's *métier* in the world – I mean, of course, civilized woman, the woman in the world as it is – is to inspire romantic passion . . . Romantic passion is inspired by women who wear corsets. In other words, by the women who pretend to be what they not quite are.

Corset-wearing women were never lacking, and he had a voracious sexual appetite. When Edith met him he had a mistress already with child, and she herself was seven months pregnant before he married her. No sooner did she introduce a housekeeper, Alice Hoatson, into their establishment, than he proceeded to father children on both her and Edith regularly. In mid-life he joined the Catholic Church, a further cosmetic touch to his old-world image, but without modifying his behaviour or even bothering to attend more than the statutory minimum of masses. By then he had become a hugely successful journalist with a particular following in the north of England, his column in the Manchester *Sunday Chronicle* proving so popular that it gave him a secure income for life.

Whatever the lesson to be learnt from bogus Bland, when Edith met him she saw the ardent, handsome, poetry-loving young man, the great talker who was to persuade Bernard Shaw along to his first Fabian meeting and who seemed an ideal literary collaborator. Even when he had come to seem less ideal, he was still the only person who could talk her out of her 'blights' – the black moods that descended on her when she had too much to do, or when she felt slighted; they enveloped the entire household, and only Hubert could relieve the misery. It is scarcely surprising that she was subject to them, on a diet of ceaseless hack work to pay the butcher's and baker's bills – a formidable bibliography attests to this – plus pregnancies leading to several stillbirths as well as three living children and, on top of this, an unrequited passion for Shaw.

'Unrequited' is not exactly the right term, for Shaw did initially get in quite deeply, as his notebook entries, with their little accounts of shilling and pence, show. For a while there were taxis and first-class carriages when Mrs Nesbit was in question (the extra fare might ensure privacy); these are followed by the usual Shavian manoeuvres of hasty, determined disentanglement. She suffered, and held it against him; and he felt *something*, if not remorse at least enough to lead him, years later, to pay a contribution towards her stepson John's university education. The two best, wittiest, strongest letters in this book were both penned by Shaw; his power to upstage all his women friends posthumously would have pleased the old fox infinitely, no doubt.

Shaw was of course a feminist, while Edith wanted love; the two things are a puzzle to fit together even when one partner is not reluctant. But for a while Edith found the way of life that suited her, and inspiration too, according to Briggs, when, about the year 1890, she met a young journalist called Oswald Barron, who began to collaborate with her. He was one of a band of her 'courtiers', recent Oxford graduates who joined the Fabian Society and were fascinated by the Blands, and notably by Edith. For she was beautiful in her own style – lots of hair and a strong face, trailing Liberty dresses, ropes of beads and dozens of bangles on her arm, incessant cigarettes in a long holder – and the parties she and Hubert gave were famous, with huge meals, wine and games played all over the house.

Julia Briggs credits Edith with a very large number of 'lovers' among the young men who gathered about her, some acting as her secretary, more joining in family holidays in Kent or in France. It is never clear whether they were lovers in the modern sense, and, while perhaps it does not matter too much, the picture of Nesbit is undoubtedly changed if she was holding court like Messalina, or on the other hand simply receiving sentimental homage. Whichever was the case, Edith enjoyed the adulation of many young men, but Barron gave her something more; he was erudite, possessed a historical imagination, and 'his way of looking at the world came to colour hers strongly'. Barron acted, says Briggs, as her 'muse or midwife'; and of course she gave his name to Oswald Bastable. Sadly, when he married in 1899 he walked out of her life without a backward glance, and was at great pains in his respectable old age to persuade Doris Langley Moore to omit his name from her book, which seems sad and silly too, if Briggs is right in her assessment of his role.

In fact, her first real literary success was not until 1899, with *The Treasure Seekers*, which means that Barron's influence was almost entirely retrospective; but it persisted, and from now on she was firmly established as a favourite. Kipling wrote her fan letters, and she believed he stole her plots. Numbers of young women and children also wrote and, when permitted, visited and worshipped. She earned large sums, and she spent freely. For a considerable time she kept three households going: Well Hall, the large family house at Eltham in south London, a cottage at Dymchurch on the Romney Marsh, and a flat in Dean Street for herself. Like many rich people, she also indulged herself in a totally absurd hobby, keeping a researcher called Tanner in her London flat for years while he worked on 'an arithmetical cipher of Francis Bacon' which proved not only Bacon's authorship of Shakespeare's entire works but also his prominent part in Freemasonry.

The story of the quarrel between Bland and Wells over his attempt to run away with Rosamund (Hubert's and Alice's beautiful daughter) for a weekend of healthy sexual fun has been told many times, and nothing new emerges here except perhaps Rosamund's loyalty to Wells's memory in the novel she wrote later. But far worse than any incestuous inclination of Hubert's is the simple fact that both

Rosamund and John, the two children he had by Alice, were brought up to believe that Edith was their mother until they were adult. Alice was known as 'Auntie'. This was presumably out of deference to the system of Victorian virtue. Not surprisingly, the Bland children were bitterly divided in their loyalties, some worshipping the memory of their vigorous father, some despising him for his behaviour towards women.

He died first, leaving Edith overwhelmed with grief and indignation at the obituary article by St John Ervine, which failed to mention her at all and instead heaped praises on Alice (in whose arms he had in fact died, Edith being away in her country cottage). She soon cheered up when another admirer appeared, Thomas Tucker, or 'the Skipper', a 'fat little Cockney robin', Captain of the Woolwich ferry, a widower of sixty with strong socialist views, who dropped his aitches and wore no collar. Collar or no collar, 'I feel as though someone had come and put a fur cloak round me,' wrote Edith to her brother Harry, announcing her remarriage in 1917. It was the Skipper's assured fidelity that entranced and comforted her: she had never encountered such a thing before, among her journalists and Oxford graduates. The next five years were accordingly the happiest of her life, she said, even though the money was running low.

For the last two years her smoker's lungs were eaten by cancer, and she ended her days, still devotedly cared for by the Skipper, in an air force hut on the Romney Marsh. Noël Coward was an admiring visitor; he had saved up his pocket money as a child to buy the instalments of her stories, and even pawned a necklace of his mother's for an entire book by her. He showed her his plays, and said she was 'the most genuine Bohemian I had ever seen'. Many years later, one of her books lay beside his own deathbed.

*The Times Literary Supplement*, 1987

# London Innocents

*Dear Girl: The Diaries and Letters of Two Working Women 1897–1917*
edited by Tierl Thompson

Here is a little gold mine of information about the lives of two Edwardian women. They were neither famous nor notorious; their world was the world of third-class railway carriages, terraced suburban houses and dingy offices. They were not even ladies, as then defined. But they were articulate and finely alert to the social questions of their time. Ruth Slate was the daughter of a City clerk, her friend Eva Slawson the illegitimate child of a baker's daughter; they were born in the 1880s, and met through the Nonconformist chapel attended by their families at Walthamstow. Both, after leaving school at thirteen, worked as clerks for companies that exploited them; both kept diaries, and corresponded with one another until Eva's early death in 1916.

They were attractive and gifted young women, keen readers, given to self-examination in the Methodist tradition, and eager to serve the community: girls who should have gone to a university, who should have had proper medical care (Eva died of undiagnosed diabetes) and decently paid jobs. Instead, they struggled with unpropitious circumstances, using much of their precious spare time to work with the children of still less fortunate families.

They were passionately eager for culture and passionately interested in debating moral questions. They read *The Women Who Did* as carefully as they read George Eliot, they idolized Edward Carpenter, they went to see Isadora Duncan and thought her splendid, they were excited by articles in the *New Age* and tried to visit its offices (Orage would have loved them). They queried the necessity of marriage, and, like D. H. Lawrence, thought it too exclusive, requiring the adjunct of close friendship with a member of one's own sex. They were interested in the state endowment of motherhood, and gave support to an unmarried mother (in Ruth's case) and a widow with children (in Eva's). They believed that the question of women's emancipation went deeper than the suffrage.

Their writings are thrilling to anyone who likes to enter the past through living voices rather than through theoretical or generalized versions of history. We feel the pulse of the age as we read. Ruth's first lover and then her younger sister Daisy die agonizingly of tuberculosis; we follow Daisy's slow climb from seventy-fifth to the top of the Brompton Hospital waiting list, only to find when she gets there that it is too late to help her. Pathetically, the family moves away from its roots to the south of London in the hope that the air will be better for damaged lungs; the breadwinners, Ruth and her father, have to travel up on the early workers' train every day to save on the fares.

Ruth's second lover, the dreadful Wal, puts up anti-suffrage posters in his lodging window to tease her, and warns her that socialism is against family life. Eva's friend Minna imagines a community of women untroubled by men; at the same time she lets the minister, Mr James, seduce her in the front parlour. Minna's little daughter has to appear before the Poor Law Guardians to beg for a few shillings when her mother is confined of a fourth, posthumous child. Eva notes that poverty, not ignorance, is the cause of much of the sickness she observes.

Ruth is jilted by Wal – the reader heaves a sigh of relief – and an admiring American pays for her to be trained at a Quaker centre outside Birmingham, where she qualifies as a social worker. So, to a certain degree, her life is a success story.

But that is not the point of these documents, which she preserved until her death in 1953 and which her husband handed on at his. No one who values the quieter voices of history should miss them. They light up a great area of English life that is usually ignored, and they do so with complete and haunting innocence and honesty.

*Observer*, 1988

# No Consolation

*Freud: A Life for Our Time* by Peter Gay

Halfway through this 800-page biography I thought Peter Gay had succeeded in the nearly impossible task of making Freud dull. Gay is a super-efficient scholar, summarizer and sifter of material, but he has little feeling for character or narrative, and there is something leaden about his tone. He uses words like 'epoch-making', tells us that Freud, if offered the Nobel Prize, 'would have grabbed it with both hands', that 'the 1920s proved a stormy decade', that a short visit to Athens was 'unforgettable' (and so on). It makes a long, long plod, compared with Paul Roazen's *Freud and His Followers*, a book with the sparkle of life on every page (and about which Gay is rather censorious).

Yet Gay's *Freud* is packed with material of extraordinary fascination, some of it new; and as I proceeded I found myself drawn in and held. A solid and convincing portrait does emerge, as though from a rough, enormous piece of rock: a figure overwhelmingly ambitious (the conquistador, as Freud described himself), tyrannical, quarrelsome, and abusive in quarrel, overbearing, unable to face up to his own neurotic traits; at the same time generous, subtle, humorous, brave and stoical. A great archaeologist of the human mind who nevertheless knew and cared to know little about the female half of the human race, in practice or theory; but whose wisdom reached into innumerable corners of the world.

Two examples of his political prescience are given by Gay: in 1930 he wrote, 'One asks oneself uneasily what the Soviets will do after they have exterminated their bourgeois.' In the same year he wrote to Einstein, apropos Zionism, 'I can muster no sympathy whatever for the misguided piety that makes a national religion from a piece of the wall of Herod, and for its sake challenges the feelings of the local natives.' Freud's scepticism is always more impressive than his certainty. The bravest and most profound words he ever wrote may be his confession, in *Civilization and Its Discontents* (published in

1930, when he was seventy-four), that 'My courage sinks to stand up before my fellow humans as a prophet, and I bow before their reproach that I do not know how to bring them consolation – for that is fundamentally what they all demand.'

Gay traces Freud's intellectual development through detailed summaries of his written work – good and useful to a general reader such as myself, although less interesting than reading Freud's own words. He intersperses passages of historical background and discussion of Freud's character and quarrels – these last two being almost synonymous, for Freud could never let a difference of opinion stay on the intellectual plane, it was always converted into an emotional storm. Like a child, he made people into angels or demons, and readily converted them from one to the other.

Two subjects that have attracted attention recently are confined to a bibliographical essay at the end of the book. One is the question, raised by Jeffrey Masson, of Freud's change of mind about the sexual abuse of children. He began by believing his patients' accounts, then decided they were fantasizing. Masson thinks Freud was right the first time but lost his nerve; Gay rejects the idea that Freud would, or could, act untruthfully. But there is truth and truth, and the recent scandals in England on the subject of child abuse make one pause a bit longer over Masson's suggestion.

The other allegation, that Freud had a love affair with his sister-in-law Minna Bernays, cannot, as Gay says, be proved or disproved at present. The important point here may in any case not be the sexual one, but that he did undeniably grow much closer to Minna, intellectually at any rate, than to his chosen wife, who did not care for his theories. Like many a good bourgeois, Freud lived in a state of emotional polygamy, and when his daughter Anna became his chief companion and greatest love, he had three wives. And why not? The arrangement was acceptable to them all; and on the occasion of his golden wedding anniversary, he wrote to another woman friend, Marie Bonaparte, that his fifty-year association with Martha 'was really not a bad solution of the marriage problem'.

Gay emphasizes Freud's 'last attachment' to Anna strongly, and suggests that, although he worried about her failure to find a husband or lover, his own need for her was too great to allow him to let her go. He, as a man who believed that women found their best fulfilment in motherhood, worried about this, but there is no reason why we should, for her life seems to have been richly satisfying.

The other emotional centre was with his disciples. Gay finds Wilhelm Fliess the most significant of these by far. The two men met in 1887, just after Freud's marriage, and Fliess became the loved and trusted confidant of all Freud's rapidly developing ideas as well as the most intimate details of his personal life. In 1894 Freud hailed him as 'the only Other', and the sight of Fliess's handwriting on a letter made him 'forget much loneliness and privation' – this was written when Freud's sixth child had just been born. It was also Fliess who prescribed cigars to Freud, to clear up his catarrh, establishing the addiction that killed him: a point that can't have been lost on the discoverer of the Oedipus complex.

The intensity of Freud's fascination with Fliess, which included covering up a serious medical mistake he made, meant that the break when it came was all the more bitter, and subsequent 'betrayals' were often referred to as 'Fliesslike'. Freud took to calling him 'a hard, wicked human being', but never forgot or ceased to worry about him, and made great efforts, thwarted by Marie Bonaparte, to have their correspondence destroyed.

Gay writes from an agnostic position as to the curative value of psychoanalysis and the truth of Freud's fundamental theories of infantile sexuality, the sexual basis for all neurosis. He is shocked when he catches Freud out using psychoanalytical terminology as a crude weapon of abuse, and he is slyly insistent on his failure to come to terms with his own neuroses, the addiction to smoking being the most blatant: Freud, a doctor, ignored his own pre-cancerous symptoms, and went for his initial treatment to a barely qualified cosmetic surgeon, who botched his work. And nothing would make him give up his cigars.

'Psychoanalyst, cure thyself!' is not quite to the point. The failures of the great are likely to be on the same scale as their other qualities. Freud's personal life may have been a little strange; but it makes no difference to the fact that he changed the world. The talking cure, even if it turns out to be no more than a variant on the confessional, is established.

More important, the way we think about ourselves, our relations with other human beings, our vocabulary, have all been transformed by him and his disciples. However well you know his story, when you come to the last chapters of Gay's magisterial book, with the bestial madness of the Fascists providing a background for the fortitude of the great 'infidel Jew' who had devoted his life to showing how reason is not master in its own house, it is hard not to have tears in your eyes – tears for Freud, and tears for humanity.

*Observer*, 1988

# A Hate Affair

*A Far Cry from Kensington* by Muriel Spark

This is a novel about a hate affair. It is told with a sort of black good humour and a boldness approaching violence; if the object of the narrator's hatred were a real person instead of a fictional one, he would be blasted into the ground by the unswerving force of the contempt he attracts.

For us, the effect is admirable. The divine Spark is shining at her brightest, neither prolix nor, to my relief, too gnomic either. There was a period when her books required the offices of academic soothsayers to be understood, but in *A Far Cry from Kensington* this is not the case. Nothing is obscure, and she writes sentences so good that I have been reading them over and over, silently to myself and aloud to friends, in pure delight at their wit and confidence.

Love arises from the heart, says the narrator Mrs Hawkins, and hate from principle. (She is given to making pronouncements.) Her story is about principles, literary and other, though love makes a gentle entry too. The time is the mid fifties. Mrs Hawkins is a war widow; she had been a landgirl with bookish inclinations, now she is a hugely overweight publishers' dogsbody. She lodges in a pleasant boarding house in Kensington and takes an interest in her fellow lodgers as well as her colleagues at work. She has a reputation for being capable and reliable; people turn to her for help, and she is good at finding them jobs, and giving practical advice on anything from when to intervene in a row between husband and wife in the next-door house to how to write novels. Some of her advice seems so good that readers may be tempted to take it direct. Mrs Spark would, amongst her other virtues, make a very classy agony aunt.

Mrs Hawkins is a Catholic, and a member of what she calls the ordinary class; meditating on this at a grand dinner, she concludes 'it was better to belong to the ordinary class. For the upper class could not live, would disintegrate, without the ordinary class, while the latter can get on very well on its own.' Read on after this, on

p. 95, for one of the best accounts ever written of the bafflement produced by certain aspects of English etiquette.

The plot moves in two directions at once. Mrs Hawkins is looking back from the 1980s at the way she changed from a very fat, useful person into something quite different. At the same time she is showing up the horrible pretensions of the man who became her *bête noire* at that time, Hector Bartlett, a hanger-on of the literary scene whose worthlessness and villainy she divines from the start. '*Pisseur de copie*' she hisses at him at an early stage of their acquaintance, and '*pisseur de copie*' she continues to hiss whenever his name or work is in question, or whenever he heaves into view himself. It means, she explains to a disconcerted friend whose French is not up to hers, that he pisses hack journalism.

Bartlett is pushy and without literary talent. He writes vindictive articles in cheap newspapers about literary friends who have got into trouble. He is unkind to animals and uses women to further his ambitions, in particular a successful novelist named Emma Loy for whom he does research, and whose name he later blackens. He affects upper-class manners, and he produces a manuscript entitled *The Eternal Quest: A Study of the Romantic–Humanist Position* (a title that may well be found in the British Library). When Mrs Hawkins, who rises to a position of influence as an editor with the publishers Mackintosh & Tooley, refuses to handle *The Eternal Quest*, Miss Loy gets her the sack. This is not all: Bartlett is also a dabbler in black magic, and makes a demonic intrusion among the lodgers in the Kensington lodging house.

Bartlett is a fairly ludicrous but not at all unbelievable figure, with his black box and his literary pretensions. The glee with which Mrs Hawkins goes into battle against him is spectacular. So is her commitment to the emotions of the past. There is a marvellous vignette of the experience of a war bride, ephemeral as a dream, sharp as a nightmare. Then the world of fifties' publishers who, though occasionally crooked, were still gentlemen – dotty, charming and exploitative of clever women – is beautifully recognizable to those with memories of it. That well-known publishing maxim that 'the best author is a dead author' puts in an appearance, although it is not the view of Mrs Hawkins herself.

When Mrs Hawkins makes casual allusion to the books she has been reading for pleasure, which are *Villette* and *Frankenstein*, she places herself quite deliberately in a tradition of women's writing which is intense and highly principled. And when later she tells her lover the nursery rhymes and fairy-stories his education has denied him, she is showing her faith in the other power of literature, to delight and console. What she loathes and rejects is the fakery of a Bartlett, who uses 'literature' and the literary world for his own base, factitious ends. It's a point that needs to be made regularly, and it's made here with the charming ferocity that is Mrs Spark's particular and cherished hallmark.

*Independent*, 1988

# An Imagined Life

*The Truth about Lorin Jones* by Alison Lurie

When someone starts researching a biography of Alison Lurie – born Chicago 1926, grew up New York, educated Radcliffe College; married, three sons, divorced; currently professor of English at Cornell University, dividing time between New York, London and Florida; began publishing novels in 1962 to sustained acclaim, and in 1988 published her eighth, *The Truth about Lorin Jones* – this eighth novel is the one they may look at a shade nervously. Its theme is biography, and the subject of the imaginary biography at its centre is an American woman painter born, as it happens, in the same year as Alison Lurie. It cautions biographers to be wary, first of their own impulses to hagiography or blame, and then of the testimony of all those who knew their subject personally: family, friends, ex-husbands and lovers, professional colleagues.

I'm not suggesting that Alison Lurie has written a warning, or even a treatise on the writing of biography, good as she is on the subject; but she has clearly grown more and more interested in the long view, in the interlocking of characters over a period of many years. Her early novels looked like brilliant episodes, paced and cut with virtuoso precision, notable for sudden dazzling changes of perspective: shifts of this kind are at the heart of the comedy of *The Nowhere City*, *Imaginary Friends*, *The War between the Tates*. She has lost none of the virtuoso skill, but it is now clear that each novel is part of a whole picture she has had in view for many years; and that *Lorin Jones*, which turns out to be one of her best yet, is a subtle web, weaving together strands from all her earlier books.

It continues the mapping of the manners and mores of modern America at which Alison Lurie excels, and its comedy has the brilliant, biting edge we have come to expect; but there is something freer and warmer in the air too. The classical values of order and moderation, so firmly celebrated in her first novel, *Love and Friendship*, have taken on some elasticity over the years. There Miranda Fenn remarked that romantic love 'deals in false images and false expectations'. Here, Professor Fenn (as she now is) sits and cries unashamedly in public for a dead friend, for a lost past. Eccentric emotion and behaviour are shown as not always dangerous but sometimes promising and fruitful.

Lorin Jones herself, it appears, was not interested in any emotion but that embodied in her painting; and everything ceased to be fruitful for her when she died in 1969. Now, in the mid eighties, she is still able to arouse passions of admiration, remorse, greed, anger, resentment and love. It's a particularly remarkable technical feat to have created this complex and ambiguous character entirely through the talk of other characters; and she does come across as a real person and a real artist, dedicated to her work above all things, unscrupulous in most ways, charming when it suited her, shy, eccentric, beautiful and possibly damaged by a mysterious trauma of her childhood; never able to forgive her father for remarrying after her mother's death; vulnerable to drugs; and, finally, fascinated by death. Where have we met Lorin before? Like most women, she has been disguised under different names at different periods, starting life as Laura (or Laurie, or Lolly) Zimmern – a name all Lurie readers will recognize.

Polly, Lorin's biographer, is twenty years her junior and never met her. She starts her research from the position of passionate admiration for Lorin's work, a degree of identification and a suspicion that her early death can be blamed on the men in her life – or rather, on their failure to cherish her as they should have done. Polly has two failures behind her, in her marriage and as a painter; but she is currently doing well in the New York art world, and bringing up her teenage son, to whom she is devoted.

If the book has a flaw it is that Polly is a shade schematic as a character: Alter is her second name, and she obediently spends a lot of time identifying with Lorin. But her story is just too good, too subtly told and too engrossing for this to matter much.

At thirty-nine, moved by soothing women friends and fashionable distrust of the male sex, she is ripe for induction into lesbian society. Much of the comedy of the book arises from the devastating observation of Polly's gay circle; but it is not all unkind. Here again there is an imaginative sexual sympathy which only a very fine writer could risk and achieve. Still, I don't suppose radical feminists will be delighted by Polly's slow discovery that manipulation, betrayal, bullying and selfishness are not the prerogative of one sex.

The play of wit and observation, light, glancing and deadly, is maintained on every page, and, as always in Lurie, there is a precise counterpointing of thought and feeling with the mundane activities of life. In the clatter of dishwasher-loading after Thanksgiving lunch, mother and daughter exchange intimacies that would shock them both at any other time. A broken teapot, a borrowed thesaurus, hair combings in the sink, a husband who suddenly sits down on the art deco chair that is only there to be looked at – all these are signposts to impending change, but never heavy symbols. They have no more than the weight of life, though highlighted by an exceptional percipience.

Alison Lurie has never repeated herself in a novel; each has started out in a new direction. She has given her readers one surprise after another, perhaps the biggest being her move away from classical values and language into a freer dimension and demotic speech. The first page of *Lorin Jones* could almost be promising an ordinary woman's magazine story; its last page could almost be finishing one. What's between, though, is less simple; and perhaps its greatest triumph is in the dialogue – if that's what you can call reported interviews in which we hear only answers, without questions – where characters are unpeeled, one after another, like ripe fruit.

*Observer*, 1988

# Family Nightmare

## *The Fifth Child* by Doris Lessing

Few writers spring such surprises on their readers as Doris Lessing.
She trusts her own feelings absolutely, and has the rare power of
putting feelings straight on to the page, more directly perhaps than
any other contemporary writer, so directly that the effect is sometimes
like a physical blow. This new novel is terrifying and, one wants to
say, unfair; yet there is no reason why art should be fairer than life.
It taps a basic human fear – the fear that one will give birth to a
child who will prove a disastrous burden instead of a source of joy
and promise – and offers no crumb of comfort.

The whole of *The Fifth Child* has the intensity of a nightmare. It
is one of the most chilling books I have read, a horror story poised
somewhere between a naturalistic account of family life and an
allegory that draws on science fiction. You could compare it with
George Eliot's *Silas Marner*, in which a child of unknown origin
brings happiness and redemption to a miserable man into whose
home she stumbles. *The Fifth Child* is this story in reverse. It starts
with a happy family, beautifully and credibly established in a very
small number of words (an appreciative grandparent describes the
happiness of the household as 'like being in the middle of some
bloody great fruit pudding', a wonderfully exact English simile). It
then shows how one child by its inherent nature destroys the happiness of the family – destroys the family. No one is to blame, the
good parents and the good siblings follow their natures, just as the
bad fifth child follows his nature.

This is what makes the book shocking. Little Ben is not the victim
of his environment. On the contrary, he is born to exceptionally
loving parents who wish for many children, and wish to do the best
for them. Lessing is at pains to insist that Ben demonstrates his
nature before birth, by excessive activity in the womb, and emerges
large, super-active and hostile to his mother and everybody else. His
siblings are soon so terrified of his violence that they lock themselves

in their rooms. He strangles animals and snatches up raw meat. He appears to dislike everyone. His mother, Harriet, thinks of him as a troll, a changeling, a hobgoblin, a gnome. His father says 'He's probably just dropped in from Mars,' his voice 'full of cold dislike' for Ben.

Harriet bears the brunt of the situation, because her instinct as a mother who must protect her own offspring is in direct conflict with the wish of all the other members of the family, that Ben should be got rid of, even at the cost of sending him off to an institution from which he is unlikely to emerge alive. Although Harriet saves him and trains him into a semblance of good behaviour, she also comes to believe that Ben is not human. At one point she asks 'Authority' (in the shape of a specialist) for confirmation of her belief, but 'Authority' is almost always dangerous and untrustworthy in Lessing, and this representative dodges the issue, leaving Harriet isolated, and feeling like a criminal.

If this were all, there would be no question about the wholly devastating impact of *The Fifth Child*. It shadows hideously what is a real experience for families with autistic or other seriously disturbed children. A problem of response does arise, it seems to me, when Harriet's heroic measures to civilize Ben bear fruit, and he becomes a viable member of society and goes to school. Although he remains alien to his family, his class and intellectual background, he is no longer alien to humanity, because at school he finds kindred spirits. At school he is no worse than a large number of boys with low IQs and criminal tendencies.

At this point the book changes gear, and seems to be making a different type of statement, one that will worry some people, and delight others whom Lessing may possibly not want to delight. What we get is a cry of bewildered horror at the delinquent subculture of our civilization – unteachable children with bad homes, drifting aimlessly, sustained on junk food and petty crime, entertained by endless representations of violence on video, acknowledging neither authority nor love, without moral or social sense.

Let us be honest and acknowledge that there are such children. When children are frightening, they are much more frightening than adults, because they confound our expectations. A couple of years ago I went into a classroom of boys at a London school, with a motherly smile on my face, and found myself confronted by blank or hostile stares. Not a single smile met mine. It was weird and also terrifying. I left the school feeling shaken, and the image of that room full of inhuman-seeming boys (I know they weren't really inhuman) has stayed with me, so that I understand what Lessing is writing about. But this is a different story from the story of Ben the goblin, Ben the Neanderthal throwback, Ben the innocently evil changeling. By combining two entirely different strands, she has weakened the impact of her tragedy. If Ben is a monster of nature who cannot be accommodated by even the most loving family, that is one thing. If he is just a boy who doesn't fit in, because he looks ugly and behaves badly and is stupid, that is something else again: he is not a monster, but someone in the wrong setting, who might be happily placed somewhere else.

This being said, *The Fifth Child* remains a hypnotically powerful account of the unpredictable nature of evil and the impossibility of excluding it from even perfectly balanced, sane and virtuous lives. Read it and tremble.

*Independent*, 1988

# Sentimental Education

*Lewis Percy* by Anita Brookner

The speed with which Anita Brookner has established herself as a writer of classic reputation is easily demonstrated by turning to the fifth edition of the *Oxford Companion to English Literature*, which came out in 1985, and in which her name does not figure. Today, this seems incredible; but her first novel was published only in 1981, with the modest title *A Start in Life*. It didn't take long for readers to understand that something remarkable and wholly original had made its appearance; a cool, dry and irresistible hand had been laid on the English language, and on us.

A start in life it certainly was. With her fourth novel she won the Booker Prize in 1984. She has written another each year since then, and is now publishing her ninth. We all have favourites, and the Booker winner was never mine; but it seems to me that she is writing better than ever in 1989, extending her scope with delicacy but also with absolute certainty of aim.

The characteristic flavour of a Brookner novel is an extreme fastidiousness; no one is so good at making you feel your own fingernails are slightly grubby. Through the eyes of her protagonists, who used to be women but lately have become men, the world is perceived as mainly gross and cruel. Greed rules: greed for food, for romance, for presents, for shopping, for a good time. Those who don't push forward for their share of the good time find themselves relegated to silence, frugality, dignified resignation. Loneliness, and the manoeuvres whereby the lonely cheat panic and lethargy, is superbly delineated.

Some readers have complained of too much despondency in her work. Pain is not glossed over, it's true. You might even say that pain is what she does best, the pain of headache, of misplaced hope, of nursing a sick parent, of being mistaken in someone else's intentions. But pain is not all. Her last novel, the subtle and beautiful

*Latecomers*, followed a businessman who overcame the painful part of his history to make a modest triumph of his life.

*Lewis Percy* also traces the path of a young man, a scholar, through years of abnegation into something riskier and warmer. There is a partly familiar Brookner background: the library, the London suburb, the mild adventure of a trip to Paris. There are some awful women too – an anthology of these might be made from her work – one giving herself away by sporting a brooch in the shape of a tennis racquet, with a small pearl as the ball; a second revealed trying to lure a pet dog from its jealous owner at a neighbouring restaurant table. Then there is the well-observed contrast between literature and life. Lewis Percy produces a thesis on the concept of heroism in the nineteenth-century novel, and the shades of Julien Sorel and Lucien de Rubempré are there to throw into relief his own brand of heroism, which is much quieter, and gentle; sometimes desperate but never careless.

In the foreground there is something quite new, however. Percy starts as a mother's boy, and when his mother tells him to remember that 'Good women are better than bad women. Bad women are merely tiresome,' it sounds like an aphorism that has the author's endorsement. In fact his story involves unlearning, or rejecting, this rule, breaking out of his cautious and lonely cocoon, daring to prefer adventure to the 'fatal lack of joy' he diagnoses in his wife and mother-in-law.

The time span is long, and used to real effect as people are shown in shifting perspectives, changing their shape and habits and significance. A dislikeable character is seen to possess redeeming charms and gifts; a shy, virtuous girl develops into something sly and selfish. Percy, who dreams of women as ministering angels, begins to sort out dream from reality towards the end. It is a sentimental education but not brutal in the manner of Flaubert.

Clamorous superlatives seem out of key when speaking of Anita Brookner, but honesty compels me to say I read *Lewis Percy* with the most intense enjoyment. It's partly that she has the best teachers' knack of making the world seem transparent as long as you are in her company. Yes, you think, now I see, now I understand. She also makes you laugh, not at an occasional joke but through the steady play of wit dealt out by that cool, dry hand of hers. How many living novelists can match her for sustained intelligence? Very few.

*Observer*, 1989

# Monster

*Jean Rhys* by Carol Angier

When you feel you've had about all you can stand of Jean Rhys's behaviour – a feeling that comes over you pretty regularly as you progress through the seven hundred pages of this remarkable biography – try turning to her short story, 'The Lotus'. Written when she was seventy-six, it describes an evening when a batty middle-aged woman, Lotus Heath, emerges from her basement flat in Notting Hill to cadge a drink – several drinks, as it turns out – from her upstairs neighbours. He is a kindly man, ready to pour whiskies until the bottle is empty, to listen to her recite a poem she has written and talk of how she is working on a novel; but his wife observes only that she seems half cracked, has the reputation of an old tart locally and is made up like one, with red nails, blotched lipstick and a grey stain of powder down the front of her unsuitably sleeveless black dress. The wife will neither take an interest in Lotus nor pity her because she knows that 'when people have a rotten time you can bet it's their own fault'. And of course she's right; Lotus gets drunk, so drunk that the evening ends with her rushing naked into the street and being carted off to hospital by the police.

There were many evenings like this in Jean Rhys's life, many appearances in magistrates' courts, nights in police cells, threats of committal to private asylums, even a spell in Holloway Prison Hospital. The extraordinary thing is that she wrote 'The Lotus', and made it funny. She saw herself, with her lipstick rubbed off and her spilt powder, her slurred insults to the wife and her invented bottle of port downstairs with which to spin out the evening. She saw it and set it down so that once read it can never be forgotten.

*Ars brevis* – five short novels and some stories – and *vita longa*: Jean Rhys's life span was eighty-nine years. She wrote like an angel and lived mostly like a monster, offering a peculiarly difficult challenge to Carol Angier, whose point of departure was her admiration for the work, and who has uncovered layer after layer of muddle, mess, squalor and horror in her investigation of the life. The challenge is so well met that this must surely be the definitive biography. It is deeply researched, subtle, sympathetic and just towards its great, appalling subject.

Jean Rhys was born Ella Gwendoline Rees Williams in Dominica in 1890, making her the same generation as Katherine Mansfield, another colonial girl whose early life provides many striking parallels with that of Rhys. Her mother came of a line of estate-owning sugar merchants and slave-owners – slavery was abolished in 1834 – and her father was a highly respectable Welsh doctor who travelled to the Antilles as a medical officer, married and stayed on. Carol Angier believes that Jean suffered very early from feeling rejected: the baby girl who preceded her in the family died, and the one after her stole all her mother's love, leaving Jean full of rage, 'a stranger on the face of the earth'.

But a very pretty stranger, eyes wide apart, sweet downturned mouth, and wilful. When she was seventeen she was taken to England by a kindly aunt, sent to school in Cambridge, which she detested, and then allowed to enrol in Beerbohm Tree's Academy of Dramatic Art. There her colonial accent proved an insuperable handicap; and after two terms, and despite the disapproval and warnings of her family, she got herself work as a chorus girl. In 1909 chorus girls needed to be tough. Jean was not tough enough, and when she was picked up and taken to bed by a rich young man of good family she fell piteously in love. Soon, by the custom of his class, he paid her off. Collapsed with misery, she drifted into an even more sordid world, for a while working as a prostitute. She had a late abortion. She felt she had died. At Christmas 1913 she considered suicide. Instead, she bought some exercise books and began to write about what had happened: the magic moment that is always excluded from her fiction, in which the heroines have no resource.

Many years passed before she published anything, while her life settled into a cycle of disasters. She married a young Dutch writer, John Lenglet; he was already married, and penniless, but they moved to Paris together, where their first baby died. The second baby, a girl, Maryvonne, was consigned to clinics paid for by a friend; Lenglet was arrested and imprisoned for embezzlement, and Jean fell in with

Ford Madox Ford, who published her stories and conducted an affair with her which humiliated her and destroyed her marriage. (Lenglet became a considerable writer himself, and a hero of the Dutch resistance against the Nazis.)

By now she had become an alcoholic. She was never capable of looking after Maryvonne, who spent her childhood in clinics and convents and then the care of her father; but she acquired two further husbands, both Englishmen. The first, a gentle publishers' reader, was able by encouraging and typing out her drafts to help her finish and publish four novels during the 1930s. They are lucid and powerful statements of what it is like to feel yourself a victimized woman in a world in which none of the strategies of the victim are going to succeed because powerful, unfeeling men will always override them. Yet the fact was that, at this point in her life, Jean was enabled to work entirely by the generosity, selfless love and understanding of her husband.

Jean's heroines have something of the slave, something of the tart in them; they are nostalgic and supremely passive, their plans rarely going further than the next hairdo, the next hand-out, the next pretty dress, the next drink. Their stories are all on one lowering note. Yet the note is struck with the accuracy and pure strength of genius. You believe that every sentence was written and rewritten a hundred times, and that for every word that has survived into the final version another hundred at least were discarded; and the books made their mark, if only with the happy few.

During the Second World War Jean wrecked her second husband's life and after his frightful death married his cousin Max. He adored her too, but turned out to be another embezzler. Max emerged from prison in the mid fifties and they sank together into the most wretched poverty, too poor to live anywhere but in remote hovels in the country; when he fell ill, Jean would sometimes batter him in her drunk exasperation, so that he had to be removed to hospital for safety. Almost unbelievably, a village clergyman who knew nothing of her writing past appeared, ministered to her, picked up the scattered scraps of paper on the floor of her cottage, took them home in a plastic bag, pieced some together and saw that she was a genius. From this (and from the patient encouragement of Francis Wyndham, Diana Athill and Sonia Orwell) came *Wide Sargasso Sea*, the novel which she had carried in her seemingly addled head for years. It was acclaimed, rightly, as a masterpiece, and brought her the fame, friends, awards, reprints and money she had never had. She was getting on for eighty by now; during the years that remained she managed to bite most of the hands held out to her.

For Jean Rhys was as much monster as she was victim. She knew everything there is to know of the woes of writers, the woes of women, and – of course and especially – the woes of women writers. She knew all about snobbery and cold respectable people, and still more of misogyny, and particularly the misogyny that prevails among Englishmen educated from preparatory school onward to distrust women and the feelings associated with women. Out of this she distilled brief, lucid, marvellous pieces of writing, poetic and disturbing; but the conduct of her life does make you see why the philistine sometimes slams his door against the artist, and doesn't mind breaking a few of the artist's fingers in the process. The artist will in any case be the one to survive, and the philistine would rather be mauled dead than alive.

*Independent on Sunday*, 1990

# The Lion and the Lady

*Henry James and Edith Wharton: Letters 1900–1915*
edited by Lyall H. Powers

If your idea of a good letter is a low, infinitely circumlocutory booming on and on, rising every now and then to a breathless twitter, and a flurry of French or even Franglais, then Henry James (or 'Jemmes' as he sometimes Gallicized it) is the answer, at any rate in his later years.

If not, you may find that this collection in which his voice is vastly predominant – there are 131 of his letters to 13 of Edith Wharton's – brings on mystified giggles or even rage. The most interesting passages have been printed before, either in studies like Millicent Bell's 1961 *Edith Wharton and Henry James* or in Leon Edel's various volumes, where they gain immeasurably by being seen in the context of the rest of James's correspondence. This selection, while it gives careful translations of *drearissime, devotissimo, à bientôt, allons, je vous embrasse* and *basta* (etc.), deals scantily with the story behind the correspondence.

Yet it is an extraordinary, and thoroughly Jamesian, story. Their correspondence began in 1900 when James was fifty-seven, an acknowledged master of his art as novelist, thoroughly Anglicized and living in Sussex. His fellow American, Edith Wharton, was twenty years younger and just embarking on her writing career; she was what was called a society matron, accustomed to dividing her time between America and Europe, immensely rich, with a sporting husband who left her cold and spent her money on chorus girls. Teddy Wharton was possibly psychotic; Edith was clever, by now intent on leading her own life and becoming a writer. She had made several attempts to attract James's attention in the 1880s – in Paris, in Venice – but succeeded only after her first book, set in eighteenth-century Italy, attracted reviews which suggested her prose style was modelled on his.

For Wharton, he was the literary lion of his generation. He in turn admired her talent, and urged her to make her subject the American, not the European, scene; and, following this advice, she produced some of her finest novels, among them *The House of Mirth* and *Ethan Frome*. But there was much more than literature to the relationship. He was dazzled by her style, intelligence and force of personality, the limitless luxury of her life. Professor Powers writes of the 'safely controlled but invigorating element of the erotic' in his feelings for her, but this doesn't seem quite right. It is clear from his letters to others that he was sometimes alarmed as well as excited by her. 'The Angel of Devastation' he called her when she threatened a visit, or excursions in her chauffeur-driven motor (always referred to as 'She' by James). Elsewhere he called her an eagle, ready to pounce; and the 'lady who consumes worlds as you and I (don't even) consume apples'. This is not erotic language; or not directly so.

In fact for some years the tightest bond between them was a three-cornered one. James introduced Wharton to his friend Morton Fullerton, a moustachioed bisexual American journalist on the make in Europe, for whom the elderly writer entertained feelings of the greatest tenderness. Soon Wharton (too, one is tempted to write) was in love with Fullerton, and by 1908 they became lovers, on one occasion spending the night together at the Charing Cross Hotel after dinner with James, who seems to have enacted almost the exact role assigned to him in Beerbohm's famous cartoon, which shows him peering at two pairs of shoes outside a hotel bedroom.

This was not all. Fullerton was being blackmailed by a French mistress, who had got hold of letters proving his homosexual involvements, and James and Wharton between them helped to pay off the blackmail, though how much they knew about its origin is uncertain. The affair between Wharton and Fullerton lasted less than two years, and she later wrote bitterly of his habit of turning up only when he needed something; James, however, continued to ask warmly and wistfully for news of him. His excitement extended to her involvements with younger men, of which there were quite a few, and he enjoyed hovering benevolently in the background, in the know, though not too much so; he didn't like to hear about 'dirty bedrooms'. All this makes for uneasy reading at times. When you reflect how cruelly James treated his old friend Violet Hunt when she got her name into the papers in a divorce suit, you see how delicately adjusted his tastes in voyeurism were; he relished a *frisson*, but if a scandal were publicly reported he withdrew his friendship at once.

The letters in this collection at first suggest a comedy set against exactly the world described in James's fiction – a rich and cultured cosmopolites with sexual ambiguities and secrets – and then move on into something more sombre, and more touching. The balance between Wharton and James changed as his books failed to sell, and he grew frail and ill, while she enjoyed commercial as well as artistic success, divorced Teddy at last in 1913 (James wrote to another friend, 'Teddy is now howling in space') and in 1914 took up active war work for the French. Her kindness and concern for her *Cherest Maître* increased, and were increasingly appreciated by him as he dwindled and suffered, his lifelong hypochondria at last justified. In his final lucid months he wrote to her with unreserved gratitude and affection. When he could no longer write, she kept in touch with his amanuensis, Theodora Bosanquet, even inviting her to become her secretary. Miss Bosanquet, however, declined the honour, recording crisply that Mrs Wharton used too much perfume, had a 'brownish-yellow' complexion, and kept the central heating turned up too high. But to Mrs Wharton's 'all-battered but all-affectionate' Master, she was no longer a subject even for irony: she was simply 'dearest Edith', to whom he was devoted and grateful, and of whom his niece remarked, 'he merely takes the good part of her and is thankful' – a more genuine tribute to a friend than most.

*Independent on Sunday*, 1990

# Nice People

*A. A. Milne: His Life* by Ann Thwaite

A. A. Milne was a nice man. One look at his perfectly clean-cut, clean-shaven face in the photograph tells you as much; his eyes are fixed on the middle distance, almost certainly focused on a golf or cricket ball, and his lips are firmly clenched on the sort of pipe Leslie Howard, whom he closely resembled, also used so effectively to establish an impeccable English public school persona. Milne's niceness, like his looks, was of a very English kind, self-deprecating, whimsical – the word he came to hate so much – and humorous; the humour was never cruel, or even dangerous, because there were a great many things that were for ever outside its range. Rebecca West, who so often hit the nail on the head, suggested that he retained in all his work the persona of a British child, well trained and truthful, with beautifully brushed hair and clear eyes and 'knowing no fear at all save that there may perhaps be some form of existence which is not the nursery and will not be kind however good one is'.

Milne's four Winnie-the-Pooh and Christopher Robin books, all of which appeared in the 1920s, made him one of the richest and most famous writers in the world; they also brought down on his head the mockery of some formidable critics, from Dorothy Parker ('Tonstant Weader fwowed up') to P. G. Wodehouse, who suggested – not without cause – that the father of 'Timothy Bobbin' was 'wantonly laying up a lifetime of shame and misery for the wretched little moppet' by writing poems about him. There were attacks by Graham Greene and Geoffrey Grigson too, but what really hurt Milne was that his fame as a children's writer made it increasingly difficult for him to interest public, critics or publishers in his other, serious work. Even his plays, which brought him early success, lost their appeal in his lifetime.

The pattern of Milne's life follows what looks at first glance like a golden course: youngest and cleverest son of a kind, good schoolmaster, he won a scholarship to Westminster, went on to

Trinity, Cambridge, edited *Granta*, sailed into a job on *Punch*, married for love, served honourably in the first war (three months on the Somme) and became a pacifist. A year before the war ended he was attending his own successful first nights, and soon his plays were on Broadway too. The immense riches brought by the children's books did not go to his head, but left his tastes much as they had always been: he liked to watch cricket, lunch at the club, write to *The Times* and play golf with his men friends. He didn't drink much, he was careful with women, he took a Betjemanesque view of beastly abroad. There was a pretty house in Chelsea and a pretend farm in Sussex.

Always generous with his money, he continued to work at writing until a stroke stopped him. When he died in 1956, at the age of seventy-four, he had produced dozens of plays, novels, poems, political pamphlets, a detective story, dramatic adaptations of Jane Austen and Kenneth Grahame and an autobiography; just about all of which are forgotten, while Winnie-the-Pooh, adapted by Disney, now rivals Marilyn Monroe in late-twentieth-century world mythology.

Is it a success story or a tragedy? Ann Thwaite allows us to arrive at our own conclusions. On the way, she uncovers some terrific details. H. G. Wells taught at Milne's father's school, and the young Alfred Harmsworth edited the school magazine: two useful contacts, you might think, though, as things turned out, Wells remained always friendly and encouraging, while Harmsworth (later Lord Northcliffe) brusquely told Milne he should 'make his own way'. At Cambridge, Milne joined in play-readings with Leonard Woolf, Sydney Saxon-Turner, Lytton Strachey and, on one occasion, his mother Lady Strachey; but that was the last of his contact with what became Bloomsbury, and there is no suggestion that we have here new possible originals for Rabbit, Piglet, Eeyore or Kanga, although the idea obstinately presents itself to me.

And marriage: Milne seems to have been an innocent, boy and man. His Daphne, or Daff, was a rich, vivacious girl with a face like a Pekinese, who believed that a good wife should immerse herself entirely in promoting her husband's career. She adored shopping at Harrods and having the house redecorated, and thought her hats made a significant contribution to his first nights. She was for romance and against sex. Later in his life, Milne wrote that 'the doom of Holy Matrimony is the Separate Room', but Daphne, who believed that 'if you don't think about something, it isn't there', insisted on separate rooms from the beginning. Giving birth to one child was so frightful that she would not consider any more. What she did enjoy was giving interviews to the press; she was never short of opinions.

The more you reflect on the Milne story, the more disturbing it becomes. Beneath that nice surface was a tangle of heaving Balzacian monsters. Milne suspected his brother Barry of making their father change his will in his own favour, and never spoke to him again, even when he wrote to say he was dying of throat cancer. Daphne's brother Aubrey was similarly treated for fifteen years for a financial misdemeanour; shock and horror when Christopher announced that he was going to marry his cousin, Aubrey's daughter. The relations between son and parents became deeply embittered. Ann Thwaite is so discreet about this that you want to know more, but she does say Milne changed his will after Christopher gave an interview in which he stated that he had seen very little of his father as a child, and that his mother provided most of the material for the books; and that Christopher never saw his mother again after Milne's funeral, though she lived for another fifteen years.

*Vogue*, 1990

# Translating by Candlelight

*Constance Garnett: A Heroic Life* by Richard Garnett

'Alas and alack, I have married a Black' – 'Oh damn it, oh darn it, I have married a Garnett': so, according to Richard Garnett, went the legendary exchange between his grandparents, the celebrated publishers' reader Edward Garnett and his wife Constance, née Black, still more celebrated for her translations from the Russian. The Blacks and the Garnetts were both notable Victorian clans, and this is very much a family book, swimming with cousins and uncles and aunts; the sort of book in which an unexplained 'Arthur' has you wrestling with both family trees for enlightenment. Sorting out the generations must have been a daunting task even for Richard Garnett, who is the son of David (*Lady into Fox, Aspects of Love*), and named for a great- and a great-great-grandfather (the latter born in 1789), both noted scholars associated with the book collection at the British Library. Let it be said at once that he has triumphed over difficulties, and produced a wonderfully warm, sprawling and absorbing book.

He has also fully justified his subtitle; when you come to the last page you feel you have travelled through life with a peculiarly British heroine, self-effacing, frugal, honourable, clear-thinking, brave, and above all a worker on a scale that can only be called heroic. Much of Constance Garnett's translating was done when her eyes were so bad that she had to ask a friend to read the Russian original aloud to her; she listened, and then dictated her English version (mishearing may in fact be responsible for some of her slips). In 1901, when she had translated most of Turgenev and was getting down to Tolstoy, we learn that she and Edward had only one reading lamp, which he (of course) used in the evenings, while she worked by candlelight. It is a relief to learn that her father-in-law provided her with a lamp of her own.

She was then approaching forty, the mother of her one child David and settled into a marriage in which Edward also took the role of son rather than husband. Her background was this. The Russian connection went back to her grandfather, an engineer and shipbuilder who worked in the Baltic, providing the first regular steamship service between St Petersburg and Lübeck in the 1820s. Her father was a lawyer, his grim character made grimmer by a paralytic illness that struck him down in middle life, and which he wrongly believed to be syphilitic; her mother, delightful, artistic and a free-thinker, died when Constance was only thirteen. 'To live a single day without our mother seemed like having to live without air to breathe or bread to eat,' she wrote. The loss also ended any acceptance of her father's religious beliefs; thereafter she was 'increasingly sceptical of all dogma, relying upon a stoic rationalism tempered by an affectionate and generous nature'.

Constance attended the Brighton High School for Girls in its first year, 1876, and went up to Newnham College, Cambridge, with a scholarship. After Cambridge she settled in London, met Shaw and Morris and the Fabians, and became a pioneering woman librarian, living and working in the East End. Edward, who was seven years younger, had no plans for a career when they met. They became lovers, and Constance began to think of marriage only when his sister warned her not to take him seriously because he was a hopeless character and would never earn a living. If this was so, thought Constance, she might as well look after him.

And so she did; they married, she nursed him when he was ill, encouraged him in his work and formed a close affectionate bond with the mistress he soon took and kept till his death: Nellie Heath, another good and self-effacing woman. Constance was always tolerant about irregular behaviour, though she would not discuss it and dreaded gossip and scandal. Edward emerges as less admirable altogether: clever but spoilt, the sort of person who puts on a mask of artistic sensibility to cover what is more probably simple selfishness. But he introduced her to the man who encouraged her to learn Russian, the political exile Felix Volkhovsky.

The Garnetts were always adopting needy friends whom they entertained, first in a tiny cottage in the Surrey woods, later in the house they built for themselves in the same remote and leafy place, later nicknamed Dostoevsky Corner. Volkhovsky became one of the family; he gave Constance a Russian grammar and dictionary; he also earned her gratitude by taking her for long, healthy walks during her pregnancy. By the time David was born, she was already translating Goncharov pages at a time. Edward was also interested in Russian literature, though he never learnt the language, and he too encouraged her to take up the work of translation seriously; his connections in publishing were useful here. She was eager to do so, partly to be financially independent ('till women were on the same money basis as men it was hopeless to talk of their rights', she wrote) and partly because Russia and the Russians had won the heart neglected by Edward. Through Volkhovsky the Garnetts became intimate with a whole circle of exiled revolutionaries: one was Sergius Stepniak, who looked like a bear and had assassinated a chief of police, but was possessed of a gentle charm to which Constance succumbed. He died when he failed to hear an approaching train as he crossed a railway line.

In 1893 she travelled to Russia, alone, and had several talks with Tolstoy. She did not meet Chekhov, but read his work and saw its greatness at once. Three years later she wrote to him asking if she might translate *The Seagull*; he gave permission, but no one in England was then interested. Several decades later she complained of the difficulty of translating even the title, since the bird was really a *Lake* Gull: 'You can't have a heroine drawing tears from the audience by saying "I am a *Puffin!*"'

Constance had nice judgement. For instance, she saw the danger to D. H. Lawrence's work when he moved abroad and lost contact with his early environment. It wasn't only literature she judged shrewdly; all her early faith in the values of the Russian Revolution did not blind her to the true nature of Stalinism, and in 1933 she wrote an impassioned letter to the *New Statesman* pointing out that 'after sixteen years of Communist rule the disqualifications due to birth and education and the inequalities of rights (even down to the right to a food card) are far more oppressive than ever in the past (since 1861 anyway)'. It was a long and splendid political statement, which the *NS*, to its shame, failed to print. Her political sanity was matched by her tolerant humanism – she saw religion as 'a sort of contagious insanity' but admired the Gospels, especially in the beautiful English of the King James version. She did not fear death, and gardened steadily while the Blitz and then the doodle-bugs raged overhead. She was a much loved friend, teacher and grandmother. She rejoiced in the creation of the Third Programme, and one of her last acts was to discuss her work as a translator with her son David, who made notes which were used in a programme she did not live to hear. She died at eighty-four, a great woman and an example to us all.

*Independent on Sunday,* 1991

# Another Life

*D. H. Lawrence: The Early Years 1885–1912* by John Worthen

When Lawrence died in 1930, E. M. Forster praised him as 'the greatest imaginative novelist of our generation'. This elicited a sneer from T. S. Eliot, who asked Forster to define his terms. Forster wrote: 'Mr T. S. Eliot duly entangles me in his web. He asks what exactly I mean by "greatest", "imaginative" and "novelist", and I cannot say. Worse still, I cannot even say what "exactly" means – only that there are occasions when I would rather feel like a fly than a spider, and that the death of D. H. Lawrence is one of them.' As journalists say, Lawrence gives good copy. In death as in life he has generated scandal, gossip and furious controversy. It has made him a hugely popular subject for biography and polemical study.

In the 1950s the greatly pugnacious Dr Leavis carried a whole generation of Cambridge English graduates into Lawrence idolatry. Leavis felt as Forster did about Lawrence's pre-eminence as a novelist, but further claims were made for him as a prophet or priest with a 'reverence for life' who would set us all on the right path, in touch with our natural selves and enjoying 'valid' sexual relationships, in which the man should be responsible for keeping woman in a position of proper awe towards him. Relations between men and women were, according to Leavis, Lawrence's 'central interest'.

One result was that, amongst the student generation of the 1950s, marriages were entered into with the intention of achieving the Lawrentian ideal of ruling husband and passionate but submissive wife. Ted Hughes and Sylvia Plath were one couple embarked on marriage in this spirit; they even named their first child for Frieda Lawrence. Since then, the influence of Leavis has dimmed, and Lawrence's ideas on marriage have been overtaken by events: amongst them, feminism and gay power. Lawrence, who claimed he would change the world for a thousand years, was a poor prophet; but he remains a marvellous writer. He forged his own language from an intensive reading of his great predecessors; he observed the natural world with scrupulous attention and applied a bold and witty imagination to what he saw; and, at his best, he gave the same sort of scrutiny to his own responses and human relations.

This Lawrence, who wrote that 'in the moments of deepest emotion myself has watched myself', is John Worthen's subject. His book is the first of three volumes to be published by Cambridge University Press, aiming to give a definitive account of Lawrence's life. Worthen has almost certainly got the best part with the early years; and he could hardly have handled them better. He has researched deeply, reading everything even remotely relevant, and is able to be authoritative where others have conjectured. It is a warm as well as a serious book, for he clearly loves his subject, and makes us share his feeling. He is both alert and scrupulous in relating Lawrence's fiction to his life, and properly cautious in his use of memoirs and reported conversations. The theme of the development of the miner's son and sickly scholarship boy with warring parents is a wonderful one, and he grasps all its possibilities in the five hundred pages of his narrative.

Even a reader already familiar with the main facts is likely to be surprised and moved by this account of the culture of a late-nineteenth-century mining community in the Midlands, so much richer than anything found in England today, both in its forms and its aspirations. It was made up of poverty and snobbery and frustration and ambition and crude religion and repression and sexual unhappiness and violence, not always confined to the pits; but the intellectual curiosity, the passion for education, for philosophical questioning, for writing and painting and the theatre, that flourished within all this, give it the allure of a lost paradise. Eastwood was a frightful place; it was also a magnificent one.

Worthen establishes the exact social level of father, who read nothing but cheap papers but knew the names of all the flowers, and mother, who dreamed and willed herself up a social rung; and of each of the terraced houses in which they lived with their family, which grew to five for all the bitterness between them. He shows chapel and shops and schools, he gives us the dialect (particularly good, this) and the children's games and the sermons preached, the cooking and the library list, the floor-scrubbing and the skimping and scrimping when new clothes were needed. He has found that only three miners' sons attended Nottingham High School between 1882 and 1899; they were excluded from games, because the sports' outfits were beyond their families' means. He tells us that Lawrence's father called poetry 'pottery', and that though Mrs Lawrence wrote verse herself, her ambitions for her sons did not envisage any of them becoming a writer; but that Bert or Bertie, as Lawrence was known at home, signed himself 'D. H. L.' or 'D. H. Lawrence' from the age of eighteen, as though consciously distancing himself from the family's Bertie, and renaming himself for another life.

Worthen does not make villains of any of his cast. The power struggle between Mrs Lawrence and her son's sweetheart Jessie Chambers, in which Lawrence used, loved, depended on Jessie and yet repeatedly broke with her – in 1906, 1908, 1910 and twice in 1912 – is a shade less sympathetic to Jessie than she surely deserves, though it concedes that Lawrence finally behaved disgracefully and left her devastated. There is no doubt that she bore the blame for what he felt his mother had done to him with her determined refinement and rejection of the natural life; but how would he have developed intellectually without his mother? Or without Jessie?

Any full and honest account of youthful sexual adventures and experiments – and Worthen has turned up more information on this score than any previous biographer – is likely to reveal ruthlessness and treachery. Lawrence was so outstanding, so attractive, so engrossing to clever and beautiful young women, and at the same time so absorbed and exasperated by his own bodily needs, that there was bound to be a tragedy for someone. As it turned out, the tragedy became first Jessie's and then Louie Burrows's, with whom he broke his engagement; and Lawrence escaped scot-free and laughing into the arms of his German baroness.

Worthen writes as though destiny intended Frieda for Lawrence, and as though she was necessary for the development of his genius. The effect of his conviction is to make me wonder. She gave him what he most wanted at the time they met, being probably the first woman who positively wanted to go to bed with him without guilt or inhibition; she was not only older, and married, but bored with her husband, and had been encouraged to believe in the therapeutic power of sex by an earlier lover, one of Freud's disciples. Lawrence was bowled over by this, but Worthen stresses how casually she intended the affair at first, how little of an elopement their journey abroad was, how nearly she returned to her children. Whether her decision to throw in her lot permanently with Lawrence contributed positively to his development as a writer is at least open to question. There could have been a different story, in which Lawrence married someone like the intelligent Louie; in which he settled in England and lived a quiet, healthy – and longer – life, cherished by his wife and family; in which his novels continued more in the pattern of Sons and Lovers and The Rainbow, social and psychological studies of the country and people he knew best . . . etc.

Worthen does not indulge in any such fantasy, of course, but he does signal some regrets for the path Lawrence abandoned. He points to a letter Lawrence wrote to a woman friend in December 1912, in which he said he wanted to 'do my work for women, better than the suffrage'. 'That is,' writes Worthen, 'he would commit himself to writing about how women managed to break through the social and emotional barriers hemming in their existence.' Worthen points out that this would be a new theme for Lawrence, but that he did not in fact take it up. '. . . from 1912 onwards he almost always linked such a breakthrough with erotic liberation; he wrote the novels and stories which the partner of Frieda Weekley would most naturally write. Work which was "better than the suffrage" also ignored the suffrage, as Frieda ignored it.' Worthen goes on to insist just how well qualified Lawrence was, by background and experience, to write about the situation of women of his generation 'who failed to make that breakthrough; women who did not think sex was very important, however much it gratified the men who demanded it. Those were the novels which, after Sons and Lovers, he did not attempt to write.'

Lawrence is a writer who forces you think about the novels he did not write, and the life he did not live, because the break in his development is so marked. Yet at the end of his volume, Worthen declares himself convinced that Frieda became an essential part of Lawrence's creative life, and that 'a profound instinct for his own psychic health . . . demanded that he make his relationship with her the centre of his life.' Perhaps we have to try to believe this, since history cannot be changed; but I am grateful for the passing vision of that other D. H. L. who might have been.

*Independent on Sunday*, 1991

# Gnawed by Rats

*G. H. Lewes: A Life* by Rosemary Ashton

George Henry Lewes was a close contemporary of Dickens, born five years after him, in 1817, and dying eight years after him, in 1878. Both men worked themselves to the limits of their strength and endurance, and probably shortened their lives by doing so; both tend to be seen as prototypical Victorians, whereas they were formed by the Regency period and kept a certain flamboyance and a dislike of the insularity and hypocrisy to which they saw England succumbing. Dickens, the idol of the public, grumbled and was forced into secret strategies; Lewes, with much less at stake, proclaimed his atheism and radicalism and braved out his unorthodox marital situations, though even he finally destroyed the letters and journals that would allow us to understand his private history as we should like to. He is best known as the consort and enabler of George Eliot, for which he deserves our homage, but he was far more than that. Although he has been the subject of earlier biographies, he has not been written about with the depth and sympathy that Rosemary Ashton brings to him.

'Always at the leading edge of Victorian culture, innovative, even shocking, in some aspects of his life and works, but nevertheless typical of the Victorian age at its progressive, energetic best': this is Ashton's introductory claim for Lewes, which she proceeds to justify. She gives a full and entertaining picture of the world of professional writers, publishers and journalists in which he was perpetually active; and although she cannot restore those parts of his story which he and his friends determined to black out, she uses her detailed knowledge of the period to striking effect.

She can be very funny in the process. I particularly like her account of the remarks sent to Lewes by his literary friends on receiving copies of his clearly lamentable novels. John Stuart Mill wrote explaining that he needed to read the book through a second time before making his comments, though meanwhile he liked it 'on the

185

whole decidedly *better* than I expected from your own account of it'. Bulwer Lytton pronounced, 'You have not yet written a Book as clever as the Author.' And Dickens, who rarely elsewhere gives the impression of a man chewing his pen as he desperately seeks for something to say, ground out, 'I would I saw more of such sense and philosophy in that kind of Literature – which would make it more what it ought to be.' He went on, 'This may not seem much to read, but I mean a great deal by it in the writing.' On receiving Lewes's second novel, Dickens was reduced to explaining that the troubles he was having with rehearsals for one of his theatrical enterprises had 'swallowed up' the great many 'striking things' he had intended to tell Lewes about the book. Not surprisingly, that was the end of the budding novelist's career.

Lewes was the grandson of an actor and illegitimate son of a man who abandoned the families of both his wife and his mistress. He therefore grew up fatherless, though there was a detested stepfather. He learnt French as a boy through periods when his mother lived in Jersey and France; adored and attended the theatre from an early age; went to school in Greenwich, may have been a medical student, and at twenty was a radical and a convinced atheist with Shelley as his idol. Lewes actually wrote a biography of Shelley, encouraged by Leigh Hunt, though not by Mary Shelley. It was never published, he himself soon deciding it was a poor piece of work, and it disappeared. I have always regretted this lost book, but Ashton convinces us that Lewes's low opinion of it was the right one.

It was, however, a preparation for what is still a highly regarded biography of Goethe, for which Lewes became as conversant with German language and culture as he was already with French. His range and versatility were extraordinary. As a young man he turned out journalism, theatre and book reviews and plays, as well as the ill-fated novels; he translated, studied philosophy, corresponding with Comte and Mill, and produced the standard textbook on the history of philosophy, which continued to be reprinted throughout the century. Without attending a university he took up science, did some original research of his own, and wrote immensely successful popular science books. No wonder he was described as 'Windmill of the hundred arms' by a poet, attacking him in the belief that he had given her a bad review. In fact the review was not by him at all – it was by Marian Evans – and the description seems if anything laudatory. It was certainly apt; in these less heroic times, Lewes's sheer output can make you feel quite faint.

One of his most interesting ventures was the setting up, in 1849, of a weekly journal, first planned as the *Free Speaker*, though it actually appeared as the *Leader*. It had a political front half, edited by Leigh Hunt's son Thornton, and a literary back half, which makes it the model for later weeklies such as the *New Age* and the *New Statesman*. Various backers put money into it, including the remarkable George Jacob Holyoake, a self-educated working man, journalist, author, Chartist, Owenite and atheist: he boldly named one of his sons Robespierre, which must have made the boy's life hard. He had been imprisoned for blasphemy before joining forces with Lewes and Hunt, and he formed a lifelong attachment to Lewes. Other backers were less fervent politically – one was a 'Christian liberal'; but the magazine did get burnt at Oxford, to Lewes's delight: 'Our object is Truth, and quite naturally we are burnt at Oxford.' It set out to be a platform for a wide range of opinions; in its own voice it spoke out for the abolition of hanging, for divorce, for universal suffrage, for abolishing the newspaper tax and for allowing Roman Catholics to establish their own archbishopric in England. It also reported Chartist meetings and gave its backing to international republican movements. Rather surprisingly, it failed to say much about the condition of women, and Lewes even delivered himself of some frightful nonsense when reviewing Charlotte Brontë's *Shirley*: 'The grand function of woman, it must always be recollected, is, and ever must be, *Maternity* . . . What should we do with a leader of the opposition in the seventh month of her pregnancy? . . . or a chief justice with twins?'

There may have been some personal reasons for Lewes's view of women. The *Leader* was not the only possession he held in common with Hunt. The other was Mrs Lewes. Like his hero Shelley, Lewes proclaimed his belief in free love and open marriage, and like Shelley found the practice less wonderful than the theory. He married young, at twenty-four, the eighteen-year-old sister of some boys to whom he acted briefly as tutor. Agnes was well educated, charming and so pretty that she was sometimes called Rose for the brightness of her complexion. Her father, Swynfen Jervis, was a country gentleman, a radical M P and scholar; both Dante Gabriel and Christina Rossetti knew the family, where their father had also been a tutor. Agnes was the eldest child; she lost her mother young and had two stepmothers. Rossetti, a boy of twelve when he knew her, admired her looks and her good nature; she was also musical, and knew German, and in the early days of her marriage was able to help Lewes with his journalism.

There is a story that Lewes insisted on demonstrating his Shelleyan attitude by seducing his wife's maidservant on the first night of their honeymoon, and later positively encouraged Thornton, who was also married, to share his wife's sexual favours. If this is so – and we can't be sure – it is likely to have confused and depressed Agnes, and turned her against Lewes. But initially things went well enough; he was devoted, and she bore him four children in six years, before moving on to bear Thornton another four. After a while, though, Lewes became dejected. Presently he moved out, though Thornton continued to cohabit with *his* wife, who on one occasion gave birth within a month of Agnes. Later Thornton challenged Lewes to a duel when he complained that he was not paying his share of the upkeep of the children. Lewes remained generous – he wrote a tribute to Thornton at his death, and continued to provide for the children – even though his original complaisance cost him the chance of ever divorcing, or marrying Marian Evans. Agnes herself was cut out of her own father's will, and Thornton was punished by becoming a mere 'leader-writing machine' and, with the whirligigs of time, a most improbable editor of the *Daily Telegraph*.

Rosemary Ashton has gone through the gossip, of which there is an abundance, with great care; there can be no doubt of the basic facts, though we have lost the evidence of the feelings. Her most surprising story is of how, in December 1938, a biographer of George Eliot received a letter from an old lady of eighty-five, Ethel Welsh, née Lewes, confidently asserting that she was the daughter of George Henry Lewes by his wife Agnes, and that any suggestion that her mother had behaved improperly was false: 'My Mother was a most perfect Mother.' Ethel had also loved her supposed father very much:

'all children liked him,' she wrote, and offered no explanation for his disappearance from the scene when she was four. The implication of her remarks is that George Eliot stole away Ethel's father from his happy family, which we know to be untrue. Can Ethel really have believed what she wrote, or was she offering the version she thought proper and loyal? Nobody knows what Agnes, the perfect mother, thought about anything, though she outlived her lover and his wife, her husband, her husband's mistress and several of her own children. The only photograph we have of her, taken in her late sixties, in a lace cap, suggests a once pretty woman, grown comfortably stout, and placid. She died in 1902, aged eighty. Perhaps she was a woman of sensations rather than thoughts.

Lewes's association with George Eliot is the best-known part of his story. Ashton rejects suggestions that it was ever anything but happy, and in particular the unsubstantiated rumour that she discovered evidence of his infidelity after his death. Even if no couple can be expected to be perpetually delighted, they were obviously deeply congenial both intellectually and emotionally. Those who come together later in life can expect to take an interest in each other's indigestion and headaches, and they were enthusiastic about this as well as supportive about each other's work. If he seems to move towards a certain pomposity, it was a small price to pay for transforming Marian Evans into George Eliot.

Lewes was loved and respected by his peers, Trollope in particular, though he never quite escaped the patronizing tone doled out to social rebels. Being a small man made him an easy target; he was also always described as extremely ugly, except by Charlotte Brontë, who saw in him the image of her sister Emily. He doesn't in fact look at all bad in pictures. Yet the note of condescension is persistent. He was 'little Lewes', vivacious and entertaining perhaps, but in the manner of 'an old-fashioned French barber or dancing-master' (this is Charles Eliot Norton in 1869). 'You expect to see him take up his fiddle and begin to play.' Henry James found him 'personally repulsive; (as Mrs Kemble says "He looks as if he had been gnawed by the rats" ... ) but most clever and entertaining'.

He was also good, generous, lacking in either intellectual or personal jealousy, courageous in facing the tragic deaths of two of his adult sons, full of wide-ranging intellectual curiosity and free of cant. Rosemary Ashton's book makes you like the man and feel he has, at last, not only been properly placed in context but also done justice.

*London Review of Books*, 1991

# Poet Underground

*The Selected Letters of Philip Larkin 1940–1985*
edited by Anthony Thwaite

A card Philip Larkin sent me in June 1975 complains of suffering from public exposure: 'a retreat into obscurity wd be a relief all round'. No such luck, of course, either then – the year after he published *High Windows* – or now he has been dead for seven years. His *Selected Letters* are an upsetting experience, to put it mildly.

Larkin liked spring, solitude, the Queen, Mrs Thatcher, Thomas Hardy, animals, crude pornography and the idea of modest, decent, old-fashioned English middle-class life as portrayed by Barbara Pym – though when he met her, he found her 'a kind of J. Grenfell person'. He disliked family life, his neighbours, most modern poets, students, the Labour Party, foreigners, abroad, holidays – and himself. He was a supremely dutiful son and an unhappy lover, resisting marriage or commitment because they seemed 'like promising to stand on one leg for the rest of one's life'. A hypochondriac, he feared death more acutely than most. When he was only twenty-seven he wrote, 'If we seriously contemplate life it appears an agony too great to be supported.' Five years later, 'the approach and arrival of death, still seems to me the most unforgettable thing about our existence'.

If death was a terror, life was a disappointment. At forty, 'I feel I am still waiting for life to start.' In his fifties, he summed up the day-to-day round: 'work all day, drink at night to forget it'. And in his sixties, 'I spend most of my time worrying about something or other, except when drunk, which is circa two-thirds of my waking hours.'

How can this be the luminous and exact poet who wrote better than any of his contemporaries, and knew he did? Perhaps he was constructing a persona as a protection against disappointment; against bogus emotion; against the bombast and fixing of the literary life. Certainly, the refusal to falsify his responses and feelings, the scrupulous avoidance of rhetoric, is the most striking thing about this selection.

An early love letter makes the point: 'These letters are a bit difficult to write, aren't they, honey? There are so many styles to avoid.' Women had the best of his self-revelation. To one he mocks himself for 'the dear passionately-sentimental spinster that lurks within me'. Taking on a bit of household do-it-yourself, he writes to another, 'It's the sort of job you'd think needed a man: *so do I.*' I wonder if the crude, scatological and sometimes plain nasty exchanges with men may represent his go at being the man needed by the job.

The letters have been published very close to his lifetime, and there is something raw about this early exposure of intimacies. At the same time, I was totally absorbed. The self-portrait is bleak and unforgiving; there are many passages to be reread, noted, remembered. And I find my own few memories of him fit with what I read here. He always replied to no doubt tedious requests for poems and reviews courteously (when I was a literary editor); he was charming and mischievous when we met. Receiving an honour at the Royal Society of Literature, he asked me if I didn't agree that the place was full of boring farts, his voice booming out over the assembled aristocrats and fancy-hatted ladies, about ten times louder than I thought tactful. A letter from the last year of his life expressed amusement at some attacks launched on us both: 'We seem to have got inextricably confused in the mind of A. Waugh, which is not a meeting place I personally would have chosen. Has the *Sunday Times* ever thought of running a series on "Talentless Sons of Famous Fathers"?'

My last memory is of lunching with him for a poetry-funding committee in January 1985. The 'Poems on the Underground' project had just come to us from Judith Chernaik. I was in favour of it; the chairman and fourth committee member were at first vehemently against it. Philip – glum, frail, hardly eating, his deafness aggravated by the noise of the Caprice – spoke up for it. He was firm, though he was not going to enthuse; he said he thought it likely to be less harmful than the other applications we were considering. Yet he also feared it might turn out to be a scheme for plastering the Underground with left-wing rubbish. So I was deputed to meet the organizers and make sure this was not so. I carried out this quite unnecessary exercise once only. 'Poems on the Underground' have been a huge and deserved success; without Philip, they would not have got that bit of funding that helped to get them going. I remember that episode as vividly as I remember the day I bought *High Windows*, and my amazed gratitude that such miraculous poems could still be written.

*Ham and High*, 1992

# Bringing out the Worst

*The Road to Divorce: England 1530–1987* by Lawrence Stone

Eight hundred years ago, in the Christian West, divorce was virtually impossible; only the very rich and powerful might bribe or bully Rome into an annulment. Yet marriages lasted no longer than they do in today's multitudinously divorcing society. Then, death did the work that dissatisfaction and the law do today; and then, orphans became a resented burden on the parish in much the same way the children of single-parent families are a resented burden on the state today.

The English have tended to associate divorce with dangerous social experiment, feminism and revolution, particularly since the French legalized it for a short, heady period in 1792; it did not pass unremarked that three quarters of the petitions were instituted by wives. One of the subtexts of Lawrence Stone's engrossing historical survey is that marital misbehaviour has always been all right for men, and especially rich men. The history of divorce is largely the history of the double standard; when, in the 1850s, there was talk of making adultery into a criminal misdemeanour, and Gladstone insisted that it should apply to husbands as well as to wives, the proposal was dropped like a scalding poker. It's when women refuse to be patient Griseldas, and when the poor look for redress for domestic wretchedness, that moralists begin to preach and warn.

The moral question is closely allied to economic ones. In 1912 the Archbishop of York pointed out that 'the permanence of the nuptial tie is . . . of advantage to the state'; and so it will remain, until and unless the state takes a wholly different stance, and decides it is worth ensuring basic income, first-class education and decent housing for all its children – the dream of the welfare state.

Lawrence Stone points out that the study of divorce offers 'an almost unique insight into the interaction of the public spheres of morality, religion and the law'. Of these, religion, in the shape of the pronouncements of bishops, puritan zealots and pious law lords, appears as mostly unappealing and sometimes absurd. Morality's changing fashions are mapped out with fine attention to detail and the grasp of wide patterns of behaviour to be expected from this author. Here is an example: towards the end of the eighteenth century, according to his statistics, adultery became both more widespread and more interesting to the reading public – amusing rather than shameful, he writes. At this point improved techniques of stenography meant that court cases could be reported in detail, and advances in newspaper technology meant the reports could be widely sold: thus the press was set on its long, prosperous preoccupation with divorce. 'You may look upon the British public as constantly occupied in reading trials for adultery,' observed Leigh Hunt in 1820; the point was still being taken by Nigel Dempster and his friends a hundred and fifty years later.

In considering the legal aspect of divorce Stone is at his most biting, particularly in the long chapter in which he discusses 'criminal conversation' – or crim. con., as it was generally known, the abbreviation suggesting at once its status as a familiar, grubby provider of popular entertainment. In seventy brilliantly narrated pages, we are offered an elegant and devastating indictment of a legal device organized to suit the needs of the 'elite males' (the phrase is Stone's) who profited from it. They were the barristers who made their reputations through it, the judges who presided over the courts and the well-to-do plaintiffs who used and abused it.

Crim. con. began in the late seventeenth century as an extension of the law of trespass, and got into its real swing about 1730. The action was taken by an injured husband against the alleged seducer of his wife. A single act of adultery would do. The case was tried before a jury with no testimony from husband, wife or lover, but only witnesses called by the men. The expense of gathering – and bribing – witnesses could be high, but judgments were speedy and financial awards to the injured husband, and against the lover, could be still higher. Collusion between all parties was frequent, as judges knew well. Yet when Lord Kenyon became lord chief justice in 1788 he instituted a reign of terror against adulterers, insisting that crim. con. judges and juries must set an example to a nation threatened with moral turpitude by inflicting ever greater punishments. 'If he cannot pay with his purse, he must pay with his person,' he said, meaning that the defendant who couldn't pay should go to gaol until he could; later he expressed a wish that adultery should be made a capital crime.

Far from stemming the tide of sexual irregularity, Kenyon's regime led to an ever increasing number of cases; and crim. con. was the making of some notable lawyers, among them Lord Mansfield and Lord Erskine, who did a double act with Kenyon. Erskine performed successfully for thirty years in these highly publicized court dramas. A fellow law lord wrote that his speeches 'upon seduction . . . are of exquisite beauty'; sometimes he broke down in tears as he read a letter by a guilty wife, or called for an adjournment on the grounds that emotion had made him feel faint. Not so faint, presumably, as the defendant.

Crim. con. was on the way out by 1830. Collusion had become too blatant to be borne. The reporting of the cases, from which 'the foulest of French novelists might have learned something', became distasteful to the domestic Victorians. The contempt of foreign lawyers, who marvelled at a nation of shopkeepers awarding money damages for the lost honour of a wife, was felt; and the pleas of women such as Caroline Norton, that they might be allowed to speak for themselves, began to be considered. The way was paved for the 1857 divorce act; as we all know, divorce has been an ever widening stream ever since.

Thackeray, who was locked into marriage to a mad wife, wisely asked, 'Which of us has his desire? or, having it, is satisfied?' His question is one that appeals to those who have doubts about divorce. Stone invokes another question, that of Lord Hailsham, who asked in 1969 whether easier divorce increases the sum of human happiness; and Stone concludes with the remark that the hopes of divorce reformers have not measured up to their expectations. But although divorce may not be a passport to happiness, it can be an exit from unhappiness, or at least a regularization of something that has already occurred; and perhaps that is as much as the law can occupy itself with.

Divorce brings out the worst in human beings, and *Road to Divorce* is a serious book with a sombre subject. It is also, I'm afraid, magnificently entertaining. It will be supplemented by two further volumes of case histories, referred to in the text but not yet available, to be called *Uncertain Unions* and *Broken Lives*. Heartlessly, perhaps, I can hardly wait to read them.

*Independent on Sunday*, 1992

# Unbeatable

*Mrs Gaskell: A Habit of Stories* by Jennifer Uglow

Which Victorian novelist constructed this story of secrecy, deception, financial risk and sudden death? A married woman has been away from home for six weeks, first abroad, then in southern England, leaving her husband to his work in Manchester. She has not told him where she is staying. She is preparing a surprise for him, and the surprise involves her in doing things of which he, as a Nonconformist minister, particularly disapproves. She has borrowed money to buy and furnish a country house in Hampshire, and concocted a plan that he should retire there in three years' time, in defiance of his known deep attachment to Manchester.

Her daughters are in the plot, and she is taking tea with them at the secret house when, in mid sentence, she gives a slight gasp and leans forward. Or rather, she seems to lean, and then she is obviously falling. As she sits on the newly bought sofa her heart has simply stopped beating, without a moment's warning, and she is dead: in the bloom of life – she is only fifty-five – and *in flagrante* too. When the news is carried to her husband, he is grief-stricken; but he rejects the Hampshire house, and remains in Manchester until his own death, which comes some twenty years later, in 1884.

The husband's name is William Gaskell. His wife, the novelist, never wrote this story, of course, but lived and died it instead. How many wives, even today, you wonder, would hatch such a plot for (or against) their husbands?

What we learn from the story is that Elizabeth Gaskell was a far stranger person than the usual picture of her allows. A strange, strong person – the superwoman of Victorian literature, perhaps? For she was lovely, charming, clever, expansive, brave, without vices or even neuroses; and formidable. With no more education than any other nice girl born in 1810; with marriage at twenty-one, and seven pregnancies thereafter; with all the domestic and social duties of the wife of a Unitarian minister, and the care and upbringing of her children; not to mention a taste for travel – prison visiting and humanitarian work among the poor – a social life as exuberant as that of Dickens and a circle of friends as large – with all this, still, at the age of thirty-six she became an enormously successful and respected writer in a hugely competitive and brilliant field.

Compare her with other great women writers of her generation, all of whom felt absolutely obliged to protect themselves from the normal world in order to get any writing done. George Eliot (childless) refused even to keep a spare room for friends, knowing what it would do to her working schedule. Elizabeth Barrett (one late child) made herself into an invalid to get time and privacy in which to write. Christina Rossetti (childless) turned determinedly away from the pleasures of earthly life. The Brontë sisters (all childless, though Charlotte died pregnant) defended their isolation with ferocity, at the cost of any semblance of conventional womanly happiness.

But Mrs Gaskell would dance half the night; she had a hearty appetite; she played cards, went to the theatre, cared about fashion and gossip, adored her children, enchanted almost everyone who met her and was forever entertaining and being entertained. Annie Thackeray described her conversational manner as 'gay yet definite', a description that suits many aspects of her behaviour perfectly. Even when her husband, with his degree from Glasgow and his classical scholarship, put her down for 'slip-shod' letter-writing, she remained a cheerful correspondent to his sister; and when she was quite tired out from all the demands made on her, the letter-writing pen only dashed the faster. Dickens, who admired her work, but did not expect women to fight him, was driven to exclaim, in the course of an editorial battle with her, 'if I were Mr G. O Heaven how I would beat her'.

Mrs G. was unbeatable. Her range and achievement as a writer of biography, novels and stories over the mere twenty years she had at her disposal are staggering. How was it done? She was certainly not the meek, dovelike creature some earlier biographers have drawn; equally, she was not the full-blown Marxist and feminist others have divined beneath the Cranford cap. Jenny Uglow lets us see how various she was, in this warm, rich and detailed biography, and shows that she knew herself to be diverse: 'One of my mes is, I do believe, a true Christian (only people call her a socialist and communist), another of my mes is a wife and mother . . . then again I've another self with a full taste for beauty . . . How am I to reconcile all these warring members?'

She did not waste energy, practical or emotional. For instance, she felt passionately about her books, and suffered in their composition; but she decided to scorn the reviews, and took to going off on holiday, preferably abroad, when they were due to appear. And these holidays abroad, which became the high points in her life, were almost all planned by herself and undertaken without her husband. Early in the marriage, she found that he was happy to go away without her when he spent ten weeks on the Continent with friends, leaving her behind with their first two children; and in this fashion he continued. Still the marriage prospered, and she neither complained – at least as far as we know, since no letters survive from her to him – nor repined. Instead, she set about making her own arrangements, practical and financial, to go where she wanted and see the friends she liked, whether in Paris, Rome or Heidelberg.

Sons were expected to *do* while daughters had merely to *be*, she wrote, apropos the Brontë family. It was not a dictum she ever accepted for herself. As a daughter, her life was sad, her mother dying when she was just one year old; but she was taken in by a middle-aged aunt who lived, separated from an insane husband and with a crippled daughter, in the little Cheshire town of Knutsford. So her consciousness was formed among strong, odd women, and apart from her only brother. Knutsford was to become Cranford four decades later, its female society reconstituted in gently humorous prose. Jennifer Uglow suggests that the Cranford stories 'make the dangerous safe, touching the tenderest spots of memory and bringing the single, the odd and the wanderer into the circle of family and community', which is perceptive both about the book and about its origins in the life of an orphan.

Growing up, Elizabeth was not unhappy; but she saw little of either brother or father and, when she did, found she had acquired an uncongenial stepmother. The sore and empty places left in the heart and the imagination by such experiences – lost parents and siblings, false geniality – must be thought of when you ask what makes someone become a writer. Add to them the disappearance of her brother at sea when she was eighteen, immediately followed by the death of their father; small wonder if the imagination had the edge on the real world. Yet she was cheerful, popular, serene, apparently pleased enough to keep moving from one set of friends and relations to another.

Jenny Uglow is good on the various circles of cousins who helped to form Elizabeth: the Unitarians, who liked their women clever and well informed, the scientists and doctors, the businessmen; the card-playing ladies too, and the young people with picnics and dances and love affairs, in Newcastle, Edinburgh, Lancashire; and the holidays in wild, romantic Wales, which so stirred her imagination. Still better are the chapters devoted to the books, where a formidable knowledge of the period allows Uglow to say many new things. Mrs Gaskell's *Life of Charlotte Brontë*, for example, is well known as a great biography, and known to have caused scandal and threatened lawsuits because of its frankness about living people. Jenny Uglow also shows how it spoke not only of Charlotte Brontë but of the condition of all women writers: how it became the instrument through which Mrs Gaskell could say what she could not otherwise have said. She points out that a passage from Elizabeth Barrett Browning's *Aurora Leigh* is used as the book's epigraph:

> Oh my God,
> – Thou has knowledge, only Thou,
> How dreary 'tis for women to sit still
> On winter nights by solitary fires
> And hear the nations praising them far off.

And she gives the comment of another contemporary, Mrs Oliphant, who called the book a 'revolution as well as revelation' and said it 'shattered ... the "delicacy" which was supposed to be the most exquisite characteristic of womankind'.

'Revolution as well as revelation' characterized other Gaskell books, notably *Mary Barton*, with its sympathies for the oppressed workers of the industrial city, and its distaste for the masters; and

*Ruth*, with its questioning of the comfortable appointment of blame entirely to the young women who became pregnant outside marriage. The courage of these two books, written in the 1840s by the wife of a Manchester minister whose congregation saw themselves held up to criticism, was immense, though Uglow is right in showing how Mrs Gaskell's nerve failed at certain junctures. John Barton, the working man who goes too far in opposing the masters, has to die, and the 'masters' will mend their ways through pity rather than justice. Ruth is also killed off; so is the prostitute Esther, and the child of another prostitute, Lizzie Leigh: outside marriage, sexual activity in women, whether innocent or the result of economic desperation, has to be punished. But still these remain brave as well as good books.

Mrs Gaskell wrote to a woman friend, during a blissful working period quite alone at home in 1854, 'Nature intended me for a gypsy-bachelor.' Curiously, she used the same phrase as Dickens, when he spoke of setting up his 'gypsy encampment', meaning his bachelor flat. But, unlike Dickens, she made her marriage work. To be fair to Mr Gaskell, it was he who encouraged her to start writing seriously, in the aftermath of the death of their small son. And although she did mention his inability to express affection, you can't help wondering whether a certain emotional emptiness, first in childhood, then in marriage, may not have helped to form and keep her a writer. Too much intimacy, too much 'happiness', can be a problem, a distraction from the world of the imagination, a spoke in the mechanism that manufactures fiction. Had she lived, had she led Mr Gaskell triumphantly to the intimacy of the Hampshire dream house, would she have gone on writing so well? We can't tell.

*Independent on Sunday*, 1993

# The Trap: Sylvia Plath and Biography

*The Silent Woman: Sylvia Plath and Ted Hughes*
by Janet Malcolm

Something like twenty years ago, I was invited by Faber & Faber to consider writing a biography of Sylvia Plath. My response was cautious, but the idea interested me. I had published one biography of a great woman, Mary Wollstonecraft, whose story mixed personal tragedy with high achievement; and Plath was another such, a true and extraordinary poet who had also gone to a terrible death.

My very modest qualifications for taking on the task were that I was of exactly the same generation as Plath. She had been taught English literature by a remarkable teacher, Dorothea Krook, at Newnham College, Cambridge, just as I had been; although I took my degree the year before Plath arrived, and never met her, many of my friends had known her. My husband, Michael Frayn, remembers her from his undergraduate years in the mid fifties as a talkative and strikingly attractive American blonde who offered to introduce him and his friends to the editors of *Mademoiselle* so that they could earn their livings without having to take jobs. He first saw her when she turned up at a meeting of the staff of *Varsity*, a student paper, and then walked round the streets of Cambridge with him afterwards. She asked him to introduce her to another undergraduate she liked the look of, and they all three went punting on the river. Later he published two poems of hers in *Granta*, in those days an undergraduate magazine. He remembers Ted Hughes standing completely silently in her room when he called on her, ignoring their conversation and gazing out of the window. Karl Miller, who knew her only after her marriage, and published her reviews and poems, also greatly admired her work but did not like her personally; in his company it was she who was disconcertingly silent. She struck him as 'self-centred and wrapped up in herself'. Miller knew her through Hughes, and she was pregnant when he met her, so perhaps she had reason to be wrapped up in herself at that point. Or perhaps she had learnt the trick of social silence from her husband.

Thinking back now to the circumstances of her life after Cambridge, it strikes me that certain notions about male–female bonding, loosely drawn from D. H. Lawrence via F. R. Leavis, coloured many young marriages of our generation. Lawrence certainly meant much to Plath and Hughes; they called their first child Frieda, after Mrs Lawrence, and his poetic influence is clear in such poems as Plath's wonderful 'Blackberrying'. The male–female notions were to do with sex within marriage being passionate, serious and sacramental. At Cambridge we had generally enjoyed our sexual freedom before marriage, girls as much as boys, but I think we saw sex as something entirely different from the bloodless, easygoing style of Bloomsbury, and imagined we had discovered its importance in a way unknown to our parents' generation. Really we were innocents, of course, and in practice those Lawrentian marriages of total commitment worked out uncomfortably, at least during the early years.

For one thing, unlike Lawrence and Frieda, or Constance Chatterley and Mellors, we produced children. Then, as young graduates, the husbands found jobs easily and continued to live much as they had before, but the wives had to struggle to fit what 'work' they could into any space left by childbearing and rearing and domestic duties. I don't recall that many of our supposedly Lawrentian husbands took on the cooking or trimmed hats for us, as Lawrence did for Frieda. In fact one of my most vivid memories of the mid 1950s is of crying into a washbasin full of soapy grey baby clothes – there were no washing machines – while my handsome and adored husband was off playing football in the park on Sunday morning with all the delightful young men who had been friends to both of us at Cambridge three years earlier. I *had* wanted to do something with my life – I thought I had *some* capacities, and here they were going down the plughole with the soapsuds.

When I recalled this to a friend, he asked whether I was suggesting that Sylvia Plath was merely a depressed graduate housewife. The answer is that I think she was that as well as a genius. The shock of adjustment from competitive and high-achieving girl to subjugated wife and mother hit the women of my generation hard. Sylvia Plath's depression and suicide had many other sources, in her father's death and her feelings of abandonment by him, in her double nature, now bubbling and outgoing, now inturned, watchful and silent, but I would guess that the breaking of the sacramental marriage bond between her and her husband just as she was so vulnerable with the two small children was crucial.

Before I could begin to think of how to approach such a complex subject, Ted Hughes told Faber politely enough that while he had no particular objection to me, he did not want a biography done, and that was that. Friends have congratulated me on my lucky escape, and since I have read most of the books that have subsequently appeared, and followed the wretched disputes in the press, I suppose I should feel nothing but relief. It's not quite what I do feel. I keep somewhere under my skin a sisterly sympathy for that young woman who was defeated by the misery of married life, alongside awe for the creature who rose out of her own death, triumphantly, as *the* poet of her generation.

Now to Janet Malcolm, and her book *The Silent Woman*. I met her when she was planning this book; I already admired her writing, and thought she had found a good subject for her acute and witty pen in the barbed-wire tangle of recriminations surrounding Plath and Ted Hughes and his sister Olwyn, to whom he entrusted the literary estate of his dead wife. (The fact that Olwyn and Sylvia disliked one another makes this a primary knot in the tangle.) *The Silent Woman* is, like everything Malcolm writes, intensely readable. It summarizes much of the material that has been published about Sylvia Plath's life, and reminds us of a great deal of what has gone on, although not everything; she is oddly silent, for instance, about some of the more outrageous 'feminist' attacks on Hughes and on Plath's grave. And sometimes it proffers journalistic brilliance where something gentler and kinder would have been more appropriate.

After a few introductory pages, Malcolm introduces Anne Stevenson, the recent and troubled biographer of Plath – her book was called *Bitter Fame* – and proceeds to describe meetings and quote from correspondence with her. It is well known that Stevenson, a poet herself, was driven close to breakdown as she struggled with her task. The reason was the repeated interventions of Olwyn Hughes, who had made the contract for the book, and proceeded to take it over like some literary incubus. Perhaps Stevenson hoped for sympathy from Malcolm; but Malcolm was playing a very sophisticated game, and what Stevenson gets is something rather different. She is given the full interviewer's treatment, her clothes, her cooking and her absent-mindedness laid before us, her history of marital problems and drinking dredged up for our inspection. Malcolm is apparently out to demonstrate just how brutal a trade biography is by adopting these methods on the people she interviewed. It is as though she has decided to model herself on Lynn Barber and has never heard of James Boswell.

Later in this book, she interviews Jacqueline Rose, author of a fine academic and purely literary study of Plath, and again she sets to work à la Lynn Barber. She begins by telling us that Rose's face, when she visited her, was framed by 'a great deal of artfully unruly blonde hair' – signifying, clearly, both personal vanity and inauthenticity – and adds that her whole person 'was surrounded by a kind of nimbus of self-possession'. Just as well, under the circumstances, you feel. Because later Malcolm tells us she was not even attempting to be fair, on the grounds that she had already decided to take the side of the Hugheses in their quarrel with Rose, whose publication they had tried to block. Since, according to Malcolm, it is impossible to be fair-minded or detached in matters of biography, here is a demonstration of unfair and malicious reporting to back up her claim.

But Jacqueline Rose was a good fighter, and more intelligent than most of us. She 'never – or almost never – forgot, or let me forget, that we were not two women having a friendly conversation over a cup of tea . . . but participants in a special, artificial exercise of subtle influence and counter-influence'. Rose talked to her as though she were addressing a class, says Malcolm; but she also gives her 'a score of 99' on the scale of 'how people should conduct themselves with journalists'. 'She understood the nature of the transaction – that it was a transaction – and had carefully worked out for herself exactly how much she had to give in order to receive the benefit of the interview.'

Few of us are going to score 99 when being interviewed. The idea that we are engaged in a transaction in which we need to work out what we are prepared to 'give' is curious, and alien, to most people. We probably imagine that an interviewer is interested in exploring and discussing topics and events, and prepared to be open-minded about our work, even perhaps our character. Subjects who are 'good' at interviews are either so well defended that they refuse to say anything interesting, or so manipulative that they cannot be trusted. Perhaps these are the ones who score 100.

Malcolm's book is not really much concerned with Sylvia Plath, and not at all with her poetry. It is deeply concerned with the nastiness of biography, and with interviewing, and the impossibility of objectivity. There is a good deal of knockabout stuff, like the statement that biography is 'the medium through which the remaining secrets of the famous dead are taken from them and dumped out in full view of the world'. The biographer is a burglar, rifling through drawers, driven by voyeurism and busybodyism, and seeking stolen goods. Biographer and reader, each as despicable as the other, tiptoe down corridors together, 'to stand in front of the bedroom door and try to peep through the keyhole'. Sometimes they do; but then again, not always. Biography may concern itself with the shape of a life, with its human, historical and cultural context. It may wish to do justice to one who has not yet received it. It may uncover aspects of history that have been overlooked, or examine the interaction between the events of a life and the work produced. And sexual secrets may legitimately be discussed: how could Andrew Hodge's superb life of Alan Turing have been written without considering Turing's homosexuality? You don't have to be the slobbering voyeur Malcolm loves to conjure up to think that a more complete portrait of a human being is better than a less complete one.

Another of Malcolm's fixed ideas is that the 1950s were a particularly low and dishonest period. Journalists love to fix labels on decades, but it is a lazy device. We are told that Plath formed part of an 'uneasy, shifty-eyed generation', always keeping up a pretence about something; and that she looked a thoroughly 'vacuous girl of the fifties, with dark lipstick and blonde hair'. There was also, it seems, a special breed of young men who flourished in 'the Eisenhower fifties', 'thin, nervous, little, moody, sickly' young men, they were, but perversely attractive to women. Yes, I remember them well, but there are still some of them around in the nineties; there are still shifty eyes too, and people pretending, and even dark lipstick and blonde hair.

Sometimes Malcolm does hit the nail on the head. She is right when she says that the *story* of Plath is trapped for ever at the terrible raw moment of her suicide, whereas most people get through their marital storms into calmer waters. She is also honest in declaring that she has decided to take the Hugheses' side against their critics, even though Ted Hughes refused to talk to her, and even though she puts in a stinging reference to how one 'cannot help wondering about the emotions of the man for whom [Olwyn] is sacrificing herself, as he observes it from his cover'.

You can't help thinking through all this sorry mess that it would probably have been best if Hughes had published all his wife's journals, given his own account of what happened, however brief, and kept Olwyn out altogether. He may not like what he sees as grubby academics and journalists making money from raking about in the past, but he can't stop the interest either in Plath's genius or in her story.

And the poems grow and grow, but the story is still like an open wound that will not close. Around it fester feelings of shame, grief and anger, blame, jealousy and malice, and Janet Malcolm's shiny surgical instruments have done nothing to clean out the wound. I think of the words of Voltaire, who wrote, '*On doit des égards aux vivants; on ne doit aux morts que la vérité.*' In sixty years, when none of those concerned is likely still to be alive, it may be possible for someone to write a more complete and truthful biography of Sylvia Plath than has yet been done.

*Independent on Sunday*, 1994

# True Grit

*Hidden Lives: A Family Memoir* by Margaret Forster

This is a wonderful book, perhaps the best Margaret Forster has yet given us, crowning her thirty years' achievement as a novelist and biographer. She has found a perfect subject in her own family history, one that uses her historical sense, her researcher's skill, and her vivid and sympathetic imagination. A few years ago she reconstructed the life of a real servant, Elizabeth Barrett Browning's maid Wilson, in fiction that occasionally verged on the lush. Here, where the servant is her own grandmother, her narrative has the bite and vigour of truth well told.

The book sets out to do justice to the women of her family: her mother, the eldest of three sisters born at the beginning of the century, and before that her grandmother, Margaret Ann Jordan, for whom Margaret Forster herself was named. All had lives of hard physical labour. The earlier Margaret was born in Carlisle in 1869, and died there in 1936; and Carlisle, the place, is the other main theme of the book, with its markets, factories, different grades of housing estates, offices, shops, churches and schools: an almost unrelievedly grim, grey backcloth for the family drama.

Carlisle was a pretty closed world. Amongst Margaret's relatives, 'the most daring journey ever made was by my father when he went as a young man to London for the day. He went to King's Cross Station, walked round it, thought nothing of it, and came back, to boast for ever he had been to London.' When Aunt Nan moved to Nottingham with her husband, their behaviour was judged dashing and dangerous, and when Margaret went to France as an au pair in 1955, she was the first member of her family to cross the Channel.

Or so she believes. But there are mysteries in the family. They centre on her grandmother, who was, she discovered from her birth certificate, the illegitimate child of a Carlisle servant girl, and orphaned at two. There were then twenty hidden years of which she never spoke, and another mysterious birth which preceded her respectable years in service, and her respectable marriage to a local butcher. When I first read the book in proof, without illustrations, I imagined Margaret Ann as a self-effacing woman. Her photograph in the finished book suggests something quite different, bold dark eyes, smartly piled up hair and seductive turn of head, making guilty secrets seem likely enough.

Margaret Forster is not able to unravel her grandmother's story beyond the fact that her first daughter, born before she married and never acknowledged in her lifetime or in her will, actually lived round the corner and must have used the same shops and walked the same paths as her half-sisters, year after year, remaining completely unknown to them. Who her father was, and where she was born, remain a puzzle.

The grandmother's grit and strength passed to her three acknowledged daughters, all clever and enterprising, as they needed to be when their father died young. Each at first did well within the limitations placed on working-class girls in the 1920s. Lilian, the cleverest, became a clerk in the local Public Health office, Jean went at thirteen to Carr's, the Quaker biscuit factory, and Nan set up her own dressmaking business. But Jean and Nan were both pretty and, by the standards of the times, wild. They attracted boys and soon made the exchange that was imposed on every girl, giving up economic freedom for sex and babies. In due course Lilian too, driven only by her desire for children, sacrificed her good career and settled for the punishing life of a labourer's wife on a housing estate. It's worth quoting the central statement of the book:

> It would have been a comfort to both Jean and Lily to have been able to say giving up their jobs had been worth it . . . but they couldn't. The further the two of them got into the life of a mother and a working man's wife the more alluring their past careers became. The only real compensation was their sons. They doted on them and if they had not given up their jobs, they could not have had them, could they? Jobs were traded for children and that was that.

The book itself is of course an ironic demonstration of the fact that it was Lilian's daughter who achieved the success her mother came to envy, throwing off all the shackles that had weighed down grandmother, aunts and mother, using her force of character along with the great educational system of the post-war years to leave Carlisle, to go to Oxford, to decide when to have her children – to refuse the old choice, job or children – and to reach a life of luxury.

Covering the more familiar ground of a working mother's experience in London in the 1960s, the last part of the book is less enthralling, although it is a necessary part of the story; and the shifting grounds between daughter and mother, a complicated terrain made up of love, disapproval, exasperation, jealousy, bewilderment, guilt and love again, are as well charted as they could be.

When Margaret was in her teens her mother would go every Friday night to Her Majesty's Theatre in Carlisle to see the Salisbury Players, and also to the local amateur dramatic society's performances. Local theatre was an important part of education in those days, and Margaret was often taken too. Thus encouraged, she began to listen to *Saturday Night Theatre* on the family wireless, which she had to plug into a light socket in her bedroom and listen to in the dark. She never heard the last ten minutes of any play because,

> My father would come back from the pub and he had to have the wireless on. So just before he was due back my mother would come up and unplug the wireless and take it downstairs for him. I never even attempted to protest. That's how it was . . . My mother always said, as she did the unplugging, 'I'm sorry, but you knew it would be needed,' and she was right.

*Hidden Lives* is a box full of these treasures, a book to be put on the A-level syllabus, a slice of history to be recalled whenever people lament the lovely world we have lost.

*Independent,* 1995

# Tante Claire

*The Clairmont Correspondence: The Letters of Claire Clairmont,*
*Charles Clairmont and Fanny Imlay Godwin*
edited by Marion Kingston Stocking

Claire Clairmont is one of the awkward fringe figures of literary history. She has not won much approval: a silly girl who changed her name on a whim from Jane to Claire and went 'prancing' after Byron (the word was his); whose perpetual presence in the Shelley household, and closeness to Shelley, was a torment to Mary Shelley; who outlived almost all the other actors in the great drama of the Romantics in Italy, cocking a final snook at the tut-tutters by inserting herself yet again into the imagination of a great writer, as inspiration for Henry James's *The Aspern Papers*.

'She transgressed the laws of society without the excuse of either passion or conviction, but with the resolution to obtain by her adventures the celebrity which she could not obtain by her abilities': the *DNB* was at its most pompous in addressing itself to Claire, although it did concede that she was clever, and wrote 'excellent letters'. Some were to Byron, whose biographers have found her as troublesome as he did. Peter Quennell pitied her *en passant* and did not seek to defend Byron's behaviour, but Doris Langley Moore labelled Claire common, coarse, tedious and vulgar, and accused her of penning boring and cruel letters to Lord B. Even Claire's own recent biographers, the late Robert Gittings and his wife Jo Manton, adopted a cool tone towards her. I find this puzzling. Like Thomas Love Peacock, I have grown fond of Claire. (He proposed to her, and was turned down.) I have sympathized with her ever since I read her journals, edited by Marion Kingston Stocking and published in 1968. Yes, she was a silly eighteen-year-old when she ran after Byron, but he was not obliged to go along with the silliness; and she paid for it in years of the most cruel punishment imaginable, during which she showed herself to be a dignified, responsible and intelligent woman.

Now Marion Kingston Stocking has edited Claire's letters – along with some by her half-brother Charles and stepsister Fanny Imlay – and we can read all that are known complete and together for the first time. Do they change the picture? I think they do, at least in relation to the matter of Claire's and Byron's behaviour towards their daughter Allegra.

The outlines of Claire's story are these. She was born in April 1798, place and father unknown; he was not married to her mother, Mary Jane Clairmont, a bright, unshackled Englishwoman who already had a son, Charles, by a different lover. Mrs Clairmont appears not to have explained their paternity to either of her children, but she improved their situation markedly when she married the philosopher William Godwin in 1801. He was a widower, and the resulting family consisted of his daughter Mary (by Mary Wollstone-craft, who had died in 1797), Mary Wollstonecraft's older daughter Fanny (by Gilbert Imlay, who had disappeared), Mary Jane's Charles and Claire (at this time called Jane); last came a son, William, born to the Godwins in 1803. The Victorians disapproved of such a mixed bag of children, but we may think Mr and Mrs Godwin heroic in rearing them all. They were always poor, yet each child was given a good education.

Claire met Shelley in 1812, when she was fourteen. They were friends from the start, the friendship persisting when he met and fell in love with Mary two years later; and, as is well known, Claire went with them when they eloped to France, and thereafter lived more often with than away from them, to Mary's intense chagrin and irritation. This was partly caused by her jealousy of the intimacy between Shelley and Claire, and partly by the fact that the world believed Shelley was sexually involved with both of them. Whether he was or not is a point over which Shelley scholars continue to agonize, and which will probably never be established for certain. What is important is that Claire shared Shelley's views about the emancipation of women, and about marriage. She wrote, much later, when she was a governess (in 1835), 'I can with certainty affirm that all the pupils I have ever had will be violent defenders of the Rights of Women.'

Claire, probably with the idea of capturing a poet of her own, pursued Byron and became pregnant by him in 1816. She followed him to Switzerland with Shelley and Mary and their baby son William, and shared in the experiences of that famous rainy summer beside Lac Léman in which Mary first dreamt of Frankenstein and his monster, and Shelley wrote his 'Hymn to Intellectual Beauty' and 'Mont Blanc'. The Byron party and the Shelley party breakfasted and supped together and the two men became friends, although they were divided in their view of women, Shelley seeing them as intellectual companions, Byron as temporary diversions, useful for sex and copying out his verses – Claire performed both functions for him, Mary the latter only – but not to be taken seriously. The two men shared a sailing boat to explore the lake, Shelley revealing during a dangerous squall that he could not swim but did not mind drowning. After this he made a will leaving a considerable sum of money to Claire and, indirectly, to her coming child; he also took part in her negotiations with Byron over the child's future. According to Claire's later testimony, Byron first suggested that the child should be brought up by his half-sister Augusta:

> To this I objected on the ground that a Child always wanted a parent's care at least till seven years old . . . He yielded and said it was best it should live with him – he promised faithfully never to give it until seven years of age into a stranger's care. I was to be called the Child's Aunt and in that character I could see it & watch over it without injury to anyone's reputation.

There is no reason to doubt this account. Byron accepted that the child was his and appeared to want it; at the same time he took against Claire, no doubt finding her too assertive and demanding. She returned to England with the Shelley party and gave birth to her daughter in Bath in January 1817, concealing the fact from the Godwins, the more easily perhaps because it followed by a few weeks the suicides of both Fanny Imlay and Shelley's wife Harriet. It was a time of horror for the whole family. None the less Shelley wrote to Byron at once to announce the birth of 'a most beautiful girl' and continued to send him regular news of the child, as did Claire, who called her Alba and proved an ecstatic and devoted mother.

For most of 1817 they lived happily at Marlow with the Shelleys, the two *Wunderkinder*, William and Alba, equally adored. She believed she must, for the child's own future good, give her up to her father, but Byron was in Italy and there was no pressure from him; it was rather Mary, now respectably married to Shelley, who was eager to send away a child people suspected of being her husband's. Shelley did not share this view; he adored Alba, was half in love with Claire, and happy to live with an extended family. In March 1818 Alba was christened with Shelley's children. At this point Byron exerted his parental authority and insisted on her being named Allegra; Claire prefixed this with the name Clara, which was also given to Mary's new baby daughter. The whole party then set off for Italy.

The story thereafter is well known. Claire gave up Allegra to Byron: 'I have sent you my child because I love her too well to keep her.' He was not much more interested in her than if she had been a pet animal, and when she was four he put her into a convent near Ravenna to be cared for by the nuns, ignoring Claire's protest that a child under seven needed the care of a parent, and that Allegra's health was likely to suffer. Claire was right, Byron was wrong, and Allegra did indeed die of fever at the age of five, unvisited in her last illness by her father, who could not be bothered, or her mother, who was denied access and information, and would have given her own life to save her child's.

Excerpts from Claire's letters to Byron have been printed before; what is overwhelming here is to see them complete. They show her growing desperation as she was denied the visits she had been promised (one only was allowed, in the late summer of 1818). She was denied even basic news about Allegra's health, and had all her requests and sensible recommendations ignored, while Byron maligned her to others and Shelley – though sympathetic – remained ineffectual. For example, in May 1819 she ended a letter to Byron,

May you live long & happy my dearest Lord Byron. And take care of your health. Likewise pardon in me the only fault I ever committed towards you – that of Co-existence. Visit Allegra oftener than you have. You ought indeed. Your affectionate Claire.

On 23 April 1820 she wrote to him from Pisa, asking to have Allegra, whom she had now not seen for eighteen months, for the summer, and pointing out that the child's health had already suffered from the climate and conditions of eastern Italy:

> the first summer she had a dysentery, at the end of the second an ague [ – ] both of these disorders were produced by the unwhole- someness of the air of Venice in summer. Ravenna is equally objec- tionable and nothing must induce me to venture her life a third time; I have always been anxious to avoid troubling you unnecessarily and to leave you quiet in possession of the child but if she be to live at all she must be guarded from the disorders of an Italian climate . . . Though I can scarcely believe it possible you will refuse my just requests yet I beg you to remember that I did not part with her at Milan until I had received your formal & explicit declaration that I should see my child at proper intervals.

The postscript reads, 'Pray kiss my dear child many times for me,' enough to move a stone, you might think, but not Lord Byron.

He then told the Hoppners, intermediaries whom Claire believed to be friendly (she was wrong about this – they joined in maligning her and referred to her as 'this voluntary little lady'), that he would not let Allegra go to the Shelley household. At this Claire wrote to say she would have Allegra on her own:

> My letter is an appeal to your Justice . . . I have exerted myself to remove your objections & my claim is bare & obvious . . . I can find no words to express my gratitude to all those who have been kind to my Allegra.

On 4 May she drafted another letter, urging him not to put Allegra into a convent as he now threatened. The next surviving letter, dated 24 March 1821, begins,

> I have just received the letter which announces the putting Allegra into a Convent – Before I quitted Geneva you promised me verbally it is true that my child whatever its sex should never be away from

one of its parents . . . This promise is violated, not only slightly but in a mode and by a conduct most intolerable to my feeling of love for Allegra . . . Since you first gave the hint of your design, I have been at some pains to enquire into their system and I find that the state of the children is nothing less than most miserable . . . I resigned Allegra to you that she might be benefitted by the advantages which I could not give her. It was natural for me to expect that your daughter would become an object of affection and would receive an education becoming the child of an English nobleman . . .

And she went on to propose that she should be placed in a boarding school in England, chosen by him or his friends, and promising not to interfere. No notice was taken. In February 1822 she drafted a letter begging to be allowed to see and embrace Allegra. No response. In April she wrote to Mary Shelley expressing her uneasiness at having no news and her fear that Allegra was sick. By then she was considering kidnapping her daughter, a course from which the Shelleys strongly dissuaded her. Again, she was right and they were wrong. Ten days after her letter to Mary, on 19 April, Allegra died. Claire was not told until 2 May, and then by the Shelleys. She behaved with calm dignity and courage, but for the rest of her life she held Byron responsible for wantonly and wilfully destroying Allegra. It is hard to disagree with her verdict from the evidence set out here. Byron will never look the same.

*The Times Literary Supplement*, 1995

# Three Essays on Charles Dickens

## 1. Dickens and Sons

*The Letters of Charles Dickens. Volume VII: 1853–1855* edited by
Graham Storey, Kathleen Tillotson and Angus Easson

There are a thousand stories and a hundred themes in every volume
of Charles Dickens's letters. It makes them hard to survey, easy and
unfailingly entertaining to dip into. As with the previous volumes
in the Clarendon Press edition prepared by Graham Storey, Kathleen
Tillotson and Angus Easson, nothing could be better than the presen-
tation: you visit the past in a state of perfect enjoyment, safe in the
surest of editorial hands.

If you knew nothing of Dickens, you might almost fail to realize
from these letters that novel-writing was his principal activity. True,
in the two years covered by this volume he completed *Bleak House*,
wrote the whole of *Hard Times* and started on *Little Dorrit*; but he
says little enough to his correspondents about his novel-writing.
The themes of the books are barely mentioned; he did not arrive at
them, or develop them, by discussing them with his friends. When
it comes to the process of writing, he is slightly more forthcoming.
There are a few natural and cheerful expressions of self-satisfaction:
'I like the conclusion very much and think it *very pretty indeed*,' he
remarked several times as he finished *Bleak House*. The painful
business of gearing up to start a book is described to Leigh Hunt; he
is 'wandering – unsettled – restless – uncontrollable' and becomes 'as
infirm of purpose as Macbeth, as errant as Mad Tom, and as rugged
as Timon'; tired of himself, yet unable to be pleasant to anybody else.
That has the ring of truth and self-knowledge. There are some equally
natural complaints of exhaustion when he is racing to finish. At the
conclusion of *Hard Times*, he is 'stunned with overwork' and 'three
parts mad, and the fourth delirious, with perpetual rushing'. One may
think perpetual rushing was a routine condition for Dickens.

Yet so many of the letters seem to be written in high or holiday spirits that you would hardly guess that the books under way were three novels of social analysis in which he dwelt insistently on the wrong-headedness, inefficiency and cruelties of his country. In the first, the judicial system was held up to contempt, and one woman's existence shown as senselessly blighted by her having once borne an illegitimate child. In the second, a group of characters was shown to be morally stunted by an educational system that cut them off from the life of the imagination and pressed them into a commercial mould. In the third, the contrast was again drawn between the spontaneous and generous world of art and imagination and the rigid, money-driven values controlling society. 'Nobody's Fault', Dickens's original title for *Little Dorrit*, expressed his disgust with the condition of England. They are passionate as well as melodramatic books, driven by a tragic sense of things being rotten and wrong. In all three, Dickens insisted on society being indivisible: as he saw it, you do not – you cannot – cushion and protect the rich by excluding, neglecting or punishing the poor, because the poor will avenge themselves one way or another, through disease or crime if in no other way. There is no need to press the remarkable relevance to today's Britain.

These powerful themes remain inside the books and hardly appear in the letters; although one, not published before, written in August 1854, after completing *Hard Times*, offers a square statement of Dickens's view of the moral and propagandist aspect of fiction. 'One of Fiction's highest uses,' he wrote, was to 'interest and affect the general mind in behalf of anything that is clearly wrong – to stimulate and rouse the public soul to a compassionate or indignant feeling that it *must not be.*' What he meant by 'the public soul' and 'the general mind', and how he thought they should express themselves, is not specified; but the following year he was writing to John Forster to say he thought 'representative government is become altogether a failure with us, that the English gentilities and subserviences render the people unfit for it, and that the whole thing has broken down . . . and has no hope in it'. Evidently the general soul was not capable of being roused enough to indignation, to the determination that certain things *must not be*. Dickens was a reformer, but always impatient with the realities of politics.

In these years of the mid 1850s he grew exasperated by the government's failure to run an efficient war in the Crimea, or to deal with London's dangerous drainage system; and he used his magazine, *Household Words*, as well as his novels, to campaign against things that were 'clearly wrong'. He was also deeply involved in continuing his private charitable work. He raised money for various working people who had fallen on hard times – the actress Mrs Warner, dying of cancer, was one – but his chief work was aimed at reducing the particular wrong of prostitution, clearly observable every day and night on the London streets, through the running of a Home for Homeless Women. It was otherwise known as Urania Cottage, and was set up at Shepherd's Bush with the financial backing of the philanthropic Miss Coutts. His letters to her about its organization are mostly well known already; but they remain extraordinary in their vivid attention to detail and commitment to the enterprise, which plucked a few bedraggled, sometimes grateful, sometimes mutinous creatures from the streets and prisons and did its best to turn them into self-respecting young people who might live useful and happy lives. Emigration to the great Victorian dustbin of the colonies was the favoured path; Dickens hoped some would marry, though Miss Coutts's Christianity did not allow her to go as far as that. A hitherto unpublished letter (8 February 1855) suggests that he also believed she would be upset should any of the inmates be 'in the family way': 'the matter would necessarily be painful to Miss Coutts'. He directed that the girl should be removed from the Home if she were pregnant as feared, but does not go into any consideration of what her fate might then be.

Considering that these were the years of the height of his fame and achievement, Dickens's involvement in the Shepherd's Bush Home stands as one of the most striking manifestations of the energy that drove him. He continued to keep a close eye on its affairs even when spending long summers in France, as he did in 1853 and 1854; the several cross-Channel dashes from Boulogne back to London to make sure *Household Words* was not in trouble allowed him also to check on Urania Cottage and its staff and inmates.

Boulogne pleased him so much that his summers there extended from June to October, and one of the themes of this volume is his steadily growing love of France and the French way of life. In July 1853 he was writing like any schoolboy, 'J'ai si longtemps demeuré – on the Continent – que j'ais presqu'oublié my native tongue'; by the winter of '55, when he took the family to Paris for a stay of six months, he had mastered the language well enough to be able to go regularly to the theatre with perfect enjoyment.

He also decided to send four of his sons to boarding-school in Boulogne. They were there over a period of seven years, an arrangement which one of them at least (Henry) did not find as delightful as his father believed it to be; the food was bad, and served on tin plates, and the boys were encouraged to spy on one another. Perhaps this was because the headmaster was an English clergyman; and perhaps Dickens, whose letters to the headmaster speak of dancing lessons and extra porter, did not realize the drawbacks, and credited the place with the French virtues he had come to love. Education was a matter he was often uneasy about.

So was the question of his sons. His relations with them become increasingly interesting – and depressing – in the course of this volume, the first that does not contain the birth of a little Dickens. Edward Bulwer Lytton Dickens, the youngest, appeared in Volume VI, and is still delightful to his father through the pages of Volume VII. Catherine Dickens observed how much her husband liked babies, a view that is borne out by his frequent boasting of Edward's physical splendour and bestowal of preposterous pet names, starting with 'Plorn', proliferating into the 'Comic Countryman', 'the Plornishghenter', 'Madgenter', 'May-Roon-Ti-Goon-Ter', and rising to a baroque 'Plornish Maroontigoonter', under which style the infant appeared on stage at Tavistock House, wearing top-boots, in a play directed by his father, at the age of two.

Of the six others, Henry, who turned out far the most able, is said by his father to be 'deficient in originality'; whereas Sydney is reported to be slow in learning, but praised as an 'original'. Frank, described by Dickens as the cleverest of all the children, is suddenly discovered to have a horrible stammer, which his father complains 'they have kept . . . from me'; he exercises Frank to help overcome the problem, evidently without much success. As the boys get older, Dickens's enthusiasm for them wanes. Walter, intended for the East India Company from the age of ten, is found at thirteen to be lacking in the abilities that might have got him into their Engineers; at fourteen his return to school is a cause for celebration, apparently because he walks about in noisy boots. Six months later Dickens discovers he is deaf, and rather ominously tells Catherine, 'I am going to try a simple remedy of my own on him', though he adds that he will send him to 'the best Aurist', should his treatment fail. Walter did go to India two years later, at sixteen, boots, deafness and all, and died there.

But it is Charley, the eldest, who takes pride of place in this volume. He is sixteen at the start, and has just left Eton, to which his godmother, Miss Coutts, had insisted on sending him. Dickens had his doubts about 'the Eton system'. While still there, Charley had disturbed him by telling him he wanted to go into the army; Miss Coutts offered him a cadetship, but after Dickens told him he doubted if the army 'would bring him to much self respect, contentment, or happiness, in middle life', and 'set before him fairly and faithfully the objections to that career', Charley changed his mind and decided instead to become a merchant. Dickens then arranged for him to go to Leipzig to learn German and business methods: a slightly Gradgrindian arrangement, perhaps, for charming Charley, who made friends among the musicians and artists of Leipzig, and was found to lack the determination to become a merchant, or the application to form correct business habits. Too eager to be amused, perhaps?

Some of Dickens's most self-revealing remarks occur in this volume, when, apropos Charley, he wrote: 'I think he has less fixed purpose and energy than I could have supposed possible *in my son*' [my italics]. He went on,

When I told him this morning that when I was a year older than he, I was in the gallery of the House of Commons, and that when I was his age, I was teaching myself a very difficult art, and walking miles every day to practise it all day long in the Courts of Law; he seemed to think I must have been one of the most unaccountable of youths.

Add to this, 'with all the tenderer and better qualities he inherits from his mother, he inherits an indescribable lassitude of character', and you can see the coming tragedy of the whole Dickens household. The sons have eaten sweet grapes, and the father's teeth are set on edge. Further, he blames the mother. No son of Dickens could have properly satisfied him unless he had been himself again; or, to put it another way, David Copperfield was the only son in whom he could take real satisfaction.

Dickens brings Charley back from Leipzig, and hopes to place him in Birmingham – 'it would be an unspeakable satisfaction to me *if I could associate myself with the town through my boy*' [my italics]. Then, finding Birmingham unsuitable after all, he looks for a London merchant house. At least that will keep Charley at home, to be 'armed against the Demon Idleness'; again, there is the faintest echo of Gradgrind in his father's tone. Charley enjoys being with his sisters at home, joins in the family theatricals and is good at them. Did Dickens never think of putting him on the stage? It seems not.

Charley was the only son to be sent travelling in Europe. All but one of his younger brothers were packed off to the colonies with much the same efficiency as the reformed inmates of Urania Cottage, and with the same partial success.

Parental love is one of the most delicate subjects, and looking at Dickens's behaviour towards his children like this, through the medium of his own letters, is a procedure he would have found unacceptable. A letter in this volume (not published before) shows him refusing to publish a paper containing biographical details about Charlotte Brontë, shortly after her death: 'I have a particular objection to that kind of interest in a great mind, which prompts a visitor to "take a good look" at the mortal habiliments in which it is arranged, and afterwards to catalogue them, like an auctioneer.' The objection is well put. On the other hand, Mrs Gaskell (one of his correspondents and contributors, with whom he quarrelled a great deal) did 'take a good look' at the details of Charlotte Brontë's life, and made from them a marvellous and important biography. Dickens was right and also wrong, as is always the case with this particular debate. No one can own their own life once they are dead; everything depends on tone; and it is not easy to defend the view that some bits of history are allowable and others not.

*The Times Literary Supplement*, 1993

# 2. Carlo Furioso

*The Letters of Charles Dickens. Volume VIII: 1856–1858* edited by
Graham Storey and Kathleen Tillotson

Outrageous as the characters Dickens created could be, he was
himself capable of behaviour as disconcerting as any of them, as
Volume VIII of *The Letters of Charles Dickens* amply demonstrates.
At the age of forty-four, this most quintessentially English of writers,
adored by his public as no other writer had perhaps ever been,
perched himself in France and shot monthly darts across the Channel,
in which he attacked the narrow-mindedness of his countrymen
and women, the pompous slowness of their bureaucracy and the
meanness and crude social divisions that crippled their national life.
The darts were in the form of instalments of *Little Dorrit*; and
although *Blackwood's* magazine called it 'Twaddle' and Thackeray
said it was 'dead stupid', the public rushed to buy in unprecedented
numbers.

Dickens, installed now in Paris, now in Boulogne, was finding the
French, quick-witted and serious about their pleasures, intensely
congenial, for he too was fast on his mental feet, and relished good
food and drink, the theatre, the streets, the excitements of city life.
The French admired him greatly in return. In 1856 Hachette arranged
for a complete French-language edition of his works to date to be
published. On 17 April Dickens reported, 'I am going to dine with
all my translators at Hachette's.' A year later the work was finished.
The quality of the translation may have been variable, but as a
publishing coup this was impressive.

The grand gesture, dear to Dickens, came easily to Second Empire
Parisians. When the newspaper editor Emile de Girardin gave a
banquet in Dickens's honour, it culminated in

> a far larger plum pudding than ever was seen in England at Christmas
> time, served with a celestial sauce in colour like the orange blossom,
> and in substance like the blossom powdered and bathed in dew,

and called in the carte (carte in a gold frame like a little fish-slice to be handed about) 'Hommage à l'illustre écrivain d'Angleterre.' That illustrious man staggered out at the last drawing-room door speechless with wonder, finally; and even at that moment his host ... remarked 'Le dîner que nous avons eu, mon cher, n'est rien – il ne compte pas – il a été tout-à-fait en famille . . .'

Three months later Dickens took his family, or at least his women-folk – wife Catherine, sister-in-law Georgina Hogarth, daughters Mary and Katey – to dine at a favourite restaurant, Les Trois Frères, where, he wrote to Wilkie Collins, everyone was surprisingly abstemious, with one exception: 'Mrs Dickens nearly killed herself,' remarked her husband. If this was meant as a joke, it was not an affectionate one. The marriage, never passionate although abundantly philoprogenitive for many years, was no longer even that; the tenth child, 'Plorn', was now four years old, and there were to be no more.

Dickens was still addressing his wife as 'My Dearest Catherine' at the start of a letter in November 1856, but this seems to have been the last time. By then he was back in England, and he and Wilkie Collins were already embarked on their plan to put on a new play, *The Frozen Deep*, written by Collins, acted by both, and cast, designed and directed in every detail by Dickens himself. *The Frozen Deep* became the engine which broke up the Dickens marriage. There is a certain neatness about the process, for the theatre was always Dickens's passion, and this play brought him something he could not resist, in the shape of a family of young actresses who spoke deeply to his imagination, Fanny, Maria and Ellen (Nelly) Ternan. They were three sisters, they were orphans, they had worked hard for their living since childhood, and they were girls of spirit, intelligence and charm. What's more, they represented Art, Imagination, Fantasy, Music – all the things Dickens connected with the dead mother of the hero of *Little Dorrit*, a poor young singer who had been hounded to death by respectable people.

Once it had been Catherine's family that had represented Art and Music, and she too had charming sisters; but now the Hogarths were demonized by Dickens, to be replaced by the Ternans as worthy recipients of his bounty. The spectacle of Dickens – the good, the great – going mad for love of a little actress, was extraordinary and terrible. A French writer – Victor Hugo, for example – could take in his stride wife and mistress. An English aristocrat – Lord Gardner – could defy public censure by fathering five children by Julia Fortescue, an actress friend of Dickens, and then marrying her – this in 1856. Even Wilkie Collins managed his irregular arrangements lightly enough. But Dickens was driven to take his affair with deadly seriousness, and when he could not preserve his privacy, he was impelled to justify himself, if necessary by large lies. In the process he turned his life upside-down, and behaved with inexcusable injustice and cruelty to a wife whose only faults seem to have been that she was dull and fat.

Carefully as the letters covering this period were destroyed and cut, the remaining evidence, well known as it now is, is still enough to make you wince. On 11 October 1857 he wrote to his wife's maid about having a separate bedroom blocked off for himself, thereby exposing Catherine to humiliation within her own household. Two days later he wrote to the theatre manager Buckstone of his interest in Ellen Ternan's stage career, enclosing a cheque for £50. In May 1858 he turned out a tissue of lies to Miss Burdett Coutts about the relations between Catherine and the children; in fact, it was Dickens himself who was eager to be rid of his sons. He had written of Alfred, in December 1856, when the child was eleven, 'I have always purposed to send him abroad'; and poor Walter was dispatched at sixteen to India, in the middle of the Mutiny, to die there six years later without seeing either parent again.

Back to May 1858: at the end of the month Dickens wrote to beg his manager, Arthur Smith, to show to 'anyone who wishes to do me right, or anyone who may have been misled into doing me wrong' his letter stating that Catherine suffered from a 'mental disorder' and that she wanted a separation; and denying that the separation was in any way connected with 'a young lady for whom I have a great attachment and regard'. He was having to battle with rumours about his relations with both his sister-in-law Georgina and Ellen Ternan, who is not named but clearly indicated. Later, Dickens denied the document he gave Smith was intended for publication – it became known as the 'Violated Letter'; but his own written instructions speak against him. In June he published, in his magazine *Household Words* and in *The Times*, an equally extraordinary public statement about the separation. These days, such a statement might be part of the banal scandalmongering of the tabloids, but then its effect was like a thunderbolt; and it led to a breach with some of his old and dear friends, who simply could not take it.

Next he wrote to a Mrs Gore, claiming that his eldest son, Charley, remained with Catherine at his wish, whereas in fact it was in defiance of it; Dickens cracked the paternal whip over the children by insisting that it was to their advantage to stay with him. For good measure, Georgina joined in the campaign of lies about her own sister.

This orgy of self-justification leaves the reader with the sense of a giant raging against his own vulnerability. A giant he remains, even though one embarked on a course of self-destruction. There are still two of his greatest books to come – *Great Expectations* and *Our Mutual Friend* – and still twelve years of his life to run. But from now on there is much more shadow than sunshine. A desperate fighting energy keeps him going, replacing the warm confidence of the young man who had seemed invincible when he captivated the whole country with his humour and his wrath.

*The Times Literary Supplement,* 1996

# 3. Dickens at Fifty

*The Letters of Charles Dickens. Volume X: 1862–1864*
edited by Graham Storey

On 7 February 1862 Dickens was fifty. There was no great celebration. On this day, as on so many others, he was on the move. Two letters written on his birthday are printed here, one written from his London office in Wellington Street, opposite the Lyceum, where he kept a set of bachelor rooms; the other from his Kentish house, Gad's Hill. Never a man to settle for long, now he seems driven. He had just finished a long reading tour, which brought him £1,000 a month, a great deal more than a novel. A novel earned only about £5,000 for more than a year of steady work. There was no novel in hand.

The separation from his wife Catherine, precipitated by his passion for a young actress, Nelly Ternan, had brought him neither happiness nor calm. Rather, it had made him suspicious of any intrusion into his privacy. Amongst the letters printed for the first time here – the editorial team has discovered many hitherto unpublished – is one of February 1864 to the artist Richard Lane, commiserating with him over the 'disgraceful publication' of some private letters. Dickens wrote, 'The extraordinary abuse of confidence in the posting about of private letters which I have of late years constantly observed, has moved me to two courses; firstly, to destroy all the letters I receive from private friends, as soon as I have read them; and secondly to write as short letters as I possibly can.'

Lane was an old friend of the actor Macready, and moved in the same theatrical circles as Dickens. The 'disgraceful publication' that upset him is now untraceable, but Dickens's letter shows just how embattled he had become against prying eyes. This means his letters are fewer and shorter than in earlier volumes, and no longer a reliable guide to his whereabouts. Like his fellow novelist and friend Wilkie Collins, he was making himself mysterious. Both men did a good job of it. Collins's two common-law wives were unknown to the world for decades, and would probably have remained so had there been no children. We have to wait for 1867 for letters in which Dickens's love for Nelly Ternan – 'my Dear Girl', 'my Darling', 'drearily missed' – is spelt out from America to his assistant and confidant, Wills (whose failure to destroy them would have enraged his boss).

For the moment we see nothing of this. In the present volume Dickens appears as a man who is not prepared to squander emotion on others. The death of his mother is noted with no softening recall of the past. The sudden death of his young son Walter in India does not move him to write even a line of comfort to Catherine: 'a page of my life which once had writing on it, has become absolutely blank', he explained to Baroness Burdett-Coutts when she suggested he might. On the death of his mother-in-law he sends Catherine a note that could have been penned by a tradesman. The arrival of a first grandchild prompts no more than a terse joke.

Within the family, only Georgina, the sister-in-law who took his part against his wife and became his housekeeper, got through Dickens's tough shell when she declared herself ill, suffering from a 'heart complaint' for which several doctors, summoned by Dickens, ministered to her. He was frightened into taking her to Paris for three months. It was an unorthodox cure, but it worked. Having grabbed his attention so successfully, Georgina made a complete recovery, and outlived Dickens by many decades, dying at ninety in 1916.

Georgina's practical and emotional support was important to Dickens, but the person who most moved him was undoubtedly himself. In June 1862 he asked Forster for sympathy, evoking his childhood as a measure of his present unhappiness: 'The never to be forgotten misery of that old time, bred a certain shrinking sensitiveness in a certain ill-clad, ill-fed child, that I have found come back in the never to be forgotten misery of this later time.' When he heard *Faust* performed in Paris, he was so painfully moved that he could hardly bear it, because the story of a rich man who seduces a girl with his wealth echoed his own story: no need to name Nelly either to Forster or to Macready and Georgina, who knew all about her.

Dickens was also moved to frequent self-admiration. Here he

is boasting about Macready's reaction to his reading of *Copperfield*:

> when I got home after Copperfield I found him quite unable to speak, and able to do nothing but square his dear old jaw all on one side, and roll his eyes . . . 'No – er – Dickens! I swear to Heaven that as a piece of passion and playfulness – er – indescribably mixed up together, it does – er – No, really Dickens! – amaze me as profoundly as it moves me. But as a piece of Art – and you know – er – that I – No Dickens! By God! – have seen the best Art in a great time – it is incomprehensible to me. How it is got at – er – how it is done – er – how one man can – well! It lays me on my – er – back . . .'

More than one correspondent is treated to these Mr Toad-like accounts of his own brilliance; the old exuberance lights up his language like fireworks.

You can't help liking Dickens in spite of his vanity and his harsh, unfeeling treatment of others. His response to the death of Prince Albert is a perfect piece of good sense. 'With a sufficient respect for the deceased gentleman, and all loyalty and attachment towards the Queen, I have been so very much shocked by the rampant toadyism that has been given to the four winds on that subject, and by the blatant speeches that have been made respecting it, that the refuge of my soul is Silence.' Pressed to contribute to the Prince's memorial, he refused, describing Albert briskly as 'neither a phaenomonon [*sic*], nor the Saviour of England', but 'a good example of the best sort of perfectly commonplace man'. The Prince of Wales, for good measure, was characterized as 'a poor dull idle fellow'. Dickens, like Beethoven, knew that genius took precedence over rank, and would not pretend otherwise.

*Sunday Times*, 1998

# Dead Babies

*Angels and Absences: Child Deaths in the Nineteenth Century*
by Laurence Lerner

At once meditation, anthology and critical discourse, Laurence Lerner's book considers the way in which child death became a popular literary subject in the nineteenth century; how poets and novelists presented and used it as a theme in their work; and how this use related to the deaths of real children. A sombre theme, and Lerner never forgets that real children died and real parents suffered, most of them in silence, and that 'a book about the words that deal with grief should respect silence'.

Amongst writers, the Shelleys, the Coleridges, the Wordsworths, the Dickenses, the Tennysons, even Byron all lost children. Mrs Gaskell's only son died early, all six of Margaret Oliphant's children predeceased her, and the Brontës saw two elder sisters die young. There are private letters of great poignancy, and poems and passages in novels relating to all these losses, among them Helen Burns's death in *Jane Eyre*, Tennyson writing of his stillborn son and Wordsworth's great sonnet 'Surprised by Joy', said to refer to his daughter Catharine, which carries a charge of emotion so great that, as Lerner notes, most readers assume it is addressed to the memory of a wife or sweetheart. 'The difference between writing about sexual love and about parental love is simply irrelevant to the expression of this emotion,' he notes. It is an important point that is not often made: that love for one's children may be at least as passionate as sexual love.

Dickens did not pretend that the death of his infant daughter Dora was a great tragedy to him; he felt he had too many children already, and she was the ninth. All the same, it was Dickens who made a runaway success of literary child deaths. The entire population blubbed into their handkerchiefs for Little Nell in 1841 and then again for Paul Dombey six years later. Since then we have had Oscar Wilde's 'One must have a heart of stone to read the death of Little Nell without laughing', and Huxley's remarks about 'sticky overflowings of the heart'; Leavis on Dickens's self-indulgence, and John Carey on his sickliness. But not all the handkerchiefs have been put away. Phillip Collins told Lerner that when, quite recently, he read the death of Paul Dombey aloud to a teachers' conference, 'the chairman was reduced to tears so overwhelming that he couldn't give the vote of thanks'. And Gavin Ewart's poem 'Sonnet: How Life Too is Sentimental' takes up the question from a different perspective, and in doing so defends Dickens powerfully. Ewart described the near-death of his infant son, removed to hospital, and his little daughter looking into the cot and saying 'Baby gone!':

> A situation, an action and a speech
> so tear-jerking that Dickens might have thought of them –
> and indeed, in life, when we say, 'It couldn't happen!'
> almost at once it happens. And the word 'sentimental'
> has come to mean exaggerated feeling.
> It would have been hard to exaggerate *our* feelings then.

Just so. On the other hand, you have only to compare Dickens's pathos with Mrs Gaskell's lines about her son (in a letter of 1848) to feel the difference between pasteboard and painful truth. This is Gaskell:

> I have just been up to our room. There is a fire in it, and a smell of baking, and oddly enough the feelings and recollections of three years ago came over me so strongly – when I used to sit up in the room so often in the evenings reading by the fire, and watching my darling *darling* Willie, who now sleeps sounder still in the dull, dreary chapel-yard at Warrington. That wound will never heal on earth, although hardly anyone knows how it has changed me. I wish you had seen my little fellow, dearest dear Annie. I can give you no idea of what a darling he was – so affectionate and *reasonable* a baby I never saw.

Dickens, writing for the public, brought out all the religious rhetoric – the idea that young children were instantly converted into angels, thanks to God for Immortality, glimpses of Heaven and Christ –

where Gaskell, the wife of a minister, could only rehearse her memories and her unassuaged grief. There is the faint suggestion that her wound might be healed somewhere other than on earth, but it seems perfunctory. The reality for her is 'the dreary chapel-yard at Warrington'. Angels and immortality do not enter into it.

Mrs Gaskell did not, like some of the women Lerner cites, try to convince herself that God had been testing her faith and obedience to his will by killing off her child and requiring her to submit. Some of the religious strategies used in the course of the nineteenth century to account for God's will in the suffering and death of children, not to mention the grief of the parents, make curious reading. The testing of the mother's faith by demanding she give up her child meekly and without complaint, as Abraham sacrificed Isaac, is perhaps the most horrible. There was also the view that, since Heaven was such a pleasant place, parents could be consoled by looking forward to being reunited with the dead child there; although the idea of being eternally reunited with an infant seems less than blissful, unless they imagined angelic nursemaids too.

Another popular consolation was that God wanted to turn the child into an angel before its innocence could be sullied; Coleridge was keen on the idea, and wrote some epitaphs celebrating it. In this argument it becomes *better* for a child to die than to live. And in fact Dickens used it in *David Copperfield* when he made David say it would have been better for Little Em'ly to fall into the sea and drown as a child rather than grow up to be seduced by Steerforth.

More acceptably, in real life Dickens welcomed the death of his severely handicapped nephew; the boy's mother was already dead, and Dickens did not mind saying what he felt – that the boy was better dead too – with a frankness a twentieth-century writer would be less likely to display even in a private letter. Lerner mentions neither of these episodes, but he does suggest that it is uncertain whether Dickens himself believed in Heaven, and points to the ambivalence in the description of Paul Dombey's last moments, when Dickens writes of 'the old, old fashion – Death!', and goes on, 'Oh thank GOD, all who see it, for that older fashion yet, of Immortality! And look upon us, angels of young children, with regards not quite estranged, when the swift river bears us to the ocean!' Lerner, who is agnostic but not irreverent towards Christian faith, comments,

> The reason for the enormous emotional impact this had on contemporaries may be its ambivalence about Christianity. It does not actually profess belief in immortality: by calling it, so lovingly, a 'fashion', the writing offers it as a beneficent invention, a doctrine devised to help us bear the pain of death . . . And so the angels of young children could be seen as a human invention, a way we have taught ourselves to speak of dead children, and all the finer for that. What weakens the theology strengthens the consolation.

Lerner looks at all sides of the question, citing a robust twentieth-century Christian rebuttal of the notion that a mother can be fully comforted by the idea that her child has become an angel, from C. S. Lewis, who pointed out that even if it was good for the child, it was no good to her as a mother. 'The specifically maternal happiness must be written off. Never, in any place or time, will she have her son on her knees, or bathe him, or tell him a story, or plan for his future, or see her grandchild.'

Neither Paul Dombey nor Little Nell had a mother to grieve for them, of course. They also pass effortlessly from life, and this is one of the reasons Dickens has been accused of sentimentality. Not only is he luxuriating in pathos, and encouraging his readers to join him in an enjoyable wallow; he is also denying the reality of illness and pain, as Flaubert and Dostoevsky did not in their accounts of children's deaths.

Paul Dombey's death was a replay of the death of Little Nell, and Nell's death was, we know from Dickens himself, associated with the death of his sister-in-law Mary Hogarth four years before: 'Dear Mary died yesterday, when I think of this sad story,' he wrote to Forster. Dickens made Nell a child, no more than fourteen when she died, while Mary was nearly seventeen, old enough to be married; his interest in child brides and the age at which a small girl might be found erotically stimulating, as Quilp finds Nell, comes into play here. Lerner does not share the view of the American critic James

Kincaid that Paul Dombey and Nell are both 'pedophile pin-ups', but he suggests that Dickens used a process of 'idealizing desexualization' on the many infantile women or nearly nubile little girls who appear in his work, not only Nell, but Amy Dorrit, Rose Maylie, Dora Spenlow, Little Em'ly, Florence Dombey and many more. It is certainly striking that Florence is already being imagined as a bride at the age of twelve; and that Little Dorrit looks like a child, and that Arthur Clennam takes her in his arms 'as though she had been his daughter'. The Lolita tendency in Dickens is pervasive, and not always related to early death. While Mary Hogarth may be partly responsible, it could also relate to his interest in girl prostitutes.

Lerner's excursions around the literature of child death are well conducted, and his comments good. I cannot, however, let him get away with saying that children figure 'as little more than a nuisance' in Jane Austen's work. It is true that she told her niece that, in fiction, 'one does not care for girls until they are grown up'; but you have only to turn to *The Watsons* to find the most perceptive and affectionate portrait of a ten-year-old boy you could wish for. The Austen family falls, in any case, outside Lerner's territory, in that they were notably successful child rearers, and all eight of their offspring made it into adult life. The fact that Jane, the genius of the family, was the first to die is one of Fate's ironies; but she was too old to be rememered as an angel, and no one has ever presumed to speak of her in those terms.

*The Times Literary Supplement*, 1998

# Tame Animals

*The Gentleman's Daughter: Women's Lives in Georgian England* by Amanda Vickery
*A Governess in the Age of Jane Austen: The Journals and Letters of Agnes Porter* edited by Joanna Martin

Amanda Vickery teaches history in London, but, as she tells us on the first page of *The Gentleman's Daughter*, she grew up in Preston, and the archives which formed the basis first for her Ph.D. and now for this book are held in the north. In the record offices of Lancashire, Yorkshire and Cumbria she has found a gold mine in the realm of women's history: letters and pocket-book diaries kept by the daughters, wives and mothers of gentlemen of the eighteenth and early nineteenth centuries, allowing us to hear their voices as they experience courtship, marriage, motherhood and widowing, and to enjoy direct accounts of their domestic and social preoccupations. Material of this kind is precious, and she is to be congratulated on her discoveries, and on her careful handling and publication of the material.

Her chapters are thematic, covering marriage, children, servants, shopping, social life within the home and outside it; and she orders and tabulates her material strictly. Certain characters nevertheless burst out of these categories to dominate the narrative with the force of their personalities. One is Elizabeth Parker ('Parky' to her friends, 1726–81), a lesser landowner's daughter whose letters and diaries chart most of her life, starting with a seven-year wooing by a cousin of whom her father disapproved. Her lover tried every line of attack, urging her to clandestine night-time meetings, and won her in the end by the old ruse of telling her he was preparing to marry someone else. At this she persuaded her father to relent, and they were married. But she was soon left a widow with small sons to bring up alone; and after another seven years she eloped – to Gretna Green – with a young man eighteen years her junior. This marriage was a disaster for both parties. She was dropped by her most important living male relative, her brother. There were no children, her husband soon came to resent and indeed hate her, and he took to drink. Although she struggled to keep her dignity, she sank in the social scale as he wasted their money, roistering in the kitchen with tenants and servants (sometimes it sounds almost like *Wuthering Heights*). Meanwhile her brother improved his status, marrying a baronet's daughter. *His* son went into Parliament; Elizabeth's sons became tradesmen. All this is documented in her own hand, with records of her hiring and management of servants, her dinners and tea parties, her snobberies and wounded feelings, her husband's blows and curses; as well as a surprising touch, her successful marketing of an anti-rabies medicine developed by her first husband, which she sold all over the north of England at one shilling a bottle until her death. (It was presumably never put to the test on an actual case of rabies.)

Elizabeth's jolly cousin Bessy is another striking character. She lodged in London with her brother until she was nearly forty, when she married a fifty-year-old bachelor schoolmaster. The marriage was deeply satisfying to both, and they paraded their satisfaction in their cosy domestic arrangements in letters to relations, Bessy proclaiming she was 'not ashamed of my passion' for her 'lord and master'. In spite of her age, there were four babies, and she breastfed them all. In fact little Betsy was shod before she was weaned, and 'My Littel Boy has not for this three week been from my Bed or lap half hour at a time. For to my shame (Tho' happy it was for him) I still suckel him.' This was in the 1760s, about the same time Jane Austen's mother was weaning her infants briskly at two or three months and sending them to be reared in the village. The decision to breastfeed or not seems to have been much more an individual choice than a matter of fashion. Bessy was by no means tied down by her maternal and domestic duties; she went out as much as she pleased to enjoy the pleasures of London life, 'frolicking' to the theatre or gawping at the royal family. And her good-humoured husband respected her taste for gadding: 'came the Coach to the Door and away whisked Madam to the Assembly as usual'.

Then there is the heiress Anne Wilmer, also from the middle of the eighteenth century, who condescended to give her hand to a rich mercer's son, William Gossip, manager of the York Assembly

Rooms. He was clever and charming, and theirs was another demonstratively affectionate marriage. They hated to be separated and wrote to tell one another so, often invoking the marriage bed: 'I wish I had my poor Dear in his own bed with me. I think you would be beter [sic]', etc. A rich, handsome and happy couple, they built a mansion on their large estate in Wharfedale in addition to their solid town house in York, and he became a J P and deputy lieutenant for the West Riding. Only the fates of their eleven children were disappointing. Most died young, and the heir outraged them by marrying down, a secret match, the daughter of a poor Halifax mantua-maker. He was disinherited. One son studied medicine, others were apprenticed to hosiers or went into the army.

The women figuring in these records were not aristocrats. They came from middle-class families, genteel, proper and prosperous for the most part; some married landowners, some professional men, some tradesmen. And their children took divergent paths, as we have seen. One thing that emerges strongly from Vickery's account is the high degree of mobility of late Georgian life, as men and women moved themselves up or tumbled down the social snakes and ladders board. This certainly tallies with observations of the Hampshire families amongst whom Jane Austen lived made in my own work.

What is very clear is just how individual and unpredictable each life and each family was, and how they refuse to conform to the generalizations of historians. Part of the purpose of Vickery's book is indeed to attack the theses of academic historians who have constructed a narrative of 'decline and fall' in the status of Englishwomen, following some notional golden age in which they are said to have been powerful working members of society. This golden age has been variously set from the Middle Ages to the years immediately preceding the Industrial Revolution; but whether or whenever it was, there is pretty general agreement that the nineteenth century was a nadir for women in which their lives were 'drained of economic purpose and public responsibility'.

Vickery's thesis is that women in the Georgian period – which extended through the first third of the nineteenth century – were in truth more confident and more autonomous than is 'usually allowed'. She suggests that the Victorian women who fought for the right to education, suffrage and professional training were seeking 'to extend yet further the gains made by their Georgian predecessors'. She supports this by claiming that Georgian women enjoyed responsibility and a significant amount of economic power in the domestic sphere; had considerable freedom in choosing their husbands; participated in the expanding social world of the Assembly Room, public gardens, music meetings and theatres; and in charitable and reforming groups such as the anti-slavery movement.

Whether these activities were really the forerunners of the feminist activities of the nineteenth century is open to argument. For one thing, the later-nineteenth-century struggles were fired by bitterness against the status quo, and taken up by middle-class women who specifically felt they lacked autonomy over their lives. The bitterness certainly had its roots earlier. Leaving aside Mary Wollstonecraft and her circle, there is the experience of the Lancastrian Ellen Weeton (1776–1844?), whom Vickery actually includes in her book. For Weeton there was little enough autonomy, shortage of money forcing her into governessing, and a tyrannical husband taking her child from her and reducing her to the point of starvation. Vickery concedes that Weeton suffered almost dehumanizing ill-treatment, but does not quote or even refer to her private writing about the situation of her sex. For instance, Weeton recalled as a child hearing her father express the wish that all his children should be boys, not because he did not love girls as well, but 'unless a father can provide independent fortunes for his daughters, they must either be made mop squeezers, or mantua makers, whereas sons can easily make their way in the world'. This thoughtful sea captain was killed young fighting the Americans, and his clever daughter had to become, not a mop squeezer it's true, but a governess; and when she married, her husband turned out to be a brute. She expressed the view that the sexes were equal, and that society would be better organized were they treated equally. Thus in 1809 she wrote to her lawyer brother,

Why are not females permitted to study physic, divinity, astronomy, &c., with their attendants, chemistry, botany, logic, mathematics, &c. To be sure the mere study is not prohibited, but the practise is in a great measure. Who would employ a female physician? who would listen to a female divine, except to ridicule? I could myself almost laugh at the idea.

The crucial point here is poverty. Weeton, like Wollstonecraft, was bred to be a lady but then found herself thrown on a world which offered no decent alternative to marriage. Before them, Richardson had meditated (in *Sir Charles Grandison*) on the difficult situation of unsupported ladies, and whether Protestant nunneries might be a partial solution to their problems; an idea Sheridan also took up. But even rich and married ladies expressed their discontents at times. In the (unpublished) letters and diaries of Eliza Chute, wife of a Hampshire M P at the end of the eighteenth century, there are clear expressions of dissatisfaction with the position of wives:

> Mr Chute . . . seems to think it strange that I should absent myself from him for four & twenty hours when he is at home, tho' it appears in the natural order of things that he should quit me for business or pleasure, such is the difference between husbands & wives. The latter are sort of tame animals, whom the men always expect to find at home ready to receive them: the former are lords of the creation free to go where they please.

There are other cases that support Vickery's view of course. Charlotte Smith (1749–1806), married in her early teens to an uncongenial and errant husband who became bankrupt, displayed extraordinary energy and was able to maintain herself and her many children entirely by her pen, becoming a successful poet and novelist. Was she a model to nineteenth-century women writers? You think at once of a later Charlotte (Brontë, 1816–55), admonished by Robert Southey to give up the idea of becoming a writer and stick to her needle and domestic duties. Fanny Burney wrote for money and kept what she earned in the 1790s, when she was married; William Gaskell in the 1850s pocketed his wife's earnings as the cheques arrived. And it was in 1848 that Geraldine Jewsbury wrote *The Half Sisters*, her impassioned attack on the way in which English ladies were infantilized by their upbringing. Mary Shelley, struggling to make a living by her pen, wrote in 1843 that she abhorred and shrank from 'a public life for women'.

Vickery points to many ladies amongst her sample who felt satisfaction at their own position in life, and it is true that a polite husband, a sufficient income, obedient servants and access to some company and amusements did appear to meet the needs of most who enjoyed these blessings. But one message that emerges from her material is the very great difficulty of making general statements about the behaviour of genteel women or their view of their own position, either in the eighteenth or the nineteenth century. Consider that Jane Austen's paternal aunt Philadelphia, an orphan, travelled to India alone in the 1750s to get herself a husband, but a generation later Jane's careful parents did not dream of letting her travel across the southern counties of England without an escort. Does this represent a general shift in attitude, or was it rather that Mrs Austen decreed what her daughters might do from the traditions of the family in which she had grown up?

It seems likely that traditions running through the female line are responsible for many such features in the life of a family; but because they were not formalized or written down, but simply passed on verbally from mother to daughter, and taken for granted, it is impossible to be certain about them. So it is for childbirth practices, the feeding and weaning of babies, ideas about contraception and sex, all very poorly documented. Sets of family letters are precious in these areas, and Vickery's book is full of fine details and discoveries. There is an especially good chapter on women's dealings with their servants, how they thought of them, how they were hired, how some were petted and indulged until they seemed almost friends; and how many ran away or made trouble. We are given the feeling of life as it was lived by her ladies, as they express their status through furniture and china, make careful note of food prices, take pleasure in discussing new fashions, grumble about an ungrateful maid or an inconsiderate man who smokes over the table, or lets off his gun in the next room; or the joy of having a small daughter, 'all over so fat and soft'. Again and again their words surprise and charm. The eighteenth was of course the great century of increasing female literacy, in which the women of England discovered they could not only enjoy reading novels and poems but write them too.

After this rich brew, Agnes Porter's journals and letters in *A Governess in the Age of Jane Austen* are weak tea. Although she was a well-read and intelligent woman, there is something desolating about the resignation that breathes from her writing, resignation to the meagreness of every aspect of her life, emotional, financial and spiritual. A clergyman's daughter, Edinburgh-born in 1745, she was devoted governess to two generations of the family of the Earl of Ilchester. Sydney Smith, meeting her when she was in her fifties and he in his twenties, described her as 'I daresay a very respectable woman . . . but I confess in my eyes she is a very ordinary article.' And so she seems from her diaries, in which her pupils are always dear or darling, and her employers almost always charming. There are tea parties, card parties, sermons, a lot of indifferent weather and some disappointing men friends. But, as her editor points out, she established herself as a professional woman rather than as a mere drudge, and she did manage to organize her finances success- fully enough to avoid destitution, the common lot of governesses too old to work on. She gave notice when she was displeased, and she chose to move about when she was not working in the mansions of the aristocracy, settling in towns as various as Yarmouth and Swindon. She enjoyed travel, and there are some lively accounts of cross-country coach journeys, unescorted, in which she strikes up conversation with grocers and glovers with views on female accom- plishments. There are also visits to the London theatre, and to see the massed charity children, and other treats. Joanna Martin has done a fine and patient job in transcribing, editing and annotating the journals and letters, and filled in the background in a long introductory essay; you end by thinking Miss Porter has been more fortunate in her editor than she ever was in life.

*The Times Literary Supplement*, 1998

# Carpe Diem

*The Diary of Samuel Pepys* (eleven volumes) edited by
Robert Latham and William Matthews

If the authenticity of Pepys's *Diary* were in doubt, what a piece of fiction it would seem – the work of a novelist of genius, more inspired than Defoe, franker than Smollett, deeper than Dickens, subtler than Proust. To support the theory, begin by pointing out how carefully the *Diary* is structured. It covers the ten years in which a young man is making it. His narrative charts a steady upward curve as he rises from nothing – just a clerk, with barely £25 saved up against trouble – to a position as a supremely successful administrator, courted, envied and admired, trusted and valued by the King; a man about town boasting a fortune of £10,000.

Then look at the choice of decade – the 1660s – with its unparalleled sequence of public events: the Restoration of Charles II, the Great Plague, the Fire of London, the wars with the Dutch, when their fleet struck panic into the English by sailing up the Medway, burning and seizing ships. Next, the panoramic account of London, laid out in brilliant flashlit views, with its river and river craft, streets and horses, alleys, hurrying servants, shop people, Members of Parliament, sea captains, beauties, theatres, gardens and palaces. Place, time and season follow one another in vivid novelistic sequence. Now it is the heat of summer, and a sweaty Pepys is stealing an afternoon off to take one of his unofficial ladies to Highgate for a fumble in a hired coach. Now it is freezing so hard that the streets are emptied of horse traffic but have filled up with football games instead; a woman slips on the ice and breaks her thigh as he walks past. Now it is May, and – certainly too good to be true, this – Nell Gwyn herself, 'pretty Nelly . . . is standing at her lodgings door in Drury Lane in her smock-sleeves and bodice'. Now it is July, and Pepys is by the river near the Tower, feeling ineffectually sorry for a group of women whose husbands have been taken by the press gang: 'Lord, how some poor women did cry, and in my life I never did see such natural expression of passion as I did here.' And now it is March 1668, and he is to address the House of Commons in defence of the Navy Board, having worked late into the night in preparation, giving himself last-minute courage with half a pint of mulled sack at the Dogg and a dram of brandy in Westminster Hall. So warmed, he addresses the full House for three hours and, according to the solicitor-general, 'spoke the best of any man in England'.

Pepys appears as a brave, not a prudent hero. At twenty-two – before the start of the narrative – he had married a penniless French girl of fifteen; love always hit him hard and he declared later that he had been literally sick for her. When the *Diary* ends, although they are sharing a fine house with what he calls his 'family' of servants, his marriage is in tatters because of his persistent unfaithfulness, culminating in a passionate affair with Elizabeth Pepys's young companion, Deb Willet. On discovering this, Mrs Pepys's anger and grief are such that she does not wash for five weeks, a fact Pepys notes not unsympathetically, although he himself was relatively keen on soap and water. There are no children to distract her, and she swears vengeance, threatening to slit Deb's nose, and extracting repeated expressions of penitence and promises of reform from her husband. Pepys has not only to dismiss Deb and swear never to see her again, but also write and tell her she is a whore. This she is not: it was he who corrupted her, and who is now responsible for the precariousness of her situation. Frightful as these events are to him, in his account of them he gives both sides of the case, like the good civil servant he is: he loves Deb, longs for her and fears for her future, but he also acknowledges that his sin is great and his wife is justified in her rage.

When he ends his diary, depressed and believing his eyesight is failing, he notes sadly that, although he has been seeing the beloved girl secretly, 'my amours to Deb are past'. Within months of laying down his pen, his wife died, of a fever. What novelist would dare to shape events so?

But every word is true. And while many of the events that crowd one after the other through the pages are thrilling, the supreme feat of the *Diary* is its laying out of private human feelings and experiences, the whole spectrum from the grossest to the finest-spun. Pepys's openness shocked the nineteenth century and is still disconcerting. Are we to laugh at a man who describes how he goes out to look for a woman and then praises God for not letting him find one? Or feel contempt for the way he uses Mrs Bagwell (a novelist's name if ever there were one), the wife of a ship's carpenter, for his purposes, while giving Bagwell contracts, all three well aware of the nature of the exchange? Are we to cheer him for his healthy sexual appetite, or pity his ill-used wife? The answer is, all these things, as in life.

The oddity in his accounts of sexual transactions is that, after the early years, he wrote of them in a private language made up of French, English, Spanish and Latin words: 'jo haze todo which I had a corason a hazer con ella'; 'I did the cosa con much voluptas'; 'toccar ses mamelles', etc. Since the whole *Diary* was protected by being in shorthand, there seems no reason for this special language, particularly as it is so easy to follow. It looks as though he adopted it, not as a protection but as a distancing device, out of some inner embarrassment. Something in his conscience – or his masculine pride – made him keep the record of his adulteries; yet he seems to have wanted to suggest that the Pepys who did those things was not entirely the same as the Pepys who recorded them – whether they were recorded only for himself, or for God, or for posterity. It remains a puzzle, if a comical one.

One of the greatest attractions of the *Diary* is that it is the voice of a young man, full of good humour, optimism, energy, ambition and commitment to his career. The buzz of enthusiasm sounds on every page. He is a meritocrat on the make, yes, enthusiastic in his hatred of certain colleagues, sometimes nervous of his great masters, but also scornful of their laxities. Often he works far into the night, but how he enjoys the great range of pleasures outside his work: music, which he composed and performed; the theatre, a passion; pictures, which he bought and also commissioned; books, devoured and collected; even science, for he was a member of the Royal Society. To these add his taste for rearranging his house and possessions, plate, clothing, furniture and money-boxes; an enjoyment of good food and good conversation, a discriminating interest in sermons, and an eye for landscape when he rode out of town. Few people have felt the fullness of the world's possibilities so keenly.

He was also blessed with the sense that his life had a shape and a meaning. Each year he kept the anniversary of his operation for the stone, which he knew he was lucky to have survived. He records dreaming of his mother, and being much affected by the dreams, both before and after her death. When he visited Ashtead at the age of thirty, a large part of his enjoyment lay in his recollection of being there as a small boy, and walking in a particular wood where he first consciously experienced pleasure in a woman's company. Nothing is known of the woman, a Mrs Hely, who may have been simply a servant, but in his galaxy she has her allotted place, part of the pattern of his life.

Pepys's origins were humble, though the larger clan of Pepys had its successful lawyers and other well-to-do members; but he was the son of a mere tailor and a quite uneducated woman, and one of eleven children. Still, he was a bright enough boy to be noticed and plucked out of the family, sent to a grammar school, to St Paul's, and on to Cambridge. As a schoolboy he watched the execution of Charles I and applauded it, which caused him some anxiety later. He was a thorough pragmatist in politics, and when a cousin, Edward Mountagu, became his patron, and was concerned in the Restoration, for which Charles II gave him an earldom, Pepys, who had clerked for him, was rewarded by being appointed to the Navy Board. There his efficiency, diligence and passion for understanding how things work made him the outstanding public servant he became.

After the end of the *Diary*, Pepys lived a long and richly interesting life. He did not lose his eyesight, but seems never to have attempted to renew writing in the same form. At his death he left it with all his books and papers to a nephew, with instructions that they should go to his Cambridge college, Magdalene, for the benefit of posterity. The *Diary* remained unread until 1819, when a scholar, one John Smith, was paid £200 to decipher it. Although he did it well, the editor, Lord Braybrooke, hashed and cut it severely for publication in 1825. This edition was reprinted several times, with additions over the years. Two larger, newly deciphered editions followed in the 1870s and 1890s.

Robert Latham's eleven-volume edition of 1970 was the first complete one, based on his study of the original over a period of thirty years, and is surely as near definitive as can be hoped for. The *Companion* and *Index* volumes add significantly to the pleasure. Pepys's language is surprisingly close to ours and presents few real difficulties; and whoever he thought he was addressing, it turns out he has something to say to all of us, even across three hundred years. What is it the best writers do? They infuse the world with their energy, making it more real, more immediate, more troubling than most of us can be bothered to notice most of the time. That infusion of energy, quite as much as the historical record, is Pepys's great gift to us.

*Guardian*, 1995